# Vanishing Act

## A Jamie Richmond Mystery

Mark Love

Vanishing Act
Copyright © 2015 Mark Love
All rights reserved.

ISBN: (ebook) 978-1-939590-60-2
(Print) 978-1-939590-67-1

Inkspell Publishing
5764 Woodbine Ave.
Pinckney, MI 48169

Edited By Amanda Roberts
Cover art By Dawne' Dominique

# DEDICATION

For Kim, who stole my heart all those years ago and
refuses to give it back.

MARK LOVE

# PROLOGUE

Malone was going to kill me.

There wasn't a doubt in my mind. He was going to kill me.

I knew it in my heart, in my soul—right down to the marrow of my bones. From the top of my wavy red locks to the bright, red polish on my toenails, I knew without a doubt that it was a sure thing.

Malone was going to kill me.

But first, I had to get out alive.

He'd warned me time and again to mind my own business. Why didn't I listen to reason? How could it be that less than four months after I narrowly escaped certain death at the hands of a psychotic bikini-bar waitress, I found myself in another situation where my chances of survival were slim? Only this time, it was not just my life on the line. I had somebody else counting on me.

Now it was up to me. I needed to figure out a way to get us out of here, fast, because right now, time was rapidly running out on me. Make that us. There was no way I was leaving alone, but there sure as hell was no way I wanted to stick around. Right now, all I really wanted was to be back in my cozy little home, curled up on the plush sofa I affectionately call "The Jewish Aunt," waiting for Malone to come home from work. But I knew that was not going to happen.

We were trapped. And waiting on the other side of that wall was someone who would rather see us sliced open on a coroner's slab than walking out the door. And to help them make that wish come true, they were setting the wall on fire.

Malone may have to wait in line to kill me.

# CHAPTER ONE

It was the day after Christmas when my cell phone rang. I flipped it open without even a glimpse at the screen. "No refunds, no exchanges," I said.

"Jay Kay, where the *hell* are you?" a sultry voice demanded.

"Linda!"

"I'm standing here in your apartment building, freezing my cute little ass off. And your door is locked. You never ever lock your door."

"When did you get back in town?"

"Two hours ago. Logan and I couldn't wait to see you. So where are you?"

I gave her directions to the new place. Linda was on her way.

Someone far smarter than me once told me that if we're lucky, we'll get to have one true friend who will always be with us, no matter what's going on in our lives. They may not be in attendance each day, and there may be months when you don't speak or get to see them face to face, but deep down you know they will always be there for you. And you'll be there for them. Turns out, I found my true friend when I was six years old.

Linda and I met in the first grade and we became inseparable. A teacher once remarked that we were 'twin daughters of different mothers'. I honestly had no idea what she meant. It was years before I took it as a compliment. Linda and I bonded. We cried on each other's shoulders. We flirted with the same boys, all through elementary school, high school, and college. I was her maid of honor when she tied the knot, and the first person she called when she was getting divorced. We never bothered with pinkie swearing, a blood oath, or the spit-in-your-palm-before-the-handshake routine. We didn't need it. We just knew.

As I ran from room to room doing a quick clean up from the sexual romps Malone and I had enjoyed before he went to work his shift at the State Police post, I realized Linda and I had a lot of catching up to do. On my way past the bathroom, I grabbed a damp bath towel.

In early October, Linda had taken a leave of absence from her job as a history teacher at the high school in Northville. Her mother, Gracie, had fallen and broken her hip. Years ago, Gracie moved to Raleigh, North Carolina to get away from the Michigan winters. Gracie had no desire to live in Florida, an area she considered nothing more than 'God's waiting room', but she liked the warmer climate of Raleigh just fine. Knowing that her mother would need assistance following her surgery, Linda hadn't blinked twice about taking the time off to be with her. The school agreed to her absence. She was due back at the blackboards with the first classes in January.

I heard the thump of a car door and a great deal of noise. Opening the front door, I was nearly bowled over by Logan. His enthusiastic greetings can be overwhelming. Kneeling in the doorway, I wrapped my arms around him as he covered my face with wet, sloppy kisses.

"Logan, baby, I've missed you."

He didn't verbalize a response, but I could tell he was happy to see me. Logan's a golden retriever, the most, well-behaved dog I've ever known. I rubbed his coat with the towel, and then wiped his paws so he wouldn't track snow or mud through the house. Once I released him, he scurried off to investigate.

"Jay Kay, you look fantastic," Linda said as she swept me into her arms.

We hugged for several minutes without saying another word. Good friends can do that. At length, we went into the kitchen to make some tea. There was so much to talk about I didn't know where to start.

On Christmas Eve, while Malone was at work, I had dismantled my cherry kitchen table and brought it from the apartment in stages. There was no way I wanted to have our first, true meal, Christmas dinner to boot, while sitting at a card table and folding chairs. Linda got cozy, shedding her scarf and winter coat, while I got the kettle boiling.

I took a good look at her. As happens every so often, a flare of jealousy flittered across my mind. I couldn't help it. She was so damn gorgeous.

Linda is about five feet, five inches tall, which is two inches shorter than me. But there's no mistaking the physical differences between us. Where I have a narrow body and very meager curves, Linda is blessed with both va-va and voom. She's slender and curvaceous, a result of great genes, which makes her hourglass figure that much more incredible. Topping it off is a thick mane of curly, dark brown hair that rolls about her shoulders every time she turns her head. When the humidity is up, the curls just intensify.

If she wasn't my best friend, I'd probably hate her strictly on principle.

But it's Linda's face that can stop traffic, or halt conversations mid-word. Her features are the envy of fashion models. A narrow, aquiline nose, sparkling, baby blue eyes, and a Cupid's bow mouth complete the package. There is nearly always a hint of mischief on her face, as if she's in on a secret that if you're really lucky, she'll share with you. And her eyes can look right through you and touch your soul.

"Jay Kay, this is so unlike you. When we talked two weeks ago, you never said anything about moving."

"What can I say? I suddenly had the urge to get out of the apartment."

While the water was boiling, I gave her a quick tour of the house. Linda's eyes widened when she saw the size of the master suite and the marble fixtures in the bath. Logan padded along with us, sniffing at everything that caught his attention. When we returned to the kitchen, he sprawled under the table. I set out a bowl of water for him within easy reach. Kicking off my slippers, I began to rub my bare feet on his fur coat. It was heavenly. We both enjoyed it.

Linda waited until we had our mugs of tea and a plate of Christmas cookies between us. Then she propped that lovely chin in the palm of her left hand, fixed those dazzling, baby blue eyes on me, and began the interrogation.

"I saw men's clothes hanging in that closet, Jay Kay. There's a razor on the sink and two toothbrushes. And you've been dodging my questions long distance about a new romance. But one look at you is all I need. You've been getting laid. A lot! So start talking."

I felt the color rush to my face. Linda has always been direct. In some ways, she reminds me of my stepfather, Bert.

"Not much to tell," I said, stalling for time. "He's just some stud I picked up by the side of the road. He reminded me of Logan, so I couldn't resist."

"Logan's a great dog, but he sleeps on the floor, not with me. I'm not buying this line of shit, Jamie," she said with a gentle smile.

"Tell me about your mom," I said.

Linda sipped her tea and took a minuscule bite out of a cookie. "Mom's fine. Her recovery is right on schedule.

She insisted we fly out early this morning, so I can get back to my normal life before school starts. I think she's got a boyfriend and she wanted to get busy with him for New Year's Eve. Now stop trying to change the subject and tell me."

She looked so serious I burst out laughing. Linda threw the rest of her cookie at me. It bounced off my shoulder and landed on the floor by Logan's nose. Before I could pick it up, he'd taken care of it.

"His name is Malone," I said when the laughter faded.

"Is that his first or last name?"

"He only goes by Malone."

Linda raised her eyebrows. "He sounds mysterious. I like him already. Tell me more. Tell me everything. I want to hear every juicy morsel, especially the sex parts."

So I told Linda everything about Malone. It was dark when my story ended. I let Logan outside to do his business. We decided to drop him off at Linda's place and go out to Mexican Village for the best Mexican food around. I realized we'd been talking for three hours, but there was still so much more to tell her.

\* \* \* \*

I started the fire in the hearth an hour before Malone was due. It was more for atmosphere than anything else, since I knew he would keep me warm on our temporary nest on the floor where the air mattress and sleeping bags waited. The majority of my furniture was still at my apartment. I could easily picture the big sofa on the wall, facing the windows. The rocker could go near the front door. There was room for the entertainment center on either side of the fireplace. I wiggled deeper into the down sleeping bags, wishing for Malone to come home.

A few minutes later, I heard the key in the door. He entered through the side door by the kitchen, leaving his boots on the landing and his coat on a convenient hook.

He came through the arch from the kitchen and stood there, looking at the fire and me.

"Hey, Jamie."

"Hello, Romeo. Come warm me up."

"No way could I refuse such an invitation."

He paused long enough to peel off his sweater and jeans. Then he was inside the sleeping bag, drawing me into his arms. The fact that I was only wearing perfume made him pull me that much closer. Apparently, confessing all the details to Linda earlier had made me realize how aroused Malone could get me. He was busy kissing his way down my body. Okay, so I was horny. Can you blame me?

"So, how was your day, dear?" I gasped between kisses.

"It was business as usual. No homicides, no shootings, a couple of accidents, and a few tickets, but a relatively calm day." Malone brought his face closer so that I could see how his cobalt blue eyes danced in the firelight. "You really want to talk now?"

I took his face in my hands and started kissing him back. "Talking is greatly overrated. But I did have some excitement today."

"Want to have some excitement now?"

I pushed him onto his back and slid on top of him. "We can always talk later."

"Much later," Malone said.

\* \* \* \*

We never did get around to talking. It must have been after four when we dozed off. I remember Malone throwing a couple more birch logs on the fire, and the image of his naked body framed in the firelight. The next thing I knew, there was a buzzing noise by my head. It took a few seconds for my brain to connect enough neurons to realize it was my cell phone.

It was the moving company I had lined up to haul my

belongings over from the apartment. Apparently they had a cancelation and would be able to squeeze me in tomorrow if I was interested. As much as I liked playing campfire with Malone, the idea of cuddling up in my own bed was a winner. I made arrangements to meet them at the apartment at eight the next morning.

As I closed the phone, I glanced at the little display that showed the time. It was almost ten. Linda was due any minute! And I had never told Malone about her. Realizing that we were both naked inside the sleeping bags gave me incentive to move. Malone was on his back, snoring softly. I had been sprawled halfway across his body, luxuriating in the feeling of my legs brushing against his. Now I leaned up and nibbled his ear.

"Malone, we need to get dressed. We're having visitors any minute."

He didn't wake up. Instead he slid his left hand down my body and cupped my ass. I could feel certain parts of his body start to respond. Reluctantly, I pushed him away. Sneaking a peek at the window, I hoped no one was looking. I crawled out of the nest and scampered into the bathroom for a quick shower.

Ten minutes later, I donned a robe and dried my hair with a towel. Quickly, I ran into the bedroom and pulled on some clothes. I was just brushing out my hair when the doorbell rang. Logan let out a couple of friendly barks. I got to the front door just as Malone began to rise from the sleeping bag.

"Stay put, Malone."

"What's going on?" His voice was a hoarse rasp. Obviously, he wasn't fully awake yet.

"It's a long story, but a good one."

I opened the door and Logan leaped into the room. He swiveled his head, checking out the surroundings then bounded onto the sleeping bags and began to nuzzle Malone. Linda stepped into the foyer and closed the door behind her. She gave me a hug.

"I think Logan wants to play," she said with a laugh.

Malone snapped both eyes open at the sound of her voice. Did I mention before that she has a sultry voice? It's been compared to Kathleen Turner, the Hollywood actress whose voice was even used in an animated film for a sexy character. Malone pushed Logan's snout to the side and worked himself into a sitting position, keeping everything covered from the waist down. He glanced at me, and then moved his eyes over to Linda.

"Malone, meet Linda Davis, my best friend."

Linda flashed a smile. "Think I'll wait until you're dressed to shake hands."

Logan was now curled on top of the sleeping bag beside Malone. He reached over and rubbed the dog's head. "Maybe I'd better grab a shower."

"Clothes would be good too," I said.

"Don't go to any trouble on my account," Linda said with a wicked grin.

I grabbed her hand and pulled her into the kitchen. Once we were in by the stove, Malone scrambled from the nest and ducked into the bathroom. Linda caught a glimpse of his muscular reflection in the window.

"He's gorgeous," Linda gushed excitedly. "I'm so happy for you!"

We sat in the kitchen, waiting for Malone. He didn't take long to shower and pull on the jeans and sweater he'd been wearing last night. His hair was still slightly damp as he walked into the kitchen. He paused beside Linda's chair and extended a hand.

"I'm Malone."

She looked at his hand and slowly shook her head. Linda rose from her chair, slipped her arms around his waist and gave him a hug. She even leaned up for a quick peck on the cheek. "Thanks for taking such good care of my Jamie."

"It's been a challenge, but mostly, it's been a pleasure," he said.

I reached over and took his hand, pulling him closer. There was a brief wave of jealousy that rippled through my stomach, seeing Linda with her arms around him. I glanced up at him. Malone's eyes locked on mine and I got one of those low voltage smiles of his that I love.

Linda went to the side door to let Logan out.

"She's beautiful, isn't she?" I said.

"I hadn't noticed."

"Are you in a coma? Just look at her!"

Malone pulled me from the chair and dipped me backward. "I don't need to look at her, Jamie. If I want to see beautiful, I just need to look at you." Still dipping me, he bent down and gave me a long, hot, wet kiss. He only straightened up when Linda cleared her throat.

"Apparently things are heating up in the kitchen. Maybe I should come back later," she said with a wide smile on her face. Even from here I could see her eyes sparkling with delight.

Malone shook his head. "No, we're fine. That's just how we say good morning."

I knew my face was flushed from his attentions. But Linda's response cranked it up even more.

"If that's good morning, I can only imagine what 'good night' looks like."

\* \* \* \*

We went out for brunch at a diner that specialized in breakfast. Linda left Logan curled up on the front seat of her car. With his permanent fur coat, we knew he'd be toasty warm since it was in the low forties that morning. Over brunch I told them about my call from the movers. We decided to go to the apartment and bring over a load or two of incidentals and my computer equipment.

Malone checked his watch. "What time are the movers coming tomorrow?"

"Eight. We'll have to get up early and drive over."

"Maybe you should spend the night at the apartment. Your last night, for old time's sake," Linda said, giving me an exaggerated wink.

Malone glanced at me and shook his head. "Actually, I was going to crash at my place tonight. I have to be in court first thing in the morning."

"Why, Max, don't you want to sleep with me?" I asked, batting my lashes at him.

"You know I do, but by the time I get home, the odds of us sleeping are greatly diminished."

"Jay Kay, can't you control your urges?" Linda asked, trying to keep the grin from her face.

"Of course I can. See how politely I'm behaving right now."

Malone made a show of picking my hand off his lap and raising it above the table, before setting it beside my coffee mug. Well, I thought I looked innocent. Linda just shook her head at me and laughed.

She knows me too well.

I turned to Malone. "Max, are you trying to get out of helping me move into our new place?"

"I'd be happy to take over some things before work today, but I have to be back at the post for my shift at three. Somehow I don't think the other residents of the apartment building would look very kindly on you if I'm tromping up and down the stairs at two in the morning."

"Jay Kay, you did spring this on us fairly quickly. We'll take over as much as we can today and leave the heavy stuff for the guys with the muscles," Linda said.

I winked at her over the rim of my coffee mug. "You certainly are quick to take Max's side on this."

She looked closely at Malone for a moment. "Is Max really your name?"

He shook his head. "I only use Malone. Jamie's been trying to figure out my first name since we started dating. Each day I see her, she gives me a new name, in the hope that someday she'll get the right one."

"Jay Kay, you really are a piece of work," she said with another laugh.

Malone waited until the waitress removed our dirty dishes and refilled our coffee mugs. His eyes kept moving between the two of us. I saw one of those low voltage smiles playing at the corners of his mouth.

"So why do you call Jamie Jay Kay?" he asked.

Linda looked down, her eyes trying to find an escape route under the table. I had to bite my lip to keep from giggling at her. Exasperated at being caught so soon after meeting him, Linda drew a deep breath and composed herself.

"It's her initials."

"No, her middle name is Rae. So her initials wouldn't be Jay Kay."

"I've called her that since we were about ten."

"But why do you call her that?" Malone asked again.

I felt like I was at a tennis match, watching the volley go back and forth. This was good and it was too much fun to intervene. Nobody flusters Linda.

"Okay, it's not really her initials," Linda said, taking her time to add a dollop of cream to her coffee.

"I know," Malone said softly, "but you still didn't answer my question."

Linda looked at me. "Is he always like this?"

"Like what?"

"Determined, focused, single-minded in his pursuit of an answer."

I shrugged. "He's a cop, Linda. It comes with the territory."

She looked back at him and made a production out of sipping her coffee.

"So?" Malone asked again.

"Better tell him, Linda, or we'll never get out of here."

"Fine! I call her Jay Kay, and it is for initials. But they're not her initials. She was awkward as a kid, always bumping into things, tripping over her own two feet. I

13

used to tease her and say she'd gotten an extra dose of the klutz gene. So I started calling her 'Just a Klutz', but I was afraid I might slip up and say it in front of other kids, who would pick on her. So I changed it to 'J A K', and then shortened it to 'Jay Kay'. I've called her that ever since."

"I see," Malone said.

"And I call her—"

"Don't you dare say another word!" Linda snapped and grabbed my arm.

"It's only fair, Algae. You told him the basis for my nickname, so I should get to tell him yours."

"Algae?" Malone asked with a bewildered look on his face. "Like seaweed?"

She let go of my arm and slumped back in the booth. "LG. As in Linda Gail, which are my real names and my real initials. It just sounds funny."

"You started it," I said, linking my arm through Malone's.

"You two are something else, a klutz and seaweed. What a pair. And they say guys have strange nicknames."

Linda proceeded to kick his shin under the table. "Shut up, Malone."

# CHAPTER TWO

I was back at the apartment for one last night. Linda was having dinner with Crystal, a friend from college who had just returned from her own holiday vacation. Malone was working. I walked slowly around the apartment, pausing here and there for reflection. After so many years of living in the same place, you'd think my memory banks would be overflowing with special occasions I was going to miss.

But that wasn't the case.

It turns out that most of those fond memories were all from the jammed packed last four months. And they all included Malone.

I sat on the Brentwood rocker with a mug of tea. The room was filled with cardboard boxes. Everything that wasn't nailed down was ready for the movers. Linda and I had hauled what we could from the kitchen and bathroom earlier. Malone had taken my computer and stored it in the house. I'd emptied the closets in stages, moving linens and towels and my hang-up stuff before Christmas. Even the refrigerator was empty.

I looked at the "Jewish Aunt," if two people should sit on it, the sofa automatically pushes them together. If I stretched out on it, I could sink down into the cushions and disappear. Sleep would follow shortly.

I was more restless than tired. Moving out of the apartment was a decision I'd made weeks ago and was already accustomed to it. After only a few nights, the little house was already feeling like home. Now that Linda was back, I could begin to make new memories there with Malone and my best friend. I realized now how much I'd missed her the last few months. The fact that I never even told Malone about her shows how preoccupied I'd been. Guess I could blame a big part of that on him. I thought about how quickly things were moving for us. I tried, unsuccessfully, to remember the last night we hadn't spent together. How was that possible? Now I started feeling sorry for myself, missing him.

As I was finishing my tea, my cell phone rang. It was almost midnight. I didn't even bother to look at the display screen. "Hi, Max."

"Hi, Jamie. You'd better get some sleep. It will be a busy day tomorrow with the movers." Malone's deep voice softly tickled my ear.

"Yeah, well, I've kind of gotten out of the habit of sleeping alone."

He chuckled quietly. "It's only one night, Jay."

"What can I say, Max? You've spoiled me."

"Jamie, what am I going to do with you?"

"I've got a few ideas." I got out of the rocker and started toward the bedroom.

He was laughing now. "Such as?"

"Well, there's the kitchen counter, the 'aunt', the shower, the hallway, the…"

"Jamie," Malone said.

I realized his voice was right behind me. He was standing in the doorway, the cell phone in one hand, keys in the other.

"Malone!" I ran to him and threw my arms around his neck. "You missed me so much…"

"Jamie," he said, scooping me up and carrying me to the 'aunt'.

"Yes, Max?"

"No more talking."

Who could argue with logic like that?

* * * *

It seemed like only a moment after he'd swept me up in his arms that Malone was gently nudging me awake. I pried open one eyelid and stared at his profile. He was nuzzling my neck, his lips moving closer to that little spot behind my ear that drives me crazy. Suddenly I was very awake. Just as I was reaching for him, the rat slid out of bed.

"Time to get moving, Jay. I need to run home, shower, change, and get to court."

"Malone, that's no way to start the morning," I groaned.

I got a brief flash of his buns as he pulled on his jeans. "Technically, we started the morning when I got here last night. Or have you forgotten our passion?"

Blushing, I turned over so he couldn't see it. Thinking back, it would be difficult to determine who was attacking whom last night. I do remember we started on the sofa. Since I'd packed all the towels, we'd skipped the shower. Malone found the box with the quilt in it and we'd swiped the cushions from the 'aunt' for pillows. Somehow, he'd coaxed me into a warm bath, where things got very steamy. We'd wrapped up in the quilt, slightly damp, but mellow around two-thirty.

"What time is it, Ramon?"

"Quarter to seven. If you hustle, you can get things back in the boxes before the movers get here."

I turned back to face him. "Have you ever known me to 'hustle' in the morning? Do I spring out of bed, fresh as a daisy and ready to face the day, particularly when it's still cold and dark outside?"

Malone drew me close for a long kiss. "I've got to go. The movers will be thrilled if you're still naked when they arrive."

I watched him slide off the bed and head for the door. Wrapping the quilt around me, I followed him out into the hallway. He stepped into his boots and pulled on his winter coat.

"Thanks for spending the night, Ramon."

He flashed me one of those low voltage smiles that I love. "Nowhere else I'd rather be, Jay. I'll see you tonight."

As he went out the door, I wondered if I'd get a discount from the movers if I didn't get dressed. Chances were, they'd probably charge me extra.

\* \* \* \*

Home. What a cozy, comforting sound those four little letters make. I was home now, with everything moved in from the apartment and everything in its place. I hoped Malone would like the new arrangements. I wondered if he'd be pleased with what we'd accomplished today.

After he'd left, I'd scrambled into my clothes, packed away the quilt, and had run down to the bakery for coffee and muffins. I'd even brought a box of donuts for the movers. It was amazing how quickly they made them disappear. By ten-thirty, they had packed the last box on the truck. Linda met me at the house. She helped coordinate the placement of the furniture. Logan had watched the activity from the kitchen, where she'd tied his leash to the table. By four o'clock, the movers were gone. We were sprawled at opposite ends of the 'aunt', catching our breath. Logan was prowling the house now, inspecting our efforts.

"I'm impressed, Jay Kay. You got everything moved in before the end of the month. This will be quite a start for the new year," Linda said.

I'd forgotten all about the holiday. Today was the

twenty-eighth. Linda and I always spent New Year's Eve together. I watched Logan come in and collapse by the hearth.

"Do you have any plans for the thirty-first?" I asked.

She shook her head. "Nothing special. I thought we'd be spontaneous and see what's going on."

Something didn't feel right. Before I could respond, my cell phone rang. Malone. Linda swiped it from my hand.

"Ms. Richmond's estate," she said in that sultry voice, "how may I help you?"

I couldn't make out the words, but Malone's voice was evident.

"Yes, I will make certain she has a nourishing meal…what's…that…vitamins…extra…towels…candles …more firewood…I'd better start a grocery list…oysters…thigh high stockings?"

I pounced on her and struggled to get my phone back. Linda put some extra sultry in her voice. "Ms. Richmond will speak with you now." She pushed me away and took Logan outside.

"Hey, Jamie," Malone said, laughing.

"Hey, Ramon, what's up?"

"Just wondering if you got everything settled in?"

"Yeah, the movers left a while ago. I think we're going to get a pizza. Should we save you some?"

"Sure. No anchovies."

"Don't worry. They give Logan gas."

"He ain't the only one."

I didn't know if he meant me or him. But I had something else on my mind. "Malone, didn't we have plans for New Year's Eve?"

There was a lengthy pause. I realized I'd forgotten something important.

"Jamie, we're going to the event at the Westin. I got the night off. I gave you the tickets Christmas Day. Remember? There's a lavish dinner, dancing to a full orchestra, watching the ball drop at midnight.

Remember?"

Now I did. He'd bought the tickets and wrapped them up as one of my presents. We had talked about going formal. Malone was even going to wear a tuxedo.

"Is something wrong, Jay?"

"No, Malone. I just got so swept up in your romantic evening that I forgot all about Linda. We always spend New Year's Eve together."

He paused again. Then as he has done so many times before, Malone surprised me.

"Can she get a date? I know I can still get tickets."

"Malone, do you remember what she looks like? Getting a date is never a problem for her."

"Then set it up, Jay, it's my treat. Listen I have to go."

"Malone!"

"Yes, Jay?"

"You're incredible."

"See you tonight."

* * * *

"Jay Kay, you can't be serious. New Year's Eve is only three days away!"

"Don't argue with me, Algae. It's all set. Look at the brochure. We're talking a lavish dinner, dancing to a real big band orchestra, champagne at midnight, and an enormous breakfast buffet at one when the band stops playing. You're going. That's all there is to it."

Linda tucked her feet underneath her and sank deeper into the cushions of the sofa. "You said you guys are going formal. I don't have a dress for something like that. And I'll need to get someone to stay with Logan. And besides…"

"…besides what?"

She looked out the window at the fading afternoon sun. "Besides, I don't have a date. I've been gone forever. And I hadn't been dating anyone seriously for a couple of months before that."

Thinking back I realized we'd both been available a lot back in the summer. We had spent a great deal of time together and didn't need men to complicate things. But now it was a different story.

"And before you get any ideas, going out with someone for a first date on New Year's Eve is too bizarre," Linda said. "I'll just stay home with Logan and watch movies on cable."

I looked at her closely. She was serious. I reached over and gently took both of her hands in mine. "Algae."

"Yes, Jay Kay?"

"Bullshit."

She tried to jerk her hands free but I held tight.

"I repeat. Bullshit. You will be going out on New Year's Eve with me and Malone. I won't take no for an answer and neither will Malone. So let's go drop fur face at home and hit the mall. We've got some serious shopping to do."

"Jay Kay…"

"…it's my treat. Think of it as a belated Christmas present. And by the way, I have the perfect date in mind for you."

A skeptical look crossed her face. "Don't even think about fixing me up with a cop, Jay Kay. You got the one-in-a-million shot."

"No, the man I have in mind is not a cop. You could say he's just what the doctor ordered. Now get your coat."

I did have the perfect guy in mind for Linda.

\* \* \* \*

We drove to Linda's house in separate cars. While she was getting Logan comfortable at home, I made the call. When I got him on the line, it took all of two minutes to describe the situation and get the answer I was looking for. I couldn't help smiling when Linda got in my car. But I didn't tell her a thing.

We headed out to Somerset Mall. In addition to the swanky stores, I knew we'd find a number of shops that would be having after-Christmas sales. Despite her feeble protests about shopping, Linda got into the spirit of things by the time we hit the second store. She found a gorgeous red dress. It had one shoulder bare, a tight bodice, and a flared skirt slit along one side, revealing a lot of leg. With her curly, brown hair, the color was perfect for her.

I had been looking for months for a little black dress. As luck would have it, I found one. It left both shoulders bare and hugged me in ways only Malone ever did. Linda's eyes widened when I modeled it for her.

"Do you like it?" I asked.

"Jay Kay, it's perfect. The only question will be how long Malone can control himself when he sees you in it."

"I'm taking that as a compliment. Now we need to keep going."

"We got the dresses we came for, why would we keep going?" Linda asked.

"Baby, everything is on sale. It's the perfect opportunity to get shoes to go with these gowns. You'll want some nice heels for dancing."

Her eyes narrowed. "But who will I be dancing with? If I get two-inch heels, will I tower over him?"

"Nice try. I told you it's a surprise. You'll just have to trust me. And I'm sure you'll get to dance a few times with Malone as well. So some shoes with two-inch heels will be just fine."

"I have shoes at home."

I shook my head. "It's my Christmas present for you. Shoes, stockings, some lacy lingerie and anything else I can think of. How's your perfume supply?"

Laughing, she gave her curls a shake. "Did you win the lottery?"

I linked my arm in hers. "Yeah, I've got Malone and my best friend came home. And that's why they invented credit cards!"

\* \* \* \*

At seven-thirty on New Year's Eve, the limousine picked us up. Malone informed Terrence, our driver, that we would be making two additional stops before heading to the Westin. The driver beamed a smile, touched his cap, and set off down the road.

It's not my nature to keep secrets, but I wanted to surprise Linda tonight. I had been on guard the last three days, expecting her to trip me up. She'd tried, but I somehow kept my mouth shut—even earlier today, when we'd been at the spa.

Malone had sprung that on us yesterday. He'd arranged for mid-afternoon appointments so we could get manicures, pedicures, facials, and have our hair styled. If there was a gold medal given for pampering, he would have won it hands down. Linda took advantage of our time together to quiz me about her date.

"So what is he like, Jay Kay? Does he have a job, live with his mother, is he kind to animals? How come he was available on such short notice?"

I took a minute to phrase my response. "He does have a job, lives alone in his own house, and I think he's very good with animals. I also have it on good authority that he's an excellent dancer, enjoys the finer things in life, and can be quite charming."

"Oh, great," Linda said with a roll of her eyes, "he's gay."

I almost sprayed Diet Coke out my nose on that one. "No, he is definitely not gay."

"So he looks like a troll," Linda said.

I shook my head in feigned disgust. "Would I set you up with a troll?"

"Maybe you would."

"If I thought he was a troll, would I have bought you a

red, satin thong to go with that gorgeous red dress?"

"Hey, even trolls need to get laid once in a while."

It had taken some effort, but I managed to steer the subject away from her date.

Now, hours later, I snuggled down in the back of the limo with Malone. Outside, snow danced across the windshield as a light swirl of flakes descended from the clouds.

The limo made our next stop and picked up her date. He looked splendid in his tuxedo, almost as good as Malone. They greeted each other warmly. I got a kiss on the cheek. His aftershave was subdued, but sexy. We chatted quietly until the limo arrived at Linda's house. He stepped out and moved quickly to her door. She opened it just as he reached the porch. Malone had put the window down so we could see her reaction and hear their conversation.

"Linda, you become more beautiful each time I see you."

There was a moment of hesitation in her eyes before her face broke into a wide smile. "Vince. You *are* the perfect date."

Linda flashed me a dazzling smile as she slid into the limousine. Vince sat beside her. I nudged Malone lightly when I saw Linda slip her gloved hand into Vince's and lean back to enjoy the ride. We chatted about the holidays and what to expect for the evening while the sleek car cruised through traffic. I felt like a fairytale princess as our carriage pulled up in front of the glamorous hotel. There was a flurry of activity as the valet raced to open our doors. I watched Vince and Linda move out, and then I took Malone's hand and followed them.

The lavish hotel was beautifully decorated for the holidays. The ballroom was enormous. We were escorted to a cozy table for four near the center of the room. From here we could see the dance floor and the orchestra. But before dancing, there would be dinner. The Westin has a history of featuring some of the most renowned chefs in the area. I had no doubt they would have spared no expense to put together a scrumptious dinner.

And I was right.

The courses flowed smoothly, from appetizers, to soup, salads, and entrees. There were two wine buckets beside our table. One held a bottle of chardonnay for Linda and Vince. The other had sparkling white grape juice for Malone and me. Since I found out he's an alcoholic, I haven't had a drink of alcohol either. Although Malone said it doesn't bother him to be with other people who drink, I decided I could do without it too. We all opted to hold back on dessert, needing some time to let our gourmet meal settle. At one point between courses, Linda crooked a finger at me. We went to powder our noses.

"Jay Kay, you could have told me Vince was going to be my date," she said with a laugh. "I probably wouldn't have objected."

"Are you kidding? I wanted to surprise you. He looks quite dapper in his tuxedo if you ask me. I even made sure he knew you were wearing red, so his tie would match."

"How did you ever con Doc Schulte into this?" she asked, leaning toward the mirror to touch up her lipstick.

"There was no con. It took me all of a minute to tell him what I had in mind. He agreed immediately. He even insisted on paying Malone for the tickets. And I know for a fact he's an excellent dancer."

Vince Schulte has been my doctor for the longest time. While he may not be as physically fit as Malone, he was nearly as tall, which would work well with Linda and her high heels when they got on the dance floor. I've always thought of him as a Dutch uncle. About once a month since I graduated from high school, we'd go out to the theater or for dinner. His presence has always been a good stabilizer for me.

"Look, I know Vince isn't as young as Malone, but with only three days to find you an appropriate date, I thought he was a good choice."

We turned away from the mirror, heading out of the crowded ladies room. Linda looped her arm through mine and leaned close to my ear. "Don't worry, Jay Kay, he's not that old."

# CHAPTER THREE

Whatever reservations Linda may have had about the New Year's Eve party quickly disappeared when she hit the dance floor. Vince swept her across the floor in a waltz and from where Malone and I followed, it looked like they'd been dancing together for years. If they missed any steps, I didn't see it. My attention was on Malone, though. Not once did he tread on my toes.

After about six dances, we switched partners. I was enjoying my dance with Vince when I realized it didn't bother me to see Linda with her arms around Malone. Perhaps my jealousy was finally getting itself under control.

"You look radiant, Jamie," Vince said as we made a turn. "Glad to see the ankle isn't giving you any problems."

"You do good work, Vince."

"I really must thank you, Jamie. This is a wonderful way to welcome in the New Year," Vince said with a wide smile on his face.

"Well, I couldn't let two of my favorite people stay home alone on such a big night."

"It's been a few years since I've seen Linda. She's even more glamorous than I remember. And she is very lucky to have such a good friend as you."

I had noticed the looks Linda drew as she twirled across the floor. I squeezed Vince's hand. "It doesn't look like the years have done her any harm."

"She's a very beautiful woman, Jamie. But then, so are you."

"That's why I love you, Vince. You're such a charmer."

We literally danced the night away. Occasionally we would stop at the table to catch our breath or share a laugh—and a quick drink. Then we were back on the floor. I realized that Vince and Linda seemed to be moving closer together. Maybe it was my imagination, but I didn't think they were looking at anyone else. I turned my attention back to Malone.

"Are you having a good time, Artemus?"

Malone guided me through a turn. "I'm having a wonderful time, Jamie. This is the best New Year's Eve I've had in years."

"You're not just saying that because of this gravity-defying dress I'm wearing?"

"Well, that's certainly part of it. But I usually work New Year's Eve. This is the first time in ten years or more that I've celebrated this way."

With my high heels on, I was almost as tall as Malone. I took advantage of that to nuzzle his ear. "If you think this is celebrating, just wait until you find out what I'm wearing underneath this dress."

There was the big countdown to midnight. The hotel had projection screens showing the ball dropping in New York City. When it touched off the New Year, streamers, balloons, and confetti rained down from the ceiling of the ballroom. The orchestra started playing *Auld Lang Syne*. Malone drew me close for a long, passionate kiss. From the corner of my eye, I peeked at Vince and Linda. I was stunned by what I saw.

I had expected a gallant kiss on the cheek, or perhaps a brief embrace. Instead, I saw Linda with her arms draped around Vince's neck. His hands were on her tiny waist, holding her steady as the crowd on the dance floor around us swayed with the orchestra. They were kissing. But this wasn't one of those Hollywood air kisses, or the drab kiss of an old couple that has as much heat as a snowball in a February blizzard. This was a 'make the girl swoon with visions of ecstasy' kiss. I don't know who started it, but I do know neither one of them was holding back.

Malone distracted me with his own amorous attentions. I quickly forgot about Linda and Vince and the crowd milling around us. I hadn't admitted it to Malone before, but this was my best New Year's Eve celebration ever. And I had him to thank for it.

When we broke the kiss, we continued to sway to the music. I had to lean close to Malone's ear to know he could hear me over the band.

"It looks like Vince and Linda are getting along well."

Malone twirled me around and laughed. "Maybe you have a calling as a matchmaker."

"Not on your life. All I was hoping for was that they would have a good time tonight." I lost sight of them in the crowd.

"I don't think you have anything to worry about, Jamie. It looks like they're having the time of their lives."

The song ended and we decided to take a break. We made our way back to the table and found Vince and Linda there. The four of us circled the table, exchanging hugs and greetings for a happy new year. I embraced Vince and gave him a brief kiss. I knew Linda was doing the same with Malone, but somehow even that didn't make me jealous. Fresh bottles were in the ice buckets. I lost count of how many bottles of wine they already had. But with all the food and the dancing, neither one seemed to be tipsy. Was it my imagination, or were their chairs closer together?

Linda signaled me that it was time to powder noses again. As she rose from the table, she gave Vince's hand a squeeze. Then she moved over to Malone, whispered in his ear, and kissed his cheek. He was smiling one of my favorite smiles as we hurried away to the ladies room.

"What's that all about?" I asked.

"Just thanking Malone for this wonderful evening. I am so glad that he surprised you with this and that you dragged me along. This sure beats sitting home watching movies with Logan."

\* \* \* \*

Just that quickly, the evening was over. We'd slowly run out of steam on the dance floor and were gathered around the table, reminiscing. Vince was entertaining us with a number of hilarious stories about some of his patients over the years. Then the staff was serving breakfast. I was amazed that I had any appetite. All that dancing had burned off a lot of calories.

Our limousine arrived right on schedule. While we were bundling up, I noticed Vince and Malone having a quick conversation. I tried to get some sense of what was going on from Malone's face, but he didn't give anything away. There was just a little twinkle in those dazzling blue eyes. I reminded myself never to play poker with him.

Malone was the last one in the limo. I smothered a yawn into his chest as I snuggled beside him. It had been a very long evening. It was almost three in the morning as our shiny carriage made its way along the highway.

"I hope you're not working later today, Malone," Vince said as he sat across from us. I noticed he was holding Linda's hand, lightly caressing his thumb across her fingers.

"No, I had a feeling it was going to be a great night. So I traded a shift with another sergeant. I'll go back to work on the second."

"Splendid," Vince said. "I can't speak for anyone else, but I am ready to kick off my dancing shoes."

Linda smiled sweetly at him. "And I thought you'd like to go for a starlit stroll around the neighborhood."

"That's what we have this lovely limousine for." Vince reached up toward the ceiling and touched a button. A section of the roof slid back, revealing a clear Plexiglas panel. The snow squalls from earlier in the evening had passed. We could all see the stars above, little diamonds glittering in the jet-black sky.

Malone activated a button on the console and gentle mood music filled the passenger cabin. I recognized Diana Krall and Tony Bennett singing a duet.

"You don't miss a trick, do you, Artemus?" I said.

"No, ma'am. I don't leave much to chance." He leaned down and kissed me, gently pressing his lips to mine. It was so easy for me to get lost in Malone's kisses. I don't think we came up for air until I felt the limo begin to slow down.

I glanced out the window, expecting to see Linda's neighborhood coming into view. Instead, I recognized my own little house, with Malone's Cherokee parked in the driveway. The car glided to a stop at the curb. The driver was already moving toward the back doors.

"Artemus, tell Terrence this was supposed to be the last stop," I said.

"Hush, Jamie. It's time to say good night."

I was confused. I looked across the seats at Vince and Linda. Her face was glowing. She leaned across and hugged me, her eyes very bright.

"Happy New Year, Jay Kay. I love you."

Not willing to trust my brain, I echoed her sentiment and kissed her cheek. Perplexed, I watched her repeat the message as she kissed Malone chastely on the lips. Vince and Malone clasped hands as Malone exited the car. Vince kissed my cheek and bade me a Happy New Year once again.

I watched Malone press an envelope into Terrence's hand. He thanked him for the wonderful service, firmly took me by the elbow, and guided me up the walk to our house. I was still having difficulty wrapping my head around the situation. Suddenly I realized what might be going to happen next.

"Artemus, we should have taken Linda home first."

"Hush, Jamie." He unlocked the door and ushered me inside.

"But, Malone, it just doesn't seem right. She and Vince…"

"…are consenting adults. And what they do in the privacy of her home, or his, or in the back of that limousine, is none of our business."

I was thunderstruck. Malone unbuttoned my woolen winter coat, then turned me around and eased it off my shoulders. I was still standing there dazed while he hung our coats in the closet and turned back to me.

"Jamie," he said softly.

"Yes, Artemus?"

"I am a very patient man. But I've been waiting all evening to find out exactly what is underneath that gorgeous gown."

"But Artemus…"

"…no buts, Jamie. It's time for you and me to properly welcome in the New Year."

I couldn't possibly formulate an argument as he literally swept me off my feet. I kicked off my shoes and wrapped my arms around Malone's neck. He had one arm behind my knees, the other around my back. Yet somehow he still managed to find the tiny zipper that held my little black dress together.

As I succumbed to Malone's attentions, one final image of Linda and Vince passionately kissing at midnight flashed through my mind. What had I put into motion?

\* \* \* \*

It was sometime in the afternoon on New Year's Day

when we awoke. Malone had been very appreciative of my wardrobe selections beneath that little black dress. I had found a strapless black bra with just a touch of padding. It matched perfectly with the black satin panties that weren't much bigger than a hankie. The silk stockings had been a nice touch as well. Remotely, I wondered if they were intact or if Malone had shredded them with his efforts. I really didn't care.

We were curled up under the quilt. My head was on his chest, listening to the steady, lazy rhythm of his heart. Malone was slowly letting his fingers play through my hair. Last night's styling was nothing more than a memory.

"Happy New Year, Jamie," he said softly.

"Happy New Year, Igor," I whispered.

Malone chuckled softly. "Where do you get these names?"

"From the internet, the sports page, the obituaries…"

"…the obituaries? That's pretty morbid."

"I'm a writer, Igor. I have to pay attention to details, wherever they might be. Some little detail might make a big difference in a character for a story. It might make them more memorable, or make it easier for the reader to identify with them."

"Couldn't you use normal names?"

I rose up to look him in the eye and shook my head. "Weren't you the guy who once said 'what's in a name'? These are normal names. Besides, think of how boring it would be if everyone had simple names, like Jim or Tom."

"Guess that makes sense."

A thought flashed through my mind. "Tell me your name isn't Jim or Tom!"

"No," Malone said, his eyes twinkling at me, "it's not Jim or Tom."

Malone distracted me for a while. I could easily imagine spending the rest of the day right there in bed with him, until my stomach grumbled in protest.

"Guess I'd better feed you," Malone said as he threw

the quilt back.

"I do need nourishment, Igor. But maybe a hot, steamy shower would be in order."

Malone scooped me up and flipped me over his shoulder. He lugged me into the bathroom using a fireman's carry. It's a good thing the shower stall in the master suite was built for two.

Half an hour later I was drying my hair while Malone ducked into the kitchen. Earlier, I started to reach for my cell phone but he managed to keep my hands occupied. Now, with him out of the room, I had my chance. I flipped it open and hit the speed dial button for Linda.

"Hello, Jay Kay," she said softly. Her voice was much huskier than normal.

"Algae, tell me I didn't wake you!"

She moaned a contented sigh into my ear. "We had a very late night, Jay Kay."

"Yes, it must have been pretty late when Vince dropped you off," I said.

There was a very brief pause. "He didn't drop me off, Jay Kay." Her voice was a whisper now. "He's still keeping me warm. We'll talk later." And just like that, she hung up the phone.

\* \* \* \*

We feasted on holiday omelets. Malone decided we needed something special for the day, so he whipped together a culinary masterpiece with shrimp, alfalfa sprouts, scallions, red peppers, and Swiss cheese inside fluffy eggs. We topped them with sour cream and slices of avocado. I managed to put the fresh rye bread in the toaster. That was my contribution to the meal.

"What's wrong, Jamie?" Malone asked after we'd eaten. He was holding a mug of coffee in one hand. With the other he tucked a stray lock of hair back behind my ear.

I shrugged. "Nothing's wrong, Igor."

"You are a lousy liar, Jamie. It's obvious something is bothering you."

I looked down at my own coffee mug. It was difficult to put into words what I was feeling. I wanted Linda to have a good time last night. I was just surprised at how good a time it turned out to be. Reluctantly, I voiced these concerns to Malone.

He was quiet for a bit. Then he got up, cleared away the dishes and cleaned the skillet from our meal. Malone came back to the table and refilled our mugs. He still hadn't said anything. I couldn't get a sense of what he was thinking. He reached over and put his hands on my waist. Just like that I was on his lap with my arms around his neck.

"Jamie, you got what you wanted last night. Both Vince and Linda had a lovely evening, as did we. I enjoyed their company. They enjoyed ours."

"Yes, Igor, and they certainly enjoyed each other's. But I wasn't expecting them to end up in bed together."

He chuckled softly. "Didn't you tell me that you bought Linda some sexy red lingerie to go with that knockout dress she was wearing?"

"Yes, but…"

"…and isn't the whole purpose of such attire to have someone to show it to?"

I blushed at the idea. "Well, it also helps make the woman feel sexy."

"And feeling sexy might cause her to be promiscuous?"

"Yes. No. I don't know, Malone." My frustration was evident.

"Jamie, what's really bothering you? Is it the idea that Linda could be attracted to an older man? Or is it that you were the one who put them together?"

Great, not only was he a cop, but a psychologist, too. I blew out a breath in frustration. "I just want them both to be happy. I really didn't expect it to happen with each other."

Malone lightly stroked my back. "Don't start picking out china patterns for them, Jamie. They have known each other a long time. Last night might turn out to be nothing more than the culmination of a very romantic evening."

Before I could voice a response, the phone rang. With a mixture of happiness and relief, I saw Linda's name on the screen as I flipped it open.

"Happy New Year, Algae."

Her voice was still husky as she laughed warmly in my ear. "I just wanted to call and thank you for everything, Jay Kay. If this is any indication as to how my year is going to be, all I can say is 'wow'."

"I'm glad you had a nice time." I turned on Malone's lap, holding the phone between our heads so he could hear as well.

"A nice time would have been if I curled up on the sofa with Logan to watch movies all night. I'll probably still be smiling two days from now."

Malone was doing his level best to keep the laughter inside. I could feel it. I tried to ignore him.

"I told you Vince was a good dancer," I said, trying to steer the conversation back to safer ground.

"Yes, you did, Jay Kay. But I think he saved his best moves for the bedroom."

I dropped the phone.

\* \* \* \*

We drove over to Linda's place to watch one of the bowl games. Vince waved to us from the sofa as we walked in, looking casual in a thick sweater, pressed jeans, and loafers. I noticed Logan had taken up a position right next to Vince. Even the dog was warming up to him. I left Malone to relax with them.

Linda had made a huge crock of homemade soup. It was simmering on the stove when I ducked into the kitchen. We hugged, as we always do. Then I held her at arm's length. The sparkle in her eyes was on full power. She couldn't stop smiling.

Glancing over my shoulder to make sure we were alone, I lowered my voice to a whisper. "Remember when you came home from Raleigh and told me that I had been having a lot of sex and that you could tell by just looking at me?"

Linda nodded.

"Now it's your turn," I said, pointing a finger at her.

She blushed and grabbed my hand. "You remember those sexy little things you talked me into getting to wear with that dress?"

"Of course I do."

"Let's just say they were very well received."

Now I was blushing. Maybe I didn't need to hear the details.

Linda hugged me again and laughed in my ear. "Don't worry, Jay Kay. We're just going to take things slow and easy. Vince isn't looking for a trophy wife and I'm not looking for a husband. But that doesn't mean we can't enjoy each other's company."

I sighed with relief. "It just seemed like everything happened so quickly last night. One minute we're all dancing, the next minute, he's taking you home."

"Jay Kay, we're adults." She hesitated for a second, making sure we were still alone. "And to tell you the truth, I've always thought Vince was kind of sexy."

Maybe it was because I had known Vince for so long that the image of him being sexy never crossed my mind. Then I remembered how he had looked in his tuxedo last night.

"I had no idea he could be so romantic," Linda said quietly. "Dancing all night long was like a slow-motion seduction. And when he kissed me at midnight, I felt like my body was on fire."

It was easy to see the impact Vince had had. Linda's face was flushed and her eyes grew wide at the memory. "I saw that kiss. I never expected that."

Linda nodded slowly. "Did you know he speaks Italian? While we were dancing last night, he would pull me close, caress my ear with his lips and whisper to me in Italian."

"What did he say?"

"He would say it in Italian then translate for me. He said '*Mi ha detto che ero la donna più bella del mondo*' that means that I am the most beautiful woman in the world. By the time I was in the limo, I was melting in his arms."

"This is incredible," I whispered. "You remember the actual words he spoke, in Italian?"

"Baby, he kept repeating them to me, teaching them to me, so later on he wouldn't have to explain what they meant," Linda said, her lashes fluttering with the memory.

"This is incredible," I repeated.

Linda squeezed both my hands in hers. "You have no idea. When we got home, there was never any doubt in my mind that we'd make love. I couldn't wait. But Vince didn't want to rush things. I think he took an hour to get me out of my dress."

"I don't believe that!"

Linda lowered her eyes demurely. "Well, maybe it was only five minutes. But he wouldn't rush. He kept touching me lightly, his fingertips were everywhere." Linda's eyes were glazed over as she brought all this back to the forefront of her mind.

"And you can remember this Italian expression?" I asked, trying to get the conversation back on solid ground.

She blinked and brought herself back to the present. "Vince kept repeating the words to me, slowly, so I could recite them as well. I may not have them down exactly, but I'll never forget. It was sexy enough just to hear him speak Italian, but when he told me what the sentence meant, I think it's embedded into my mind. It was the most romantic night of my life, Jay Kay."

Who would have ever expected such passion from my kindly old doctor? If I hadn't been buried in Malone's arms all night long, I might have been envious. I wondered if Malone could speak another language.

MARK LOVE

# CHAPTER FOUR

"Jay Kay, grab your wallet and your workout gear," Linda's voice was way too excited for my serenity. "It's time to hit the gym. We can sign up for classes tonight and start getting back in shape."

It was the third day of January and I had been writing most of the day. Now I looked up and realized it was almost dark outside. Malone had cooked French toast for brunch with crispy bacon on the side. Before he left for work, he'd put together a big garden salad for dinner. There was also half of a roasted chicken from last night's meal in the fridge. "What's wrong with the shape I'm in?" I asked, standing up and checking my reflection in the window.

Linda laughed warmly in my ear. "Nothing's wrong with you. But we could both use a little muscle toning. And if you want to keep Malone's attention, you need to get some physical activity outside of the bedroom."

"Does wrestling on the 'aunt' with Malone count?"

"Only if you can sustain your heart rate for sixty minutes," Linda said.

"But it's so nice and warm and cozy here. I don't want to go out in the cold."

"Stop being a wimp, Jay Kay. I'll be there in ten minutes."

It was pointless to argue with her. I'd be the first one to admit how stubborn I was. But Linda can take stubbornness to a whole new level. When she made up her mind, there was nothing that could talk her out of it. And deep down, I knew she was right. I had gotten lazy and the workout would probably do me some good.

After switching off the computer, I dashed into the bedroom for my gear. All I needed was a quick change into yoga pants, an exercise tank top, sweat socks, and gym shoes. Then I pulled my hair into a ponytail and dug out a hoodie. I grabbed my down jacket, wallet, and keys just as Linda pulled up in the driveway. It took only a minute to lock the doors and run out to her car. She was bundled up against the chill as well, her curls pulled back with a wide headband. In the rack on the dash were two water bottles.

"Check out the schedule on the seat, Jay Kay," she said as she focused on driving. I dug the listing out from under my leg and looked at the classes she had highlighted.

"So you've narrowed it down to these three," I said, "Yoga, kickboxing, and Latin dance. I don't know what the last two are. Which one are we going to take?"

A devilish smile crossed her face. "We're taking all three."

"You can't be serious."

"I am definitely serious. The new gym offers a variety of classes and they have a lot of equipment available that we can use as well. There's also a pool, in case you want to swim."

"But Algae, three classes are too much. Are you planning on working out daily?"

She rolled her eyes at me. "Get real, Jay Kay. Each class only meets once a week. But in order to really get the most out of the season, we can go more often. The best schedule for me is Tuesday and Thursday evenings and Saturday morning. There's no way I want to work out

Friday night and we'll consider Sunday to be off limits. So this makes perfect sense."

I had no response to that. Despite my protests, I knew she was right. It would be easier to get into the habit of working out now, to keep the figures we had, rather than waking up one day and discovering my clothes were too tight. I also had an ulterior motive. I wanted to maintain Malone's interest. He seemed to like my body the way it was, so I had every intention of keeping it that way.

Linda explained what kickboxing and Latin dance were. Apparently, kickboxing is an exercise program focusing on the body's core—building strength and flexibility without adding bulk. Latin dance is more of a party than an aerobics class, where dance moves are incorporated with Latin rhythms. Linda tried it while she was in Raleigh and loved it. She claimed it was the most fun she'd ever had working out. I didn't see how the two could possibly be mixed.

We parked at the new gym and hurried inside. At the reception desk, we registered for all three classes. We posed for gym ID badges and handed over our credit cards for the charges. Linda had even brought a padlock with her so we could secure our jackets in a locker just outside the classroom. All told, it was relatively painless, until we went into the classroom.

Inside we found a group of about a dozen women of various shapes, ages, and sizes milling about. Soon, a short girl with a thick blonde ponytail said it was time we got started. We got into orderly rows and began with a series of stretches. I was grateful for the fact she was not an anorexic model wearing a leotard that could have doubled as a cocktail napkin. This girl actually had some meat on her frame, and some very toned muscles.

"My name's Madeline and I'll be leading this class every week. We'll start out slowly and add a bit more difficulty each time." She had a way of bouncing on her toes while she talked. I wondered if she ever stopped moving.

"I teach several classes here, so on occasion I'll mix things up. I guarantee that by the time you're done with the class tonight, you'll know you've been through a workout."

True to her word, she began to put us through our paces. It turned out that since she taught both the kickboxing and yoga classes, she combined the best of both sessions. So we spent the first half-hour doing stretches and exercises that focused on the trunk of the body. When we hit the second part of the class, Madeline had us get into a yoga position.

"Yoga is about the mind, the body, and the spirit," Madeline said as she dropped to a mat and folded herself into a lotus position. "It's a way to relax, to go within. Think of it as meditation with some movement."

"If I get folded like that, there won't be any movement," I muttered to Linda.

"Don't worry, Jay Kay. I saw a crowbar out in the hall. I can pry you apart."

Obviously I wasn't going to get any sympathy from her. Somehow we survived the first class. At the end, Madeline had us all on our backs with our arms out to the side, eyes closed, trying to clear our minds. She moved around the room and lightly rubbed lavender oil on the base of our necks. It was supposed to help with the relaxation efforts. I think it worked.

Afterward, Linda and I walked around the new gym to see what else was available. It was a two-story structure with several basketball courts, a running track, four classrooms for aerobic classes, an Olympic sized pool, and more. In just about every available space there were different exercise machines, like stationary bicycles and treadmills. On the first floor, by the basketball courts, there was another area filled with even more machines as well as free weights, barbells, and other equipment. Madeline spotted our confusion and took a few minutes to show us around. Another corner even had a gymnastics room. The last stop was the adult lounge. Here were a couple of vinyl couches, a large television screen, a pool table, and several computers. Madeline led us back to the classroom, where we retrieved our coats from the locker. By now it was after six o'clock and the place quickly filled up with a mixture of adults and teenagers.

"Is it always this busy?" I asked.

Madeline smiled and raised her eyebrows. "This time of year, we get a lot of people who made resolutions to get in shape. Usually by February, it will thin out as about half of them start coming up with excuses why they don't need to work out. Mornings are better. You'll see the same crowd of people in here just about every day."

I noticed several men paying close attention to Linda. If she really came here three times a week, there was liable to be a rash of whiplash incidents.

"Most of the guys are pretty cool. Bottom line is they're here for a workout, too. Some of them are very serious about it." Madeline shrugged her muscular shoulders. "Of course, there are always a few poseurs. They just try to chat up the girls."

Linda and I exchanged a glance. "Do they take your classes?"

Madeline laughed. "Most of the guys wouldn't be caught dead doing yoga. We do get a few. Relax. Even if you get here early and want to loosen up a bit before the class, they won't bother you." With that, she waved and walked away.

"Just keep your sweatshirt on, Algae, and they won't even know you're here."

"I'm not worried, Jay Kay. Suddenly my romance calendar is filled."

Who would have thought such an innocent comment could lead to so much trouble?

\* \* \* \*

Malone was pleased to learn that Linda was succeeding in dragging my body to the gym for regular workouts. He was all in favor of physical fitness. He went to the gym about five times a week, getting in his workout before he started his shift. Since he was usually at work in the evenings, it wasn't difficult to get myself out of the house. But Saturday mornings were a very different story.

I was burrowed under the quilts, enjoying the sensation of my bare legs against Malone's. I started out last evening wearing a pair of emerald green, silk pajamas my mother had sent for Christmas. But shortly after Malone had come home from work, the pajama bottoms disappeared. The last thing I remembered, I had been innocently dozing on the 'aunt'. Then, a very amorous man was awakening me. Now, for the life of me, I had no idea where my clothing ended up.

"Otis, what did you do with my bottoms?" I whispered.

Malone's response was to turn gently in my direction and slide one hand down to cup my ass. "Here it is, Jamie, right where it should be. Just the way I like it, warm, naked, and next to me."

I giggled as he pulled me closer. "Not *my* bottom, Otis, my pajama bottoms."

He groaned and snaked an arm outside of the quilt. "Maybe they are in the hall, or maybe not. But you don't really need them now, do you?"

"I have to get dressed, Otis. Linda will be here soon. I don't want to give her ideas about what went on last night." Reluctantly, I pushed away from him and stepped out of the bed. The wooden floor was cool beneath my feet. I glanced across the room at the tri-fold mirror on the dresser. The pajama top was completely unbuttoned. It was long enough to just barely cover my buns. I wondered for a moment if that was the intention. A glance at the clock confirmed Linda would be here shortly. I pulled fresh underwear, workout pants, and an exercise tank top from the dresser. I had just enough time to wash up and brush my teeth. As I was slipping into my clothes, I sprayed perfume on the pajama top and placed it in the proximity of Malone's head.

"This will have to keep you company until I return, Otis."

He groaned again, pulling the blankets down enough to expose his face. He drew the silk top close and inhaled the fragrance. Then, before I could step away, Malone bolted out of the bed and grabbed me. He was covering me with kisses when the doorbell rang.

"I knew a Saturday morning class was a bad idea," I gasped, trying halfheartedly to get away from him.

Malone stopped kissing me for a moment. "Exercise is important. Why don't you and Linda come back here after class? I'll cook brunch."

I loved it when Malone cooked. And there was something sexy about a man who was confident in the kitchen.

"You've got a deal. Now you'd better get back in bed before Linda peeks in the window and gets a thrill."

He gave me one final kiss and released me.

I went to the front door to let Linda in while I found my coat, scarf, and gloves. She gave me a hug and started laughing at me.

"What's so funny?" I asked.

"Did you have a pleasant evening?" Linda asked as she struggled to maintain an innocent expression.

"It was very peaceful. What makes you ask?"

She pointed over my shoulder. My pajama bottoms were dangling from a blade of the ceiling fan. No wonder I couldn't find them this morning. I felt my face grow warm as Linda laughed again.

"Whose idea was it to work out on Saturday mornings anyway?" I grumbled.

Linda gave me a gentle shove toward the door. "Don't complain, Jay Kay. You're not the only one who left a handsome man in a toasty warm bed this morning."

The gym was packed Saturday morning. One of the reasons we rode together was so we wouldn't be fighting to find two parking spaces. It was below zero that morning. We ran from the car to get inside the building. After swiping our badges to enter the facility, we had to wait for a crowd that was milling around the aerobics rooms.

Apparently all of the classes on Saturdays were busy.

Today was our Latin dance class. There were about fifteen women hovering near the door of the classroom, waiting. Since we were a few minutes early, Linda and I decided to walk around the track a few times to limber up. I told her about Malone's offer to cook for us. Linda widened her eyes in delight.

"Did he say what he was making? I've got a taste for one of those omelets you had on New Year's Day. Or maybe some Belgian waffles."

"He didn't give me a clue. Do you want me to call him and place your order?"

She playfully slapped my arm. "It's not a problem, Jay Kay. I'm sure Malone will create something tasty."

"He usually does. That's why I keep him around."

"Bullshit. You keep him around because he's got your hormones in overdrive. Name one other guy who ever dangled your jammies from a ceiling fan?"

I felt my face grow warm again. "You know damn well I've never had this much fun before."

"So admit that the cooking is just a bonus."

"Okay, Malone's culinary skills are a wonderful extra. What about Vince? Do you think he'll cook for you?"

Linda's eyes were twinkling. "So far we've only been cooking in the bedroom. And that's fine with me. Unlike some people I know, I have my own talents in the kitchen. But I'm going to dust off my Italian cookbooks."

I could see the others going into the classroom. We finished our lap on the track and joined them. Inside was a willowy girl in her early twenties who didn't have an ounce of fat on her body. Her dark hair was cut very short. Her voice was a little deep and had a raspy quality to it. At least there was some part of her that wasn't perfect.

"My name is Gigi. Welcome to beginning Latin dance. We'll crank up the music and get started on the moves. I have to warn you that we'll go pretty much non-stop for the whole hour. So if you need to take a break and grab some water, go ahead."

Linda rolled her eyes at me. Somehow her description of a dance party didn't sound like it was going to match the actual class.

Gigi put us slowly through our paces. Certain music triggered certain moves. We had formed three rows and everyone was stumbling through some of the steps in the beginning. I was surprised at how quickly we were working up a sweat. By the end of the hour, most of us were laughing as much as we were moving.

We walked out with the others to grab our gear from the locker. I noticed more women waiting for the next class. There were also clusters of men, hovering around the exercise equipment, watching the women.

"It looks like happy hour at the bar," I said, flicking my gaze across the hall.

Linda pointed out that several of the women for the next class seemed to be dressed for the bar. We noticed two wearing eye makeup and one had on perfume. Perhaps this was their version of a singles bar. We pulled on our coats, oblivious to watching eyes, and ran home for brunch.

Malone did not disappoint us. When we walked in the back door, we were met with the heady aroma of freshly brewed coffee. He was leaning against the counter, freshly shaven, showered, barefoot in jeans and a thick black sweater. I got a kiss and pulled away from his arms.

"I'm all sweaty, Otis."

"Just the way I like you."

Linda laughed and pushed me toward him. "Do I have

time for a shower, or is our feast ready, Malone?"

"That depends on whether you want to take a thirty-minute shower or a five-minute shower?"

"It takes me twenty minutes just to wash this head of curls, Malone."

I saw a glimmer in his eyes as he glanced at her for an instant. Then he looked at me and gave me a squeeze.

"Let's eat."

Malone had been very busy. On the table was a basket of homemade blueberry muffins, still warm from the oven. There was also a large bowl of fresh fruit with sections of grapefruit, oranges, and strawberries. Warming in the oven was a casserole dish with three half-moon shaped omelets. We sat around the table and dug in.

"What's in the omelet?" I asked, gingerly prodding mine with the fork.

Malone glanced at Linda then gave me one of those low voltage smiles. "It's food, Jamie. Eat it."

"But I want to know what's in it, Otis."

Linda took a bite and moaned in delight. "I'll take yours if you don't want it, Jay Kay."

"I didn't say I don't want it. I just want to know what's in it."

Malone just looked at me. "Taste it and you'll find out."

He knew I would give in. There's no way I couldn't try it. So tentatively, I dug out a wedge in the center. I tasted cheese, some kind of spicy sausage, and mushrooms. I liked it. So I took another bite, and another, until suddenly it was gone.

Malone topped off our coffee cups. Then he hooked his foot beneath my chair and dragged me closer. Linda smiled sweetly and sipped her coffee.

"Can I expect a feast like this every Saturday after our workout?" she asked.

Malone slowly shook his head. "Sorry, beautiful, but if I do this every week, Jamie will get spoiled."

"You can spoil me anytime you'd like, Otis," I said.

"Yes, but I'd rather keep you guessing when those moments might happen. If I cook for you like this all the time, it will become mundane."

I raised four fingers in a salute. "I promise never to take you for granted, Malone. Regardless of whatever name I call you."

He was about to respond when his cell phone rang. Malone's face darkened briefly as he checked the display. He excused himself and stepped into the living room to take the call.

"I think that's my cue to hit the showers, Jay Kay."

"Take your time, Algae."

She pulled the headband from her locks, shaking out those luxurious curls. "If I'm washing this mop, I don't have much choice."

Malone was sitting on the rocker, facing the kitchen. I saw him smile briefly at Linda as she turned the corner and blew him a kiss. But his expression quickly turned serious. I got busy loading all the dishes in the dishwasher and wrapping up the rest of the muffins. As I was finishing up, I caught a glimpse of Malone's reflection in the window just before he drew me into his arms.

"I've got to run out for a while, Jamie," he said softly, nuzzling my neck.

"Anything wrong, Otis?" I was having trouble drawing a deep breath.

"Nothing I can't take care of."

My voice was nothing more than a breathy whisper. "You keep kissing me like that, Otis, and you'd better be planning to take care of me before you go anywhere."

Slowly, he unwound me from his arms. "I'll make it up to you, Jamie."

"Don't leave me like this, Malone."

I heard the shower start up.

A mischievous gleam appeared in Malone's eye. "You really should get out of those sweaty clothes, Jamie."

Before I could muster an argument, or even take a step, he'd pulled me close again. Only this time, Malone was intent on removing my workout gear in record time. Where did he learn those moves? When he finally stepped away, I was completely undressed, perched on the edge of the kitchen counter. He gave me a long, lingering kiss that left me flustered and flushed. And with that, Malone grabbed his coat and stepped out into the cold.

"You'd better make this up to me, Otis," I said to thin air. "It will take me twenty minutes for my heart to calm down."

# CHAPTER FIVE

I would never admit this to Linda, but I enjoyed our workout sessions. There was enough variety in the classes to keep them interesting. With the weeknight classes starting at five o'clock, we were able to go out for a light dinner or a glass of wine afterward and still get home at a reasonable hour. Saturday's class didn't start until ten, so we could sleep in a bit.

After our first Tuesday night class, we decided to try some of the stationary bikes on the first floor. We found a couple of empty ones and started pedaling away. I made Linda a bet that she'd have a guy hitting on her within ten minutes. I was long by seven. He was an older, short, round guy who had lost the battle of his receding hairline and opted to keep the rest around his ears long. Even though Linda and I were having a conversation, he jumped right into the middle of it.

"Hi ladies, you must be new here."

Linda turned to him and said "Hi." Turning back to me, she said, "So anyway, these two kids are arguing over…"

"Don't let me interrupt you," he said, moving into a spot between the two machines so he could see both of us and we could see him. "I just wanted to welcome you to the gym."

"Do you work here?" I asked.

"No, I just come in here to work out." He answered my question, but his eyes never left Linda.

"Well, don't let us keep you," I said. "So what were these kids arguing about?"

"Whether or not it's ethical to cheat on an exam if you can get the information in advance on the Internet."

The guy wasn't taking the hint. "So if you need any help with anything, just let me know. My name's Mike."

Linda blew out a breath and turned her full attention to the guy. "Thanks, Mike, we'll keep that in mind. Now if you don't mind, my friend and I were talking."

If he was embarrassed, he didn't seem to show it. Maybe he was too dense to realize it. "Oh, right. Well, I'd better get to my workout."

"You do that," Linda said, smiling sweetly.

Finally he took the hint and walked away. Not thirty feet away was another woman grinding away on an elliptical machine. He didn't hesitate. He jumped onto the machine beside her and started talking before he even got the pedals moving.

"Do you believe that guy?" I said.

"Just because he's wearing a tank top and the same shorts he's probably owned since junior high and it is four degrees outside doesn't mean he might not be a nice guy."

"He reminds me of a monk with that haircut," I said. "And he interrupted us twice within two minutes. That's got to be a record."

Linda looked at me and smiled wickedly. "Let's call him Mikeus Interruptus. Monks should know Latin, right?"

I laughed so hard I almost fell off the bicycle.

When we were kids, we started tagging people with nicknames. We never called them by those names, but it was our way of identifying the person with some distinguishing characteristic. Linda was pretty sharp at it.

She often comes up with the perfect name in the blink of an eye. Mikeus Interruptus sounded like an impatient monk. It fit perfectly.

We decided that every Tuesday we would put in an extra half hour on the bikes or some other machine, provided we could find two side by side. This would give us a chance to catch up and burn a few more calories in the process. And to give the workout some fun, we would start to name some of the regulars.

The time went by fast. We finished our half-hour, grabbed our gear from the lockers, and bundled up to face the cruel, January weather. I could see the eyes checking her out.

We decided to stop for some soup and a glass of wine on the way. Well, she had wine and I had a glass of tonic water with a lime. I had been patient, trying to give Linda the time to tell me on her own, but I couldn't wait any longer. Once we'd placed our orders, I leaned across the table and studied her closely.

"What's wrong?" she asked, self-consciously brushing her hair away from her face with the back of her hand.

"Just checking to see if you're still getting laid," I said.

Linda cupped her chin in her right palm. "That's very cute. Things are very good. We're keeping it casual; maybe one or two times a week we get together."

"So come on, tell me all about it. I want details, Algae."

She shook her head slightly. "Jay Kay, do I ask you about the sexual activity between you and Malone?"

"Of course you do!"

"And you're just crazy enough to tell me." Linda took a sip of her wine and sat back. "Vince and I are very compatible. He's very tender. And he certainly knows how to please a lady with his attentions."

"But, Algae, he's like sixty!"

She playfully flicked her fingers at me. "Actually, he's only fifty-two. And it's not so uncommon to find an older man attractive. Look at all those Hollywood guys who trade in their wives every five years to get a younger model. Did you know that in Europe it's very common for a younger woman to be involved with an older man? They say the older men are much more together. Vince is very passionate. He's charming and considerate and incredibly thoughtful. He has the energy of a man half his age. And that's all I'm going to say about that."

"Algae, are you trying to tell me he's more passionate than guys our age?"

She sighed and stared at me. "You're not going to leave this alone, are you?"

I shook my head. "I've known you forever. I've seen a lot of the men you've dated over the years. Handsome, successful businessmen, attorneys, professors, and God can only know what else. And you're going to tell me that Vince outshines all these studs?"

Linda cupped her chin in her palm again. It was a posture I've seen often over the years, accompanied by that twinkle in her eyes when she knew she'd gotten you. Just like now.

"Vince is the most romantic man I've ever been with. The other night we went out to dinner at a little café in Novi. He knows how much I like to dance, so we went dancing afterward."

"Algae, you've gone dancing with other guys before."

She smiled sweetly. "Yes, I have. But Vince took me to a little place where there was just a piano player, a guitarist, and a vocalist. They played all these old, romantic songs. And we were the only ones in the club. He booked the room just for us."

I opened my mouth to respond but nothing came out. She was right.

"And he taught me another phrase in Italian. '*Poi mi ha detto che ero l'angelo che aveva atteso per venti anni*'.

"What's that one mean?" I asked quietly.

"I am the angel he's been waiting twenty years for. I tell you, Jay Kay, he doesn't need a broom to sweep me off my feet. I am already there."

* * * *

On the nights that Linda and I didn't go to exercise classes, we usually just did our own thing. Some nights I was with Malone if he wasn't working. Since we had gotten involved, I adjusted my work schedule to match his. That meant I would sleep a little later in the morning and went to sleep around one in the morning. Okay, so he was normally home by a little after eleven.

It was a Thursday, a couple of weeks after we first started working out. Linda suggested we stop for a coffee and pastry on our way home. I was looking forward to a Creole dish Malone made, but I knew she wanted to talk about something. During our class I noticed that her smile was even brighter than normal. Apparently something had been going on.

So we pulled into a coffee shop that she likes to frequent. I got a slice of iced lemon loaf and a cup of tea. Linda got a vanilla coffee and a raspberry muffin. I waited until we were seated at a little table far from the doorway or anyone else.

"So are you going to tell me what's going on, Algae? You've been beaming a thousand-watt smile since you picked me up."

I saw the color radiate on her cheeks. She lowered her eyes and took a sip of her coffee. I waited. Finally, she drew a deep breath and raised her face.

"I think I'm in love," she said quietly.

I sat back in amazement. This was the same woman, who, not three weeks ago, had sworn that they were just getting to know each other, just going to take it slow. Suddenly she was talking love. Before I could respond, she waved a hand at me.

"Just be quiet and listen, Jay Kay. I know that's difficult for you, but please just hear me out."

I tore a corner off the pastry and popped it into my mouth, then closed my eyes to savor the lemony sweetness and let it dissolve on my tongue. I imagined this was how a sunbeam would taste. When it was gone, I opened my eyes and gazed at her. I extended my right hand and just looked at her.

"Vince came over last night. I wanted to cook for him, so I made shrimp with angel hair pasta. You know the way I do it, with mushrooms, red peppers and fresh parmesan cheese."

My stomach growled. It's one of her signature dishes. I started to comment but Linda waved me quiet.

"So we had some good, Italian wine, a white one that really went well with the pasta. The stereo was on, something soft like Diana Krall and Van Morrison. After dinner, we moved to the sofa. The fire was lit and one light was on low. I had been in a bit of rush to get dinner ready when I came home from work, so I hadn't bothered to change."

She paused to sip her coffee. I couldn't keep quiet. "What were you wearing?"

"You know that turquoise sweater with the cowl neck?"

I nodded. It does magical things for her eyes.

"That and a black wool skirt, some stockings and those black leather boots that come up to mid-calf."

Linda loves boots. She has several pairs and usually likes the ones with a two-inch heel. I knew exactly the outfit she was describing. It could stop traffic any time of the day or night. Like she couldn't do that already! I waited for her to continue. She took another taste of her coffee and then started talking quietly again.

"So we're on the sofa, sitting there, just listening to the music. He had an arm draped over my shoulders. And I mentioned that I had to get out of my boots. My feet were starting to cramp. That's when things got...different."

I wasn't sure I wanted to hear this, but there was no

stopping her now. "What do you mean, different?" I asked.

"Vince told me to move to the other end of the sofa. Then he slowly unzipped my boots and pulled them off me. My legs were on his lap. He started to massage my feet, chasing away the aches and pains. Then he moved up to my ankles. And the whole time, he just kept talking, keeping his voice very low and soft."

"What did he say?"

Linda shuddered with the memory. "He told me all of the things he was going to do to me, all the ways he wanted to please me."

I pulled back the sleeve of her jacket. Her arm was covered in goose bumps. "Do you really want to tell me this, Algae?"

"I've got to tell you because I still can't believe it happened. It was like I was hypnotized. He was in total control of me. I couldn't even move."

Somehow no words found their way out of my mouth. I just stared at her so she kept talking.

"I swear he touched on every fantasy, no matter how dark, I have ever considered. And the whole time, he just kept talking softly, massaging my legs. I thought I was melting from his charms on New Year's Eve. That was nothing compared to last night. Jay Kay, by the time he finally undressed me, I was so far over the edge, I didn't think I'd ever make it back."

I would have never believed my good and kindly doctor would be capable of fulfilling all her fantasies. And even if I had, I could never have imagined how dark these fantasies would turn out to be.

\* \* \* \*

Malone had been acting strange for the last three weeks. He seemed a little tense some days, but when I tried to ask him what was bothering him, he'd just quietly shrug, give me half a smile, and shake his head. This was not like Malone.

Occasionally, his phone would ring. Most of the time it was a friend or one of the guys from the post and he would take the call even if I was curled up next to him on the 'aunt', watching a movie. But once in a while, he'd glance at the display screen and step into the kitchen to take the call. I swore I'd heard a woman's voice, but couldn't tell for certain. Sometimes he would leave right after getting one of those calls, telling me he had an errand to run. I started thinking about that first Saturday in January when he'd gotten a call right after we'd had brunch with Linda. Was there something I was missing? Something I was too blind to see? Was I doing something wrong? I didn't want to press him, but it was a little unnerving.

My imagination was getting the better of me. As we were leaving our yoga class on a Tuesday night, I mentioned it to Linda. She pulled me aside, away from the bustling women, now dripping with sweat, racing for the parking lot.

"You're worried about Malone?" she asked in disbelief. "What could there possibly be to worry about? He's gorgeous, treats you like a fairy princess, has a good job, and can cook. What more do you want, Jay Kay?"

We stepped into the adult lounge, where several couches sat around a plasma screen television that was always turned to sports. No one else was in the room. I found the remote and clicked it off.

"I'm worried there might be another woman," I said feebly.

Linda burst out laughing. "You are so paranoid. When would Malone have the time, the energy, or the inclination to be involved with another woman?"

"I don't know," I said defensively. "It's just that sometimes, he gets really thoughtful and quiet. And it usually happens after he gets one of these strange phone calls. How do I fix this?"

Linda looked at me like I was nuts. "First off, who said there's something wrong? Second, if there is, what makes you think it's something you can fix by yourself? Third, have you tried to talk to Malone about this?"

I couldn't meet her eyes. I kicked the edge of the chair she was sitting on and then studied my gym shoes. Linda just sat there, patiently waiting. "I'm afraid if I press it, I'll ruin what we've got going."

"Jay Kay, there could be a million reasons why he's thoughtful and quiet. You just need to trust Malone. Let him know that if something is bothering him, whether it's about work, or home, or something else, he needs to know that you're there for him. Don't jump to conclusions."

"You're right," I said with a sigh. "I'm just nervous. I don't want to do anything to drive Malone away."

"Then don't start getting crazy on him. Talk to him. Get him in a weak moment, like when he's naked, and talk to him."

It was my turn to laugh out loud. "I have a hard time talking when he's naked."

Linda flashed me a devilish smile. "That's perfectly understandable."

Now I felt foolish. Maybe I was making a big deal out of nothing. But Linda knows me better than anyone else. She even told me so as she led me back out to a couple of treadmills.

"Jay Kay, think of me as an objective third party. You know I love you both. But you have to keep in mind that living together is a big step for the two of you. I know for a fact you've never done it before. What about Malone?" She strengthened her case.

"He was married briefly years ago, but has been divorced for a long time. Since then I don't know if he's lived with anybody or has always had his own place."

"So this could be part of the adjustment. Think about it, Jay Kay. You've known this guy less than six months and already you're living together. That's pretty damn quick for most people. I've known marriages that haven't lasted that long."

"When you put it that way, we have been on the fast track," I said thoughtfully.

"You keep saying you don't want to scare Malone away. Then you need to be able to give him some room. This has to be an adjustment for him as well. Nine months ago, you guys didn't even know each other. Now you're both swept up in this whirlwind romance, playing house."

"Well, he's definitely romantic."

"Jay Kay, you've gone from the occasional date to a full-fledged living arrangement. You're like a couple of teenagers who discovered a copy of the *Joy of Sex* and can't wait to try out the positions."

It's a good thing we were on the treadmills and away from anyone else. I had to bite my lip to keep from giggling at her comment.

"Am I right?" Linda asked when I failed to respond.

"I seem to have misplaced that book. Could I borrow your copy?"

She innocently batted her lashes at me. "No."

We finished up and gathered our coats from the locker. We didn't stop for coffee or soup. Linda had some papers to grade and wanted to get back home. She gave me a hug when she dropped me off and whispered encouraging words about my situation with Malone. One of her suggestions was downright sinful. I'd keep it in mind for another day.

* * * *

I waited up for him. I'd lit the fire and was enjoying the snap and crackle of the birch logs as they sizzled on the grate. I was wearing jeans, a thick sweater, and my furry slippers. There was a mug of hot apple cider on the table, but I'd lost interest in it. Malone came in through the back door. After shedding his boots and his coat, he joined me on the 'aunt'. I had been sitting up with my feet propped on the table. Once he sat down, the sofa worked its magic and we were pressed together.

"Hello, Barnaby," I said as he pulled me down for a kiss.

"Hello, Jamie. How was yoga class?"

"I feel taller and more flexible. You wouldn't believe some of the poses they make us do. I think this is how pretzels were invented."

Malone shifted, swinging his legs up onto the sofa. We were sprawled on it now, sinking deeper into those comfy cushions. I was quiet, enjoying the sensation of my head on Malone's chest, his arms wrapped tenderly around me. We were both staring into the fire, watching the flames dance.

"Are we okay, Barnaby?" I asked softly.

He kissed the top of my head. "I'd say we're light years beyond okay, Jay. Why do you ask?"

"I noticed that you seem distant sometimes, like there is something troubling you. If there is, I hope you'll tell me."

He squeezed me closer. "Jamie, it's just something I've got to work out."

"Maybe I can help, Malone."

"Do you trust me, Jamie?"

It was something he asked me at the strangest times. I gave him my standard answer. "Mostly."

There was a lengthy silence. It felt like a flock of butterflies had just invaded my stomach. I wanted him to talk to me to let me help him. But I'd made the initial offer. I couldn't force Malone to talk to me any more than I could force him to eat my cooking.

"I just need a little time, Jay," he said at last.

"Take as much time as you need, Barnaby. Just make sure you'll be right here with me. And remember that I'm right here, too."

Somehow his hands had found their way beneath my sweater. "I'm not going anywhere, Jay."

"That's what I was hoping to hear, Barnaby."

# CHAPTER SIX

It was the first Saturday morning in February. Linda picked me up at nine-thirty to go to our Latin dance class. How in the world I ever agreed to such physical activity, without Malone, I will never understand. But she can be so very persuasive. Malone mumbled a brief greeting from underneath the blankets as I pulled on my exercise gear.

After class, we went to a coffee shop Linda likes. We splurged on low-fat muffins and tea, none of those thousand-calorie ice cream flavored lattes for us today. It gave us the chance to catch our breath after class and have some serious girl talk. I reassured Linda that I had taken her advice and talked with Malone. She seemed satisfied with his responses. That gave me the opportunity to change the subject.

"So how are things at school?"

Linda smiled slyly. "School is going well. In some respects, you'd think I hadn't been gone the last ten weeks of classes in the fall. But I've got a pretty good mixture of students. And they all appear to have adjusted very quickly to my return."

"So life is back to normal for you?"

"Jay Kay, subtlety has never been your strong suit. If

65

you're curious about something, just ask me," Linda said.

"Okay, I'm curious as hell. You and Vince seem to have become very compatible. And I'm just wondering how you do it."

She actually gave me a very innocent look. "Do what?"

"Keep him interested and keep the romance going. You practically glow from within every time I see you after you've been together."

"I haven't got the slightest idea what you're talking about."

"Algae, how can you say that? Don't you notice a change when you look in the mirror?" I was starting to feel exasperated.

She took a minute to think about it, calmly sipping her tea. "I am happy. Being with Vince makes me happy. I don't analyze it, or try to figure out different ways to keep him interested. I am interested in him as a person and he's interested in me. Everything else that happens just sort of flows from that."

"So you're not going to tell me your secrets?"

"Jay Kay, it's not a secret. We like each other, we talk to each other and we're just letting things slowly take their own course. Neither one of us has a road map we're following. Some nights we're just spontaneous. And I really like that."

I looked at her in amazement for a minute. Could it really be that easy? The key to happiness is just to be yourself and let fate or nature take its course? I wondered if that would work for me. But I don't have Linda's self-confidence. Yet everything about her and Vince seemed so right.

I was still trying to figure out a way to capture some of her powers when we left the coffee shop and headed for home.

Malone's Cherokee was in the driveway, close to the garage. Linda parked and we went in the side door of the house. From here, it was one step up to the right to go into the kitchen. But if you go straight ahead, you were moving down a flight of stairs to a partially finished basement. It runs the width of the house, so a good forty feet from one wall to the other. We hung our coats on the landing. There were strange noises coming from the basement and the lights were on. Linda and I exchanged a glance then headed downstairs to investigate.

In the center of the room near the far wall was a large wooden table. It had to be at least eight feet long. Sticking out from beneath the table were two pairs of denim covered legs. I recognized Malone's tennis shoes on one set of feet. There were black and red sneakers on the other. They were talking quietly. On the floor by Malone's side was a heavy toolbox.

"Dexter, what in the world is going on?" I said.

Malone waved his right foot at me. "We're busted, kid. Guess we'd better go out and face the music."

Linda leaned against me, one hand on her hip, the other resting on my shoulder. "This ought to be good."

We watched them squirm out from beneath the table. Malone got to his feet and dusted off his hands. Beside him rose a gangly teenage boy, with a mop of thick, black hair hanging over his eyes. When he straightened up, he was almost as tall as Malone. He wasn't looking our way. Instead, his eyes remained on Malone.

"Hey, Jamie. Ian and I were just putting together our new pool table. Ian, this is Jamie and Linda."

The boy slowly turned his attention our way. He was painfully shy and his eyes were on the floor. Malone nudged him and he looked up.

"Wow!" he said in a voice that hadn't cleared puberty yet, his eyes practically jumping out of their sockets.

Linda and I were still in our workout gear. Turns out that we had both opted for the tank tops with a little extra support built in, so neither of us was wearing a bra. While my pants were nylon, they weren't as clingy as the Lycra ones Linda had worn. Hers could have been spray painted on. I started to blush and Linda let loose with a laugh.

"Where are your manners?" Malone asked, giving Ian a light slap to the back of the head.

Linda pushed away from me and moved toward the kid. "Leave him alone, Malone. That's the nicest compliment I've had all week." She reached for his hand. "I'm Linda. It's nice to meet you, Ian."

The kid's eyes were still huge as he gently shook her hand. It was an effort for him to look at me, but I'm used to that reaction when Linda's around. I gave him my hand as well and he clung to it while taking a step closer.

"Malone told me you were pretty," Ian said.

"Dexter has been known to exaggerate on occasion," I said with a smile. I realized Ian was extremely nervous as I eased my hand free.

A look of confusion crossed his face. "Who's Dexter?"

Now Malone and Linda were laughing. Malone was leaning against the table, hands at his side. Linda was perched beside him. "Go ahead, Jamie," Malone said.

I explained the situation to Ian, how I keep giving Malone different names in the hope of discovering his real first name. Ian's confusion faded. "But I know his name."

"You do?" I asked in disbelief. Could it really be this easy?

"Mister." The kid shrugged. "Mr. Malone. When no one else is around, I can call him Malone though."

Malone didn't even bother to subdue his grin. Linda let loose with another round of laughs. "Give it up, Jamie," she said.

"I will never give up." I decided to change the subject. "Malone, where did this pool table come from?"

He waved me over. It wasn't just an ordinary pool table. It was an antique billiard table. Malone explained that Leo Billings, one of the troopers he worked with, restored old furniture as a hobby. Billings found this table and stripped it down to its original mahogany. Then he'd painstakingly brought the wood to a gleaming luster. With new green felt and webbing for the pockets, he now had a beautiful table. Trouble was, Billings had no place for it at his own house and didn't even shoot pool. Knowing we had plenty of space in the basement, Malone decided to splurge and surprise me. Billings delivered the table in sections this morning. Malone and Ian were just finishing with the assembly.

Linda disappeared up the steps to grab a shower and change into some jeans. I watched the guys put the last touches on the table. Ian grabbed a broom and was sweeping the linoleum. Malone came over and gave me a kiss.

"I've got to run Ian home, Jamie. But I'll be back if you and Linda want to grab some lunch before my shift."

I looked him closely in the eye. "Lunch sounds good, Dexter."

He nodded and started to pull away. I grabbed him around the waist and whispered in his ear. "Where did this young man come from?"

"It's a long story, Jamie. But it's a really good one. Go get cleaned up. I'll be back in half an hour."

I sighed and shook my head. "Malone, I'll still be naked in half an hour."

He gave me a lecherous grin. "I'll be back in twenty minutes."

\* \* \* \*

Linda finished her shower and was using the spare bathroom to dry her hair and change. I raced to the master suite and freshened up with an abbreviated shower. Normally, I could luxuriate under a hot spray for at least twenty minutes, given the opportunity. But Malone was extremely punctual. If he said he'd be back in half an hour, I knew he'd be true to his word. For some reason, I thought that if I wasn't ready, he might use that as an excuse to not tell me about Ian. I didn't want to give him any opportunities to delay.

My hair was still damp, but I was getting dressed in black jeans and a bright gold sweater. Linda was sitting on the edge of my bed, watching me wiggle into my jeans.

"Jay Kay, maybe I should take off so you and Malone can talk," Linda said quietly.

"No way, Algae, Malone said he's taking both of us out to lunch. Besides, he knows how close we are. Whatever he's going to tell me about this young man, he knows you'll be the first one I talk to."

She nodded in agreement. By now, Malone understood the extent of our relationship. Although I hoped he didn't realize how intimate some of the details were that we shared.

"Do you think he's Malone's son?" Linda asked.

I was frozen in place. The thought hadn't crossed my mind. "No. Malone would have told me about a son before now. Wouldn't he?"

"That's not a question I can answer."

"I sure hope Malone can."

Now my imagination was running rampant. My curiosity kicked into overdrive and I tried to come up with reasonable scenarios as to who this teenage boy was and what his relationship with Malone was. As quickly as I formulated one version, I would discard it as preposterous. Linda had gotten quiet. We were both lost in our own thoughts when he finally returned. Malone suggested a new place for lunch. We locked up the house and drove silently out to eat.

We were sitting in a semi-circle booth in the back of a Thai restaurant about a mile from the post. Malone would go directly from here to work. Linda followed in her car, since we had some things we were going to do this evening. I maneuvered Malone into the back of the booth, with Linda on one side of him and me on the other. There was no way he was getting out of here without telling us the story.

We ordered Pad Thai and Bangkok noodles and a whole slew of other dishes. I knew Linda and I would probably skip dinner after this meal, so we were going to enjoy the feast. I just hoped that Malone's story wouldn't negatively impact my appetite. I really like Thai food.

With mugs of tea before us and the orders placed, Linda and I fell silent. We both stared at Malone. He calmly sipped his tea. Then he looked at each of us slowly. One of those soft smiles that usually I find so irresistible was dancing at the edge of his eyes. We waited.

"I suppose you want to know about Ian," he said quietly, as if he were discussing the weather.

"No shit, Dexter. That's why you're such a good cop." I reached over and took his hand, just for good measure. "Who is he, where did he come from, what's your relationship with him, and where does he live when he's not assembling pool tables would all be good questions to answer."

"Jay Kay, give him a chance to explain."

His fingers were rough and chapped, but Malone held my hand lightly.

"It's not what you think, Jamie."

"Malone, right now, I don't know what to think."

He took another sip of his tea and leaned back. "I told you it was a long story. Guess it's time you heard it."

Suddenly, I wasn't sure that I wanted to.

Malone took his time. I realized that he had been working up to this for quite a while, trying to find the best way to tell me. By the time we got to the restaurant, I was expecting the worst. Turns out, it wasn't that bad.

For several years, Malone had been helping coach little league baseball for the city of Northville. He became good friends with several of the coaches, many of whom had kids on the teams. Malone started out with one group of eight-year-olds and kept with them as they advanced into junior high and this year, high school.

One of the coaches he'd befriended was a guy named

Asa MacKinnon. He was a real gregarious character, full of laughter and life, and he insisted each boy on the team got a chance to play. He instilled a winning spirit, but enforced the idea that the game itself was to be fun. He and Malone hit it off well.

MacKinnon's son was Ian. He was a good outfielder, with an arm like a rocket from deep center. While he had no illusions of becoming a major league player, young Ian enjoyed the game and the connection with his dad.

Just before school started, with Ian about to enter his freshman year of high school, his life resembled a carnival ride gone amuck.

While driving home from a business trip on a rainy summer night, Asa MacKinnon's car had been crushed in a multiple vehicle accident. By the time rescue units arrived and the tangle of semi-trucks and passenger cars undone, it was too late. Asa was dead. He left behind his wife Terri, Ian, and a daughter, Caitlin.

There were no other males in the MacKinnon clan that could offer support to Ian. Both of his grandfathers had passed away years ago. He had one uncle on his father's side, but he was a career officer in the army and stationed overseas. Terri had her hands full looking for work, trying to keep the family going, and focusing more on her daughter. Ian became an afterthought.

Malone stepped in.

The recent calls he had been getting were from Terri. She was distraught, not sure how to get through to Ian. He was despondent some days, angry at the universe on others. He had a few friends at school, but with the transition to high school, he was struggling. Before we started dating, Malone had spent a lot of time with Ian. Suddenly, Malone didn't have the free time. But now, he was determined to make it up to the kid.

"I realized after the first of the year that I'd let him down," Malone said quietly. "Between work and a certain demanding redhead, I suddenly couldn't find time for Ian.

And I felt like crap because of it."

I just stared at him for a moment. "Malone, why didn't you tell me?"

"I don't know, Jamie. We're still getting to know each other. We've come a long way in the last few months, but I didn't know how you'd react to a teenage boy hanging around."

Linda chose this moment to break the tension. "She's not afraid of a teenage boy, Malone, and neither am I."

"I realize that now. But I also wasn't sure how Ian would react to the two of you. I mean, you are sort of a package deal."

I was still holding Malone's hand as the waitress brought our food. Glancing across the table, I saw a wicked grin appear on Linda's face.

"Well, if you'd told us about him before, we probably wouldn't have met him today in our gym clothes. The poor kid's eyes nearly jumped out of his head."

Malone waited until the platters were spread around the table before commenting. "Yes, I probably should have warned you. But it worked out. There's just one more thing you need to be aware of, Linda."

"What's that?" she asked, scooping some Pad Thai onto her plate.

"Ian goes to the same school you teach at."

She paused with some spicy noodles hanging off her fork. "Great. So I just flashed my body at a member of the student body. Thanks a lot, Malone."

Linda ran out after lunch to warm up her car. I pulled Malone aside in the restaurant's alcove.

"What's your plan with Ian, Dexter?"

"What do you mean, Jay?"

"Do you want to get together with him once in a while, do testosterone type things like demolition derbies and sports? Or is there more to it?"

Malone shook his head. "I don't know. I'm sort of making this up as we go along. Asa was a good friend. And

Ian and I got along well before. But his mom is struggling to keep him in line. And he feels like she's suffocating him at times. It's still an adjustment for both of them."

"And it helps them if you're around?"

"Yes. I think it smooths the water for both of them."

Malone snuck a quick peek at his watch. "Jamie, I've got to run."

I gave him a tight hug. "You're a good guy, Dexter. I'll see you tonight."

We kissed for a long minute. Opening my eyes, I realized the restaurant staff was standing on the other side of the alcove, watching us. Waving good-bye, we dashed out into the cold.

Linda and I went back to her house. We spent some time with Logan, taking him for a long walk just before dark and quietly discussing this latest development with Malone. Now Linda and I were sprawled at opposite ends of the couch at her place. Logan was pacing the floor preparing to give chase to a runaway chipmunk should one suddenly appear.

"What are you thinking, Jay Kay?"

I shrugged.

"Well, now that you know about this, what exactly are you going to do about it?"

I didn't have a clue. "What should I do about it?"

Linda leaned forward and batted her lashes at me. "It seems to me there is a perfectly logical solution."

"And what might that be?"

Her smile lit up the room. "We go shopping."

\* \* \* \*

The Bentwood rocker creaked slightly beneath me. I was debating lighting the fire, but decided to save the wood for another time. Instead, I wrapped a quilt around my legs and slowly rocked away. I was wearing a soft, flannel nightgown that draped to my knees, and a lined, satin robe that almost reached my ankles. The stereo was on low, with some mellow Motown music, Marvin Gaye and Smokey Robinson. Linda had left about an hour ago, feeling very satisfied with herself and our efforts for the day. Upon reflection, it had been a good day.

Lights from the Cherokee swept in the window as Malone pulled into the driveway. I hoped his day at work had been uneventful. And I hoped he liked what we had done.

"Hey, Jamie," he said softly, appearing in the archway from the kitchen.

"Welcome home, Dexter."

He came over to the rocker and bent down to kiss me. My arms went around his neck on their own accord. I was beginning to think that's where they always belonged. Leaning back slightly, he got his strong hands beneath me and just that quickly, I was out of the chair and sprawled on the 'Jewish Aunt' with him.

"You know, it's very sweet that you wait up for me every night."

"Linda says Logan does the same thing. But I'd like to think I'm a bit cuter than fur face."

Malone grinned. "You are definitely cuter. And you have many other attributes that a dog could never compete with."

There wasn't much conversation for a while. He easily untied the sash on my robe and was busy kissing me, one hand sliding slowly up and down my bare leg. I could have waited until Sunday, but I wanted to spring my surprise on Malone. With an effort, I pushed him deep into the cushions and got to my feet.

"Something wrong, Jamie?" His voice was a little hoarse as he reached for me.

"No, Dexter. But I just need to get your opinion." I took his hand. Malone started to pull me back to the warmth of his arms, but I slowly shook my head. "First things first," I said.

He slipped off the sofa. Still holding his hand, I led Malone down the hall.

Our little house has three bedrooms. Originally, there were four small rooms, but the owner had knocked out a connecting wall between the two bedrooms at the front, creating a master suite complete with a full bath and walk-in closets. The other two rooms were across the hall at the back of the building. The smaller of the two I had set up as my office, with my computer, desk and file cabinets. I had yet to hang all the pictures on the walls, but it was a work in progress. It was the last room I guided Malone to. I reached inside and flicked on the light.

In the center of the room was the bed from Malone's apartment. His old dresser fit nicely against one wall. But it was the new addition that I wanted his opinion on.

Malone surveyed the room for a minute. "What's going on, Jay?"

"It's a desk, Malone, the perfect size for a student. And it comes with a comfortable chair, drawers for storing pencils and paper, and a shelf for a printer."

He turned slowly and looked at me. "What are you getting at, Jamie?"

I guided him to the bed and we sat on the edge. "Dexter, this is a spare bedroom. Linda has stayed here a couple of times since we moved everything in. But for the most part, this room doesn't get used. I just thought if we put a desk here, maybe Ian could stay over some nights. He could use the break from his mother and be able to spend more time with you."

"Jamie…"

"…He could put posters on the walls, hang some extra clothes in the closet and the dresser and…"

"Jamie."

"Yes, Dexter?"

"Don't you think we're jumping the gun here? I mean, he really belongs with his own family."

I realized I was still holding Malone's hand. Squeezing

it tighter, I leaned against him. "I'm not saying he could move in completely, but it might be a nice change for him if he's got someplace outside of home where he is comfortable. You guys can play pool, watch sports or do whatever you'd like. And with your schedule, sometimes it would be easier for him to crash here if you want to do something early in the morning."

He was quiet for a long time. I hoped he was considering it. If it bothered him, I could always say it was Linda's idea. I was afraid to break the silence. It seemed like every time I was feeling confident about our relationship, I did something that made me wonder if I was reading too much into it. Or maybe it was too soon. Just about the time I was going to make some wiseass comment, Malone let go of my hand and wrapped his arms around me.

"There's just one thing I worry about with this plan, Jay," Malone said.

"What's that?"

"Sometimes when we're being romantic, you get a little loud. What about the nights when Ian stays over?"

I wiggled onto Malone's lap. "We'll soundproof his room."

Apparently Malone wanted to take advantage of the fact that I was so close. He had his arms around me. Even through the fabric of his jeans, I could feel his body responding to mine. Malone's kisses were slowly driving me crazy. With one hand pressing me close, he pulled my robe open, drawing the sash free once more. Turning, Malone eased me onto the bed, moving me closer to the headboard. My body was on fire. I wanted to shed my robe and nightgown and feel Malone's skin on mine. But he had other ideas.

His kisses were incredible. He started out slowly, tenderly kissing his way around my face. On this night he started with my eyes, lightly kissing the lids. Then he moved across my cheekbones with a little more pressure.

Then his warm breath and lips were on the shell of my ear. He barely whispered my name at this point. Then he was nuzzling behind my ear, touching with his lips a spot so sensitive that I thought my heart might explode. It was as if Malone had discovered yet another level of passion and was ready to introduce me to it. I moaned as he pushed my arms up above my head. It took me a moment to realize what he was doing.

Last week, after a particularly intense session of sex, I had been pressed up against him, dripping with sweat, gasping for breath. He held me then, kissing me tenderly, coaxing my heart back into a normal rhythm. Somehow the notion of Linda having her fantasies fulfilled by Vince jumped to mind. I told Malone what we shared was like fantasy sex, that he always seemed to know how to take me to the edge and beyond.

"We all have fantasies, Jamie," he had whispered softly, still cradling my body against his.

"What are yours, Antonio?" I asked when my voice was working.

He shook his head. "I get to live out different fantasies every night we're together, Jamie."

"I'll tell you mine, Malone." As soon as the words jumped out of my mouth, I wanted to call them back. What if my desires were too crazy? I didn't think it was anything out of the ordinary, but then, I make a living using my imagination.

He must have sensed my discomfort. "You don't have to tell me, Jay. We can just discover them together."

But since I'd ventured into the subject, I felt the need to at least reveal one fantasy. It was probably one many women have at one time or another. So I admitted that I'd always been curious about what it would be like to be tied up. Not with handcuffs or chains, but maybe a silk tie. Malone distracted me with his hands and lips after that so I thought we'd moved on to safer grounds. And I hadn't thought about it again, until tonight.

He was still kissing me, moving his lips over to mine now, toying with me. I could feel his hands sliding up and down my arms, stretching me out on the bed. And then I realized I couldn't move my arms. My eyes snapped open. Malone had a devilish grin on his face as he pulled back.

"Dexter, what are you doing?" My voice was a throaty rasp.

"I'm just fulfilling a fantasy or two."

He had used the satin sash from my robe to bind my wrists to the wooden headboard. I squirmed beneath him as the realization sunk in.

"Somehow I always pictured myself naked or wearing some sexy lingerie when I thought of this, Dexter. Not dressed in a flannel nightgown."

Malone gave me one of those low voltage smiles and shook his head. Then he rolled off the bed and began to undress. He took his time, carefully folding his jeans and sweater and placing them on the dresser. Then he turned and walked naked out of the room. I couldn't believe it! He just left me there. And I couldn't get my hands free.

"Malone, this would be a lot more fun if you were here with me."

"Patience, Jamie. I just need something to drink."

He returned with a couple of lit candles from our bedroom that he placed on the dresser. He had a tall glass of orange juice that he sipped while sitting next to me on the bed. Malone took a sip, placed the glass on the dresser and leaned over to kiss me. I felt the juice trickle into my mouth.

He sprawled beside me. Then with one hand, he slowly began to pull my nightgown up. I felt his hands everywhere. As he raised it above my hips, Malone resumed kissing me. And I sensed this was one fantasy I'd want to revisit. Now he moved the nightgown higher. Just the idea of him taking advantage of me this way was a rush. My body was thrumming like a guitar string. And Malone was a master musician.

"Jamie," he whispered in my ear. He was beside me now, lightly kissing my face while his hands continued their explorations. "How long should I keep you tied up?"

"A minute," I gasped "or for an hour or two." In my wildest fantasies, this is the part where I would make a feeble attempt at escaping. But that wasn't happening.

"I wonder how close I can get you," he said as he drew patterns on my thighs with his fingertips, long slow circles and ovals.

"I'm already going to peak, Dexter. The question is, how many times?"

Malone raised his head to look deeply into my eyes. "How many times would you like to peak, Jamie?"

"More than half a dozen will probably put me in the hospital, Dexter."

"Then you'd better keep count," he said. Malone pressed his lips to mine as his fingers worked their magic. I could only hope that my body remembered to breathe on its own. Malone's hands were busy. His lips moved down my body, pausing at certain spots. At that point, all I could do was give myself up to him.

# CHAPTER SEVEN

In order to make sure these new plans wouldn't cause any friction with the family, Malone called Terri. Sunday afternoon found the two of us at her Northville home. Terri had sent Ian and his kid sister to the grocery store just before we got there so we'd have some time alone to discuss my idea about Ian staying with us occasionally

Terri was an attractive woman, but it was obvious the last few months had taken their toll. She had thick, brown hair that wouldn't stay in the ponytail she'd pulled it into. Her eyes were red-rimmed and I noticed the bags beneath them. I doubted she was getting much sleep. She hesitated at the door when we arrived. Malone stepped over and gave her a brotherly hug. Terri clung to him for an extra moment. She waved the two of us to a couch. We both turned down offers of coffee and tea. Restless, Terri fidgeted on the edge of her chair.

Malone explained our relationship. I felt very grown up, hearing him describe our living arrangements. Terri just nodded.

"Jamie had this idea, but we wanted to talk to you first before we discussed it with Ian."

"He told me that he met you yesterday," Terri said with

a wan smile. "He was pretty upbeat the rest of the day. He really enjoyed helping you, Malone."

"And I enjoy having him around."

Malone hesitated. I caught his eyes flicking toward me. I could see how difficult this was for both of them. Malone was obviously concerned about overstepping whatever boundaries he had. I gave the quiet another beat before jumping in.

"Malone has told me what a great kid Ian is," I said, "and how he wishes he could spend a little more time with him."

Terri nodded. "He really misses Asa. But it helps when there's another man around. He just can't seem to get comfortable with me. Things we used to talk or joke about always included Asa. Now that he's gone…"

Nobody followed up on that comment. I watched Terri draw a deep breath and give a little shudder as she got her emotions under control. I couldn't imagine having your entire family destroyed in an instant that way.

"We just moved in together. We've got a nice house that's only about twenty minutes from here. That's where Ian was yesterday, helping Malone with the pool table. There's just the two of us. And we have an extra bedroom," I said.

"Jamie thought that it might be nice for Ian, if it's okay with you, if he stays over at our place once in a while. Since my schedule always rotates, there may be days during the week when I'm off and I could spend some time with him. And on the weekends, I've always got time in the morning, even if I'm working that afternoon."

Terri seemed pleasantly surprised. "You want him to stay with you?"

Malone calmly raised a hand. "Not all the time, maybe one or two nights a week, if it works out for you. The idea is that if I see him more often, it might help with his relationship with you and Caitlin."

"He was a lot happier last night," Terri said. She turned

her attention toward me. "Are you sure you want a teenage boy living with you? He could certainly disrupt your time together."

I patted Malone's thigh. "Well, Malone does need to get his rest sometimes."

* * * *

Malone had Wednesday and Thursday off that week. So he picked up Ian after school Wednesday and brought him to the house. He had a duffel bag filled with extra clothes, a backpack jammed with books, and some extra athletic shoes. When they arrived, Malone showed Ian the spare bedroom. The kid immediately dumped everything on the floor and headed for the kitchen. I was standing in the doorway of the office, watching this play out.

"Not so fast, hotshot," Malone said.

"What's wrong? I'm hungry." Ian groaned, raising his palms like it was a given.

"And we'll get some food after you put your gear away. I've seen your room at home. That's not going to happen here."

Grumbling, Ian returned to the bedroom. Under Malone's supervision, he unpacked his clothes and neatly put everything away. Then he emptied his backpack and arranged his books on the desk.

"Now can I eat?" Ian whined.

"Come with me."

I had jumped back behind the desk, pretending to be writing away. Now I snuck out and followed them into the kitchen. Malone led him to the refrigerator.

"Bottom left drawer is filled with fruit. Apples, oranges, and grapes are always there. Bananas are on the counter. You can have fruit as a snack. There are usually two kinds of cheese in the drawer. You can have some with crackers."

"I'm hungry," Ian groaned. "Can't we order a pizza?"

Malone slowly shook his head. "It's three in the afternoon. Dinner will be at five thirty. A snack will tide you over until dinner."

Ian grabbed two apples from the drawer. "What if I don't like what's for dinner?" He spied me sitting on a kitchen chair. "Is Ms. Richmond a good cook?"

I bit back a laugh as Malone leaned against the stove. "Tonight, I'll be cooking. We're having marinated chicken, with potatoes, salad, and green beans. Maybe some fresh biscuits if I'm feeling motivated and appreciated."

"I appreciate you, Seamus," I said.

Ian took a huge bite out of his apple.

"And on some days, you will help cook," Malone said.

Ian scoffed. "Cooking's woman's work."

Malone folded his arms across his chest and narrowed his eyes at the kid. This was more fun than Saturday morning cartoons.

"Do I look like a woman to you?"

The kid realized he'd put his foot in his mouth along with most of the apple. Suddenly he was shaking his head, trying to find a way out.

"For your information, most of the greatest chefs in the world are men," Malone said. "Furthermore, while you are here, you are a guest in this house. That means you will be polite, you will keep that bedroom neat and you will do whatever chores Jamie and I feel are appropriate, such as helping clean up the kitchen after dinner. Clear?"

Ian managed to swallow his apple. "Yes, sir."

"Good. Now you've got time to hit the books. Get some of that homework done before dinner. We'll have a quick billiard tournament after we eat."

"Sweet," Ian said. He finished the second apple, dropped the cores in the garbage can, and headed back toward the bedroom. I waited until he was at the far end of the hall. Malone was still leaning against the stove with his arms crossed. He winked at me.

"You were a little tough on the kid," I said, rising from

my chair and moving to him for a hug. Malone slipped his arms around me and nuzzled the top of my head.

"I'm just setting the ground rules. We all want this to work, so we may as well get started on the right foot."

"And if you want him to keep coming around, you'd better not let him taste my cooking, Seamus."

Malone hadn't mentioned to Ian that Linda was joining us for dinner. She had stopped by her place long enough to pick up Logan and switch into some cords and a sweater. But it was obvious Ian felt a little awkward being around her. He even called her Ms. Davis when he asked her to pass the chicken. Linda ignored it the first time, but when he referred to her that way again, she bit her lip and looked at me. I cringed when he'd called me Ms. Richmond earlier. I turned my gaze to Malone. He was oblivious. I saw him sneak a piece of chicken to Logan, who was sprawled behind Malone's chair, underneath the kitchen window.

"We need to set some ground rules here," Linda said as we were finishing the meal.

"More rules?" Ian groaned.

Linda was unaware of the discussion upon Ian's arrival. She looked at Malone and me for guidance. Malone merely smiled and extended a hand. It was her show. She leaned toward Ian, making certain she had his attention. Like a fourteen-year-old boy could possibly be looking anywhere else?

"Ian, do you respect Malone?" she asked.

"Of course I do."

"And do you respect me and Jamie?"

He nodded quickly. "Sure. My dad and mom taught me that it's important to show respect. You know, like calling him Mr. Malone. He said I only have to do that when other adults are around. But not you guys."

Linda leaned a little closer to him, keeping her eyes locked on his. It was hypnotic. There was no way Ian could look away.

"That's good. But here's my deal. When we're at school or maybe at a school function, like a game or a dance, that's when you need to call me Ms. Davis. It shows the proper respect. But when it's just the four of us, you can call me Linda."

His face brightened and, somehow, his eyes got bigger. I hadn't thought it would have been possible. "For real?" he asked.

"For real," Linda said.

"And you can call me Jamie."

Ian was grinning broadly now. "Can I call you Jay Kay?"

"Don't push it," I said, "only she gets away with that."

He considered it for a moment. "Sweet."

Ian got up from his chair and began to clear the table. I watched in disbelief as he rinsed the plates, flatware, and glasses and loaded them into the dishwasher. Obviously, his act before was just that. Someone had shown him around a kitchen before. When the table was cleared, he turned to Malone.

"Are you ready to shoot some pool?"

\* \* \* \*

Thursday Linda came by to pick me up for our yoga class. She seemed preoccupied when I got in the car. While the guys were shooting pool last night, we had run out to the sporting goods store. They were having a sale on all kinds of exercise clothes and shoes. Even though we were going to get sweaty, we wanted to look good doing it. I was wearing one of the new outfits under my heavy down jacket. I noticed Linda was wearing a new pair of shoes.

"Bad day?" I asked.

She gave her head a shake as if to clear it. "No, the day was okay. Sorry, Jay Kay, I guess there's just a lot on my mind."

"Want to talk about it?"

We were already pulling into the gym's parking lot. "Maybe after we work out," Linda said.

It wasn't like Linda to be preoccupied. She had the ability to keep the different parts of her life from overlapping. Obviously something wasn't right. But I knew her well enough that when she was ready, she would talk to me. We went into the gym for our class.

Normally during the workouts, Linda is pretty aggressive, holding the yoga poses longer, pushing herself to go through the various steps. But this time she seemed to be on autopilot. More than once I had to bite my lip to keep from saying something. Now my curiosity was getting the better of me. I couldn't wait for the class to end.

Since Malone had the night off and Ian was going to be there, I suggested we go out for something to eat. I even offered to treat. Linda wasn't interested in sitting in a restaurant this time. So I convinced her to get a pizza from Mama Vera's and take it back to her house. Malone could always come get me later if I needed a ride home.

So with the pizza in tow, we went back to her place. Logan was bouncing around the house as we came in. I placed the pizza on the table and spent a few minutes getting nuzzled by the dog. Then he moved across to the living room to where Linda had dropped onto the sofa. Logan took one look at her, climbed up beside her, and rested his head in her lap. Linda bent down, hugged him, and started to cry.

My imagination ran through a whole cavalcade of possibilities that could make her cry. Was something wrong with her mother? Did she and Vince have an argument? Was there a problem at the school? Was there something physically wrong with her?

I kept coming up with scenarios, discarding each one as quickly as I did. I went to her and knelt in front of her, leaning forward and wrapping my arms around her and the dog.

She wasn't wailing, not letting great gushes of air out of

her lungs. It was as if her eyes were leaking. I didn't say a word. I just held her. At length, Logan wiggled out of her grasp. Linda shifted her arms around me. I just kept holding her.

After a while she slowed down. Linda reached over to the table beside the sofa and snagged a couple of tissues. I leaned back a little. She dried her tears. Those blue eyes looked right through me.

"Talk to me, baby." Whenever one of us was struggling with something, we used the term baby. It went back to an old cop show on television, where the big tough guy would say 'who loves ya, baby'?" No matter what, our bond was so strong there was never any question about who loved us. It was a way of reassuring each other.

She sniffed, then used the back of her hands to brush her curls back from her face. "I might be in trouble in, Jamie. I'm not sure what to do. And I'm a little scared."

"Let's start from the beginning, baby. Tell me what's going on."

I moved up to sit beside her on the sofa. She turned a little, taking my hands in hers.

It started a couple of weeks ago. She came out from the school late one afternoon and found a bag of candy, those multi-colored gummy bears, tied to the windshield wipers on her car with a big red ribbon. There was no note. It was the type of bag you can buy from a bulk food store, so there was no distinguishing mark on it. At first she thought it might have been a treat from Vince. She looked around the parking lot, but didn't see anyone other than the usual group of faculty and staff heading home. Linda rarely ate candy. Since there was no note and it could have been tampered with, she tossed it on the seat of her car and threw it in the garbage can when she stopped for gas.

She thought about mentioning it to Vince, but it didn't seem like the kind of thing he would do, especially since there was no note. She chalked it up to someone playing a joke on her and forgot about it.

Until today.

When she came home from work, she grabbed her mail. Amid the bills and the advertisements was a glossy travel magazine. It wasn't something she had a subscription to. And there were several pages earmarked, showing tropical resorts with white sandy beaches and bikini-clad models. There was no delivery label on it.

"I know it's not Vince. I saw him last night for dinner. If he had left me candy, he would have mentioned it. And if it was him, he would have brought the magazine with him. Someone is following me. They know where I work. They know where I live. I'm wondering what else they know." Linda's voice had taken on a hollow quality that I didn't recognize. "Am I crazy?" she whispered.

"You're not crazy, baby. Somebody's stalking you. Do you still have the magazine?"

She gave a little shudder. "It's in the kitchen garbage can. Why?"

"It might give us a clue as to who's doing this."

"What am I going to do, Jamie?"

"I think it's time we talk to Malone."

I'd forgotten that Malone had taken Ian to a Red Wings game. He wouldn't be home until late. I was reluctant to leave Linda alone, even with Logan in the house. Wearing my gloves, I pulled the magazine from the garbage by a corner of the cover. Then I dropped it in a plastic grocery bag and tied the handles together. I put the pizza in the oven on low heat to warm it. We sat and talked quietly, trying to think of anyone who might want to bother Linda this way.

Finally, the aroma of the pizza got to her. We moved into the kitchen, sat at the table and ate. Linda even dropped a slice in Logan's dish. He made it disappear in a heartbeat. After we'd eaten, we put together a plan.

Linda gathered clothes for work on Friday. She took a quick shower and slipped on sweatpants and a sweatshirt. We put some chow for Logan in a big container, secured her house and with the dog for company, piled into her car. Then we drove back to my place.

"I'm not taking over Ian's bed, Jay Kay," Linda said as we were cruising over. "I'd rather sleep on the 'aunt'. Besides, Logan will want to be near me and it's just as easy if we're in the living room."

I could tell she was feeling better when she called me Jay Kay. "Personally, I think the 'Jewish Aunt' is much more comfortable than the spare room anyway. I'll just give the guys fair warning to be quiet when they come in."

I sent Malone a text on his cell phone, indicating Linda and Logan would be sleeping over. By the time we got situated at the house, Linda was yawning. I set up the 'aunt' with pillows and a couple of quilts. I took an old blanket and arranged it on the floor for Logan. There was a water bowl in the kitchen by the table for him.

"Comfy?" I asked as Linda settled beneath the quilts.

"I don't normally wear this much to bed, but since Ian is going to be in the house, I'd better not flash the kid. It might scar him for life."

She had me grinning. "Algae, if you flashed him he might spend the rest of his days trying to find a girl his own age who could measure up."

"I'm sorry I was such a basket case before, Jay Kay." She reached out and pulled me close for a hug. "Thanks for being there for me."

"Where else would I be?"

I left one light on low in the kitchen. Malone and Ian would be back soon. Linda needed her rest. She offered to take Ian with her to school in the morning, to save Malone the trip. In exchange, she would try and sleep now and let me explain everything to Malone. Logan would stay with me for the day. We would regroup tomorrow when she got out of school.

I took a hot, steamy shower and got ready for bed. While waiting for Malone, I tried to figure out who would possibly be doing something like this to Linda. Could there really be a stalker out there, fixated on her? And if there was, would they do something to hurt her?

I had no idea how crazy things would get.

# CHAPTER EIGHT

I was propped up in bed reading the latest James Rollins thriller when the guys came home around eleven. Ian gave me a sheepish grin as he slid silently by my door. Malone quietly eased our door shut and moved toward me. The reading light was on behind me. I realized that it made my nightgown transparent. No wonder Ian had been grinning. Malone bent down to kiss me. I think it was an hour before we separated.

"Welcome home, Frederick," I said when I found my voice.

"It's nice to be home, Jamie. Suddenly we have a full house. We'll have to keep the noise level down." He gave me a lecherous wink and reached for me beneath the quilt.

"Maybe you'd better save those ideas for the morning, Frederick."

Malone stretched out on top of the blankets and propped his elbow on the bed resting his head on his palm. "Is something wrong with Linda and Vince?"

"No, I don't think this has anything to do with Vince."

I took my time and spelled it out for Malone. He didn't interrupt, he just listened until I brought him up to date ending with Linda camped out on the 'aunt'. Malone confirmed that both she and Logan were sleeping peacefully. Now he turned onto his back and pulled me to him. I rested my head on his chest. Malone slowly began to run his fingers through my hair. It was still a little damp from the shower. I didn't mind. Neither did Malone. I had told him once how incredibly sensuous it was for me when he did that. It always made me feel special. Malone admitted he loved the feel of my hair on his fingers, how he liked the weight and texture of my locks on his skin.

"Is there anything we can do to help her, Malone?"

"It could just be a prank. Or it could be two unrelated incidents. A student from one of her classes, or someone else she knows at school, could have left the candy. But I'll check it out in the morning."

"How are you going to do that?"

He turned his head enough to give me a glimmer of a smile. "I'm a cop, Jamie. I have my methods."

"Would any of those methods have anything to do with me?" I asked, giving him my most innocent smile.

"I'm sure I could find something to do with you."

The proximity of him was getting to me. Malone sensed this. He eased me up from his chest and slid his face through my hair to my neck. Softly, he started kissing me. For a moment I seriously thought about stalling him until morning when Linda and Ian were gone. Okay, so it wasn't really a moment. And I wasn't serious.

"Frederick," I whispered, "why do you still have clothes on?"

He didn't stop kissing me. Malone's hands were in my hair, holding my head close to his lips. I was still above him. The quilts had somehow been kicked to the side. I was very warm, even though I wasn't wearing much at all. Pressing my body down on his, I could feel Malone react. My hands got busy.

His lips worked their way from my neck, to my ear, across to my eyelids, and then down to my mouth. I could taste his lips on mine the moment I worked him free from his jeans. We shifted together. Malone pressed his face into the hollow of my throat now, kissing me in a very sensitive spot. He slid his left hand up and pressed it firmly down on my mouth to muffle any noise I might make. It didn't take very long, since we were both so aroused. Gasping, I collapsed beside him.

"So much for waiting until morning, Frederick," I said when I'd caught my breath.

"Remind me tomorrow to soundproof our room."

\* \* \* \*

Friday morning I awoke to the sounds of a bustling household. Linda came in to use the master bathroom to shower and put on her makeup. Malone eased out of bed and checked on Ian. He even made the kid a lunch since he knew how tight money was for Terri. I tried to wake up and get moving, but it was an uphill battle. When I heard the shower go off, I slid from the bed and pulled on jeans and a sweatshirt. Malone was just bringing Logan back inside.

"Go back to bed, Jamie," Malone said after he gave me a kiss.

"But everyone else is up."

He chuckled and drew me close. Logan rubbed up against my legs. "But everyone else has their eyes open."

Nodding sleepily, I went back to the bedroom. Logan followed me and curled up on the floor by the window. I caught a glimpse of Ian dashing down the hall to the spare bathroom. Linda poked her head in.

"Sleep okay?" I asked.

She nodded. "That couch still has magical powers. I think I was asleep in less than five minutes. I never even heard the guys come home."

Linda looked a lot better than last night. I was glad she'd decided to stay here. While she was putting on her makeup, I outlined my conversation with Malone. She was

95

wearing a pair of tailored black slacks and a deep blue sweater with a cowl neck. The color did amazing things with her eyes. With her makeup done, she came over and sat on the edge of the bed. Logan raised his head for a few minutes of attention.

"We'll figure this out," I said. "Malone's already got a plan."

She leaned over and hugged me. "I'm glad we talked. I was beginning to think I was paranoid."

"I told Malone you offered to take Ian to school."

Linda's eyes widened. "If I play my cards right, do you think he'd go out and scrape the frost off my windows?"

"Are you kidding? He'd probably do it with his fingernails!"

She went out to the kitchen to grab breakfast. I wasn't alert enough to join the conversation she was having with Ian and Malone. Ten minutes later I heard her car start up. A few minutes after that, Malone came back to bed.

"That might make for an interesting ride to school," he said, leaning over to kiss me. "When Ian realized Linda was going to take him, he started blushing. I think it will be a while before he calms down."

"Good thing he's not in any of her classes."

"So what's your plan today, Jamie?"

I stretched my arms up high. "Well, I thought I'd take a long, hot soapy shower, have a muffin and some fruit for breakfast, and take Logan for a nice, long walk. Then I've got about six hours of work on the computer, doing research for my next novel. That should keep me busy until Linda gets home. What about you?"

Malone reached over and grabbed the bottom of my sweatshirt. Slowly he began to pull it up. "I'm going to head over to the high school, but figured I'd wait until classes were in session. So I've got a little time before I need to leave."

"Why Rocco, what do you have in mind?"

Malone didn't have to say a word. The look in his eyes

was enough for me. He kept pulling my sweatshirt up until it was almost over my eyes.

"What about Logan?" I asked, realizing the sweatshirt was muffling my voice. I felt one of Malone's hands brush lightly across my breasts. I pretended my nipples were stiff because of the cold. Well, I tried.

"Let him find his own girl," Malone said.

"So you want to have sex with an audience?" I groped blindly for Malone's sweater.

"It's probably not the first time he's seen this kind of activity."

I tossed my head, finally getting free of the shirt. The dog was resting on the floor, his muzzle across his paws, his eyes on me. Out of the corner of my eye, I saw Malone glance at the dog, then back to me.

"I don't have the heart to chase Logan from the room," I said.

He thought about it for a second. Then Malone pulled me close. "Seems to me I heard something about a long, hot, soapy shower,"

"Are you going to wash my back, Rocco?"

The gleam in his eyes made me shiver. "Among other things," he said.

It was well after nine when Malone left. We'd run the tank dry on the hot water heater. But I, for one, was squeaky clean. True to my word, I bundled up in boots, a heavy down jacket, gloves, scarf, and a hat. I clipped Logan to his leash. Outside, it was clear and crisp with temperatures in the low thirties.

By my estimation, Logan and I walked about two miles, drifting through the neighborhood. We took our time. He checked a lot of trees and fire hydrants. When we got back to the house, I gave Logan a fresh bowl of water and fixed myself a mug of tea. Then I settled in behind the computer. After a while, Logan came in and sprawled beneath my feet to keep me company. He certainly kept my toes warm.

It was almost two when Malone came back. I was in the kitchen, getting a refill on the tea. He shrugged off his jacket and settled into a chair.

"The school parking lot has video cameras mounted high on the light poles. They do a pretty good job covering the area, especially the section designated for the teachers." He paused, reaching down to scratch Logan behind the ears. "Trouble is they don't keep the video for more than a week, unless something comes up."

"Could you see Linda's car?"

He nodded. "Yes, but I'm going to suggest she park in a different spot, where the cameras overlap. I went over the last week's video. There was nothing suspicious."

"Was there anything worthwhile about the magazine, Rocco?"

"I took it to the forensic lab and asked them to run it through for prints, particularly on the pages that were earmarked. There could be hundreds of partials on that magazine. If it was on display in a bookstore, any number of people might have handled it. But we'll wait and see."

* * * *

Saturday night, I was home alone and restless. Malone was working until eleven. Linda and Vince had a date, going to a nice dinner downtown and then to hear the Detroit Symphony Orchestra. They were performing a number of selections, including some Vivaldi pieces. I was a little bit jealous. I really like Vivaldi.

Today had been a much better day for Linda. Just having confided in Malone and me seemed to put her situation in a much better perspective. And after Malone had done a little snooping around, I think she felt even more reassured. She made both of us promise not to say anything to Vince. I wasn't sure that was such a good idea, but Linda didn't want him to worry needlessly.

After our class that morning, Malone cooked brunch

for us. Then Linda dashed off to get her hair styled before her evening out. So Malone and I had some quiet time before he had to leave for work. We spent it curled up on the 'aunt', watching the flames dance across the birch logs. I was surprised that we were both able to contain our basic instincts, but I adored the secure feeling of Malone's strong arms wrapped around me, his face nestled into the hollow of my neck where he could nibble my ear if he felt the urge. We didn't talk. We just seemed to soak up the comfort of being together like that. Once he was gone, I did the grocery shopping, ran a few errands, and came back to an empty house. I tried to work for a while, but couldn't focus. Reading didn't help. Neither did music. I found myself wandering around from room to room.

We'd been in the house for about six weeks now. I realized it was more of a home than the apartment had ever been. I liked having the extra space. And I liked having the others around. In this short span of time, I'd grown accustomed to the idea of having Malone with me every night, and frequent visits from Linda and Ian. It felt like a comfortable place for family to gather. That image reminded me that I needed to call Bert, my stepfather, and invite him over.

I drifted down to the basement. There was plenty of room down here to have a party, and the new pool table fit right in. Running my fingers along the felt, I decided to see if I still had any talent. When Bert first became a fixture in my life, he taught me how to shoot pool. I'd done pretty well mastering the game. Straight pool, eight ball, nine ball, and rotation were all different billiard games Bert schooled me in. After gathering the balls into the rack, I chalked up a cue and started to shoot.

It's amazing how quickly the skills I developed as a teen came back. And I discovered that shooting pool was therapeutic. I couldn't think about other problems while I was lining up a shot. But subconsciously, I could look at things from a new angle. I was on my third rack of balls when I saw Malone coming down the stairs. I finished my shot, banking the seven off a rail and dropping it smoothly into the center pocket.

"I didn't know you were a pool shark, Jamie," Malone said as he took me in his arms for a kiss.

"There's a lot about me you don't know, Aaron."

"I'm sure that's true. But think of all the fun I can have finding out."

He pulled the cue from my fingers and propped it against the wall. Then he lifted me up so I was sitting on the table, with my legs dangling off into space. Malone leaned me back, kissing me again. His hands went to my face, to my hair, to my neck. I couldn't have said no to him even if I wanted to.

I wrapped my arms around his neck and drew him closer. Why was it that when he kissed me, everything else in the world just disappeared? It was like we were the only two people in existence. I had never experienced that with anyone before. I blinked my eyes, making sure he was real.

Malone eased me down onto the pool table. His left hand was cupped behind my head, playing with my hair. The right hand had magically disappeared beneath my sweater. I was surprised at how warm his hand was, considering it was below zero outside. A moan escaped my lips as his fingers moved higher. He broke the kiss to look in my eyes.

"Aaron, what am I going to do with you?" I whispered.

His smile was like a flash of heat striking my chest. "I have a few ideas, Jamie. Maybe you should just close your eyes and enjoy them."

"I'm too curious, Aaron. I can never keep my eyes closed for any length of time when you're around."

His gaze remained fixed on my face, but his fingers were moving. I felt him undo the snap on my jeans. I didn't want him to ever stop touching me, or stop wanting me.

"We've been living here for a while now, Jamie."

Malone's voice was a soft, steady, hypnotic whisper. "And there are still some parts of this house that we haven't...explored yet."

Now he was moving, using both hands to slide my jeans off. My mind flashed back to last weekend when Malone had bound me to Ian's bed. He moved my hips to the edge of the table as my jeans hit the floor. Malone was standing there, gazing down at me.

"I think we'd better explore this part of the house quickly, Aaron, before I get cold."

"I'll do my best to keep you warm," he said as I wrapped my legs around his hips.

"There was never a doubt in my mind."

MARK LOVE

# CHAPTER NINE

Why in the world was I so nervous? It's not like this was a surprise. It had been my idea in the first place. But I was keyed up. I wanted this to be right. I wanted him to feel comfortable. But the situation was unusual. I paced from the kitchen into the living room, making minuscule adjustments to the cushions on the 'aunt'. The logs were burning cheerily in the hearth. The place was very comfortable. I looked up in surprise when I heard the car door slam in the driveway.

Quickly I went to the front door and swung it open. He stood there for an awkward moment before that familiar snort of laughter escaped his lips and he stepped inside, pulling me close for a bear hug.

"Hello, Jamie."

"Bert. It's good to see you."

We stood there for another moment or two, and then he slowly released me. He held me at arm's length and let his eyes take me in. "You look good, Jamie Rae."

"So do you, Bert. Want the tour now, or after dinner?"

He shrugged off his overcoat and draped it on the edge of the 'aunt'. "Now sounds good."

I took my time showing him the house. He liked the

hardwood floors, the gigantic master suite, and the basement. "You could put a bowling alley in here," Bert said with a grin. He rubbed his fingers on the pool table's felt and gave me an appreciative nod. I turned away so I wouldn't blush, flashing back to Saturday night's interlude there with Malone.

I led him back upstairs to the kitchen. Earlier in the day, Malone mixed up a large crock of homemade chili for dinner. I had picked up two loaves of that thick, crusty bread from the Greek bakery in town and thrown together a large, green salad. We settled in at the kitchen table to enjoy our feast on a cold winter's night.

Bert had been married to my neurotic mother during my formative teenage years. I learned so much from him that I could never begin to catalog it all. Even when Vera filed for divorce and took off for greener pastures and a parade of men, Bert and I remained close. Sometimes we falter and a few months will pass when we don't see each other, but we're comfortable enough to pick right up where we left off.

Bert Nowalski is a captain with the state police, a grizzly bear of a man usually dressed in a suit and tie, but he is one who could just as easily step right back into a uniform. To complicate our current situation, he was also Malone's boss. It was through my relationship with Bert that I met Malone. And it was months after we became lovers that they learned that I was now something they had in common.

"This is a very nice place, Jamie," Bert said. I realized he was eyeing me suspiciously as I ladled up a bowl of chili for him. Knowing my lack of prowess in the kitchen was making him hesitate.

"Relax, Bert. Malone made the chili. I just put the salad together."

"Just making sure," he said with a grin. He gratefully accepted a bowl. Maybe it was one of my character traits to bring out the smartass in everyone.

We talked quietly over dinner. It was never my intention to fall in love with a cop, especially one who worked with Bert. But he told me once, not so long ago, that we don't get to choose who we fall in love with. I had no idea back then how right he was.

"So how are things going with you and Malone living together?" Bert asked as he wiped the last of the chili from his bowl with a thick chunk of bread.

I realized my face was split with a wide smile. "It's been good, Bert."

"You share this good news with your mother yet?"

I slowly shook my head. "I'm not sure how Vera will react when she hears about Malone. God forbid she'd want to come to town for a visit and meet him."

"No chance of that until May or June," Bert said. "Michigan is far too cold for her fragile constitution."

"That's just a lame excuse that she uses. The sad part is we both know it is bullshit."

Bert gave me a stern look. "I didn't raise you to swear."

"I'm sure it's not the worst thing you've heard today."

"No, but since I get to hear it all day long, the last thing I want is to hear it from my daughter. Beautiful women shouldn't stoop to swearing."

Rather than avert my gaze, I busied myself clearing away the dishes. I left the crock of chili to cool, wrapped up the rest of the bread, and put the salad and dressing back in the fridge. Bert eased out of his chair and wandered into the living room. I was wiping off the table when I heard the stereo click on and the beginning of a Mozart sonata filled the living room.

He was sitting in the rocker, calmly staring at the logs burning. There was a contented look on his face.

I perched on the edge of the 'aunt'. We didn't talk for a while; we just watched the fire and listened to the beautiful music. In my mind, I saw a brief overview of my life with Bert, from my early teen years to the present day. I swear he still looked the same as always. It was a moment before

I realized he was staring at me.

"What?" I asked sheepishly.

"I asked you a question, but apparently you were no longer here with me."

I grinned. "Just doing some reminiscing. I was thinking about a very cold winter when you took me ice skating for the first time."

"Seems to me that you were stunned that I could actually skate," Bert said with a snort of laughter.

"Yes, you did surprise me. But I think your approach to stopping was a bit unconventional."

Bert shook his head and laughed again. "Anybody can go forward. But it takes a certain level of aptitude to bring this much bulk to a halt."

Bert's unorthodox method was to head for the boards around the rink normally used for hockey games. He'd wait until the last possible moment, then turn around and crash back first into the boards. Using them as a springboard, he'd bounce off them and continue skating.

The flash of headlights filled the front window as a car turned around in my driveway. I went into the kitchen to warm some apple cider for both of us when a double tap knock landed on the front door. Bert did the honors. I heard a squeal of delight and another round of his laughter. I stepped into the doorway and watched.

Linda had to stand on her tiptoes to get her arms around his neck. Bert bent down slightly and with one arm around her waist was in the process of lifting her off her feet. I let them get reacquainted while pulling another mug from the cupboard. I put the mugs on a tray along with a bowl of cinnamon sticks and brought the cider out by the fire.

Bert returned to the rocker. Linda was sitting on the edge of the coffee table, one leg crossed over the other. She looked as radiant as ever, wearing a thick black woolen skirt that almost reached her knees, a pair of black leather boots and a cream-colored sweater. She bounced up, gave me a hug and accepted a mug of cider.

It was an idyllic evening, listening to the two of them catch up, sharing old memories and laughter. I may be Bert's daughter, but Linda has always been an unofficial niece. I watched her face light up as he reminded her of old tales from our youth. It was a subject we never tired of and Bert had plenty of ammunition.

If someone had told me that this comfortable scene would soon be shattered, I would have thought they were nuts.

\* \* \* \*

The events of that Thursday night will be etched in my memory for as long as I live. Not only because of what happened, but because I've been replaying that scene over and over in my head ever since, like some video recording stuck on a perpetual loop.

Linda and I had gone to the gym, as was our custom. Earlier in the day, she found a childish Valentine's card tucked under the windshield wiper on her car. There was no signature, just a cartoon character offering up their heart. It could have been from anyone. Or it could have been from her stalker. She started to throw it away, but remembered the warning from Malone. Using her gloves, she picked it up by the corner and dropped it into a plastic bag in her car. I was going to give it to Malone on the off chance there could be fingerprints on it.

So she was a little unnerved when we went to work out. But the physical activity, the pounding music, and the noise of the other women grunting and groaning through the moves helped to improve her mood. We bundled up afterward and were headed for the car. The lot had been crowded when we'd arrived, so we ended up parking at the far end.

Talking quietly, trudging through the clumps of snow and ice, neither one of us heard him at first.

"It's getting to the point where I just want to stay home," she said quietly.

"You can't hide, Linda. If you become a prisoner in your own home, then he wins. And you are much too strong a person to let that happen."

She gave me a wan smile. "I know, Jay Kay, it's just..."

"Hey!" a gruff voice snapped at us from only a couple of feet away.

Linda let out a shriek of surprise. She lost her footing on the ice and crashed to the pavement. Looking over my shoulder, I saw a blocky shape, hidden in the shadows beyond the reach of the overhead lights, gliding close to the back end of a parked car. He took a menacing step forward, one hand clutching something tightly and extending it towards us.

"Run!" I screamed at Linda for all I was worth.

"Hey," he snapped again, still reaching for us.

I took a step toward him and planted my left foot on one of the few dry patches of pavement. Then I swung my right foot as hard as I could, as if I was about to nail a fifty-yard field goal to win the Super Bowl. Without realizing it, I braced for the impact. To this day, I'd swear I was aiming for his crotch. But I missed.

Maybe the pavement wasn't dry after all. Or maybe suddenly shifting my weight to make that kick caused me to lose my balance. Or maybe subconsciously I couldn't really kick a guy in the balls. Or maybe he sensed what was happening and he took a step back. I'll never really know.

In my peripheral vision, I could see Linda scrambling to her feet, already racing toward her car, clicking the remote control to unlock the doors. My leg continued its arc and just before making contact, my left foot shot out from underneath me.

My right foot slammed into the bulky guy. I caught him square in the chest. With my body going horizontal, it must have looked like some kind of ninja move. Whatever it was, it was enough to take him off his feet, and he went down with a thud. I couldn't be sure, but it looked like his head bounced off the pavement.

I landed on my side and scrambled immediately to my feet. I was crouched in a fighting stance, anger and adrenalin churning in my gut. The guy let out a low groan. He made no move to get up.

Suddenly lights flared around us. Linda managed to start her car and pull it into the aisle. She lay on the horn, a long deep-throated wail that cut through the night. A few people who had been moving across the parking lot came running over.

Illuminated by the headlights, I looked down at the attacker. He was an older man, with a couple days' worth of stubble across his face. His left hand was pressed against his chest, roughly in the spot in which I'd kicked him. Slowly he raised his right hand in my direction as our eyes locked. His voice made a throaty rasping noise as he spoke.

"She dropped her glove."

\* \* \* \*

Malone was not happy. The look on his face told me everything I needed to know. I'd stepped over some kind of line.

"Jamie, I told you I'd take care of this. You can't be taking matters into your own hands." His voice was tense. There was none of the tenderness, the humor or the calm that I usually associated with Malone.

"But Malone, I can't leave it alone. We're talking about my best friend."

"I know who we're talking about! But you can't go running around like some renegade in a movie, trying to see that justice is done. This whole thing could have blown up in your face."

"But I…"

"No buts, Jamie." He leaned forward, looming over

me. "You put an innocent old man in the hospital, attacking him like that. And the only thing he had done was follow Linda out to her car because she dropped her glove."

"But Malone…"

He threw up his hands in disgust. "You just don't get it! You have this notion in your head that you're right and to hell with everyone else." I couldn't remember Malone ever swearing before. He couldn't look at me. Right now, I wasn't so sure I could stand it if he did.

"I'm sorry, Malone." My voice was little more than a whisper.

"Sorry might not be enough, Jamie. You could have killed that guy. And what if he'd really been after Linda? What if he was armed? Instead of just getting in your car, and calling for help, you could have been putting yourself in harm's way."

I had come by the state police post to talk to Malone. It was hours after the incident, yet he was still pissed. I knew he wouldn't show it to anyone else at work, but I didn't want to let any more time go by. So I leaned against the desk in the small office he shared with the other duty sergeants, waiting for my punishment.

"Is he still in the hospital?" Malone asked quietly.

I nodded. "It's just a precaution. Apparently he has a history of heart problems. I swear to God, Malone, I really thought he was the guy who has been stalking Linda. It wasn't until he went down that I realized what was happening. And of course, Linda was terrified when he came toward us."

Malone came over and leaned against the desk beside me. "So when a stranger approaches you in the early evening, your first reaction is to kick the guy in the chest?"

"Actually, I was aiming lower, but I slipped on the ice. I really am sorry, Malone. I told the hospital that I'll pay for whatever charges there are for the poor guy."

"What happened to the precautions I told you both to

take? Staying together, being observant of your surroundings, understanding that it's all right to call for help. What about all that?"

I kept my eyes on the floor. There was no way I could look at him. It was all I could do to shrug my shoulders.

"No more heroic moves, Jamie. I'll get you each a canister of pepper spray. But until this thing is settled, I expect you to behave. And keep your cell phone in your hand."

"We'll do whatever you say, Malone. I really did think she was in trouble."

He shook his head slowly. Then he drew a deep breath, draped an arm around my shoulders, and pulled me close. "Remind me never to sneak up on you, Jay."

"I promise to never kick you like that, Malone."

\* \* \* \*

It had been a couple of nights since I'd kicked Melvin Saperstein in the chest and put him in the hospital. As a form of penance, I'd been keeping my head down. Malone cooled off. I was trying to focus on my writing, diligently spending at least six hours a day on work-related matters. That included setting up and conducting a couple of interviews that would help me to flesh out the characters for my next story.

But during that whole time, I couldn't get Linda out of my mind. She was no longer the unflappable girl of my youth, able to take whatever happened in stride, enjoying life to its fullest each and every day. Now she was timid. She was meek. I didn't know how she was able to maintain her professional demeanor while teaching classes.

As I thought about it, I realized that in the classrooms, she was safe. Inside the confines of the school building, no harm had come to her. She could continue to function as always, a well-respected teacher. But once she set foot outside the building, it was like throwing a switch.

I turned away from the monitor and propped my heels on the edge of the desk to focus my attention on my best friend and her predicament.

Linda had been doing her best to keep everything together, but I'd seen the look on her face, the terror in her eyes when Melvin Saperstein hurriedly approached us that evening. It was dark. It was cold. His face was in shadows. All either one of us saw was a bulky man rushing in our direction, one hand clenched in a fist out in front of him. All either one of us saw was trouble. That's how tightly wired we'd become.

How much longer could she keep going like this? How much longer would the stalker continue his game? Was there an ultimate act he had in mind? Was this guy just stringing her along, trying to unnerve her? Were all of these little steps moving up to something more elaborate, something physical? So far there had been no actual contact with Linda. She hadn't been approached.

Or had she?

I had no clue who could be stalking her. Maybe it was someone she saw on a regular basis. It was possible. But unless I could shadow her every hour of every day, how could I detect a pattern? There must be a way to help her.

I was still at the desk when I heard the back door open. Time had gotten away from me. Malone stepped into the doorway of the office.

"Working late, Jamie?"

"Just thinking, Malone."

He stood there for a minute without saying a word. I could tell he knew what was on my mind. It's not like I'm working on quantum physics or the drag coefficient of a new model car. His expression gave nothing away, but his eyes slowly grew warmer. He stepped to the desk and pushed my feet off the edge. In a fluid motion Malone took my wrists and lifted me right out of my chair.

"Why, Reginald, whatever…"

"Hush." He silenced me with a kiss. Malone scooped

me into his arms. I thought we were headed for our bedroom but he had other ideas. Still kissing me, he eased me down onto the soft cushions of the 'aunt'. He broke the kiss and pulled a thick quilt over me. There was no hesitation in his movements. He knew exactly what he wanted and what he was going to do.

I watched silently while he moved to the fireplace, opened the flue, and lit the kindling beneath the birch logs. Then he switched on the stereo and dialed in the public radio station that featured jazz at this time of night. I was facing the hearth, watching the flames dance across the logs, enjoying the snap and sizzle as the fire spread. He came back to the 'aunt' and slipped beneath the quilt beside me.

"We're going to get overheated with this quilt, Reginald."

"Somehow I doubt that, Jamie."

He drew me on top of him and started kissing me again. I felt his hands slide beneath my sweater and begin to inch it toward my shoulders. Suddenly, I felt like a teenager about to do some heavy petting while her parents were away. Malone grazed a fingertip across the clasp of my bra and it was magically unhooked.

"How do you do that?" I whispered against his lips.

"Trade secrets," he said.

With a slight tug, my sweater went over my head with my bra tangled inside it. Out of the corner of my eye, I saw it sail in the general direction of the hallway. Now he had one warm hand on my back, pressing me against him, while the other slid down between us to unsnap my jeans. My arms were around his neck. My fingers tangled in his hair. I would have offered to help, but I sensed Malone wanted to take care of this on his own. Of course, with the way he was kissing me, I wouldn't have been much help at all.

Within seconds my jeans were gone and I was naked beneath the quilt. Malone was still dressed. When I tried to reach for his sweater, he caught my wrist with one hand and rolled me against the back of the couch. Still kissing me, he began to drive me crazy with his free hand, a caress here, a pinch there, a little pressure, oh yeah, right there.

"Reginald, what are you doing to me?"

His cobalt eyes were dancing with delight. "Whatever I want to do, Jamie."

What woman in her right mind would argue with that?

# CHAPTER TEN

It was early Saturday morning. Outside, the wind howled, shaking the windows in their frames, reminding us all that we were in Michigan in late February. I was grateful for the thickness of the heavy quilt that kept us warm. I was more grateful for the presence of Malone's body fitted so closely against mine. Having him next to me made the winter so much more bearable.

My phone buzzed on the bedside table. Everyone who knows me understands that I am not a morning person. So either it was a wrong number or someone was in trouble. I snaked a bare arm out from beneath the quilt and snagged the phone.

"Jamie! I need you!" Linda's voice sounded frantic in my ear.

I sat bolt upright, the quilt dropping to my lap. "Linda. What's wrong?"

"Please, Jamie. Can you come right over?"

Malone had raised his head, both eyes snapping open. He didn't hesitate, just rolled out of the bed and started pulling on his clothes.

"We're on our way, baby."

What in the world was going on?

Malone raced to Linda's neighborhood. We got there in record time. I kept her on the cell phone during the ride, just trying to find out more about what was happening. I got bits and pieces. She wanted me there. That was enough for me.

Malone slid the Cherokee to the curb two houses down the block from Linda's place. I looked at him curiously. My attention had been on the phone, not our surroundings. Malone pointed out the windshield. "It's a crime scene, Jamie."

Parked in front of Linda's house was Vince's Mercury sedan. I could see Vince standing on Linda's front porch, bundled up in his winter coat. He was slowly shaking his head in disbelief. Linda was inside, staring through the front windows. Malone directed me to the house. As I moved past Vince, I noticed his jaw was clenched. The anger was welling up inside him, looking for an outlet. I touched his arm. He relaxed slightly.

"Linda needs you, Jamie."

"Are you hurt, Vince?" I asked.

"Only my pride and perhaps my wallet are impacted. Physically, I will be fine."

I ducked inside. Linda's hug was so tight I thought she might crack one of my ribs. Logan ambled over. He must have sensed something was wrong, because he didn't bark or jump or beg for attention. He merely stood beside Linda, his head resting against her leg. After a moment she relaxed and we turned to look out the window.

Malone was slowly walking around the car. While the recent snow had melted off the grass, there was still a bit of frozen slush in the street. I could almost hear it crunch as Malone moved around the car. Still holding onto Linda, I took a good look at the Mercury.

What looked like duct tape covered each window in the form of an X. Beneath the tape, the glass was shattered. The doors and the roof had been sprayed with bright yellow paint. I couldn't make out the words from here, but

I guessed they were not kind. All four tires were flat. Malone was by the trunk now. He squatted down for a minute and peered beneath the car. I saw a flare of light and realized he was using the heavy flashlight he kept in the Cherokee. Malone got to his feet, dusted his knees off and walked toward the house. He and Vince had a brief conversation on the porch. Then Malone popped the door and stepped inside.

"Did you call the police yet?" he asked as Vince followed him.

Linda shook her head. "We thought we'd check with you first. In case it was just some kids playing a prank."

Malone's eyes were stone cold. "Call the police. This wasn't the work of kids. Somebody's deadly serious."

Linda made the call. She was full of nervous energy, so I persuaded her to make some coffee. While it was brewing and we were waiting for the cops, we congregated at the front window.

"Tell me what happened," Malone said quietly.

Vince blew out a breath in frustration. He pulled his coat and gloves off and reached down to stroke Logan's head. He did it without thinking. I noticed that the dog had taken up a position within easy reach of both Vince and Linda.

"I got up about six. I have office hours today. I got dressed and was going to just run out to the bakery before heading off to work. I let Logan out the back door around six-thirty. When I was getting ready to leave, that's when I noticed the car. I didn't hear anything during the night."

Malone nodded. "What did you two do last night?"

"We went out after work for a quiet dinner at Cherry Blossoms," Linda said. "Then we came home and watched a movie." She leaned closer to Vince. He lifted his hand from Logan's head. His arm went around her waist.

"What time did you get home?" I asked. Malone shot me a look but I ignored it.

Linda thought for a minute. "It was probably about

nine o'clock or so. Vince didn't finish with his last patient until almost seven. That's why we went out for dinner and just came back home."

"Do you think someone followed us?" Vince asked Malone.

"That's hard to say. Someone definitely knew that was your car," Malone said. "What time did the movie end?"

Vince answered that one. "It was close to eleven. I remember thinking about going home last night. But it was late and cold and—"

"I wanted him to stay," Linda finished.

Nobody said anything for a moment. Malone nodded out the window as a police car moved slowly down the street. He glanced at the three of us and headed for the door.

"Are you sure this wasn't kids, Malone?" I asked.

"I'm positive, Jamie. You guys stay here. I'll be right back."

Vince called his service and had them contact one of his associates to cover his morning appointments. Linda got us each some coffee and filled a travel mug for Malone. Immediately, she brewed another pot. I watched Malone from the window seat. He shook hands with the two patrol officers then gestured at the Mercury. One of the cops dropped to a knee and repeated the examination Malone had done earlier. The other cop walked around the vehicle, taking everything in. At one point, he stepped back to the driveway and looked out to the street. Then he looked up. Malone joined him for a brief conversation. The other cop went to the patrol car to use the radio.

Malone came in. His ears were bright red from the cold. He gave Linda a brief smile and accepted the mug of coffee.

"What's going on?" I asked.

"Farmington Police will handle it. They will talk to all the neighbors, see if anyone heard or saw anything during the night. They're going to call in their forensic people to photograph the car before they tow it in."

Malone shrugged out of his jacket and sat on the edge of the recliner. I went to him. Perching beside him, I watched Linda and Vince settle on the sofa. Logan sprawled on the floor at their feet. Vince was slowly running his hand through Linda's curly mane. It reminded me of times that Malone did the same thing with me.

"There will probably be a detective from Farmington here in a little while to interview you both," Malone said quietly. "There is a chance they might get some evidence from the car itself, once they take it in."

"What kind of evidence?" I asked.

"Fingerprints would be a start. Whoever smashed those windows took the time to secure the glass with heavy tape so they would shatter, but not make much noise. And it looks like they used a heavy cutting tool to snip off the valve stems on the tires."

Vince leaned forward, his arm now going around Linda's waist. "What did you find beneath the car, Malone?"

Malone sipped the coffee. Then he threaded the fingers of his free hand through mine. "Whoever did this isn't just some kid playing a prank. This is someone who seriously means to do you harm. I think the windows and the spray paint were a secondary plan when the primary plan failed."

"Why would someone want to do this to Vince?" Linda asked softly.

"Right now I think they were striking out at a material thing. Maybe they wanted to scare him away or send some kind of message."

"What was the primary plan, Malone?" I asked.

He held my hand a little tighter. "They wanted to blow up Vince's car."

The three of us stared at Malone in disbelief. Why would anybody want to hurt Vince Schulte? He was your friendly neighborhood doctor. He didn't perform back alley abortions or run Planned Parenthood meetings. He was the guy who volunteered at countless youth sporting events to stick around the sidelines, no matter what the score, just in case somebody skinned their knee, sprained their wrist, or banged heads with another athlete. He built his entire practice around listening to his patients, taking his time to explain to them their ailments and what the best course of treatment would be. Even after years of work, he was often the first to respond when a patient called his service after hours and needed his help. He was one of the nicest, kindest, friendliest people I'd ever known. I couldn't get my head around the idea that someone wanted to hurt him.

"Malone, what do you mean?" Linda asked.

He looked calmly at the three of us and set his coffee mug on the little table beside the chair. I noticed he set it on a magazine, so it wouldn't damage the wood.

"When I was walking around the car, I smelled gasoline. It was stronger in the rear. The car hadn't been running, so I shouldn't have been able to smell anything. That's when I dropped down to look.

"Someone punched a hole in the gas tank. Not huge, but big enough to cause the gas to drip down onto the ground. There was a good sized puddle beneath the tank, on top of the ice on the street."

Vince rose from the sofa to look out the window. Two other people had joined the police officers. One was busy with a camera. "But poking a hole in the tank wouldn't cause it to blow up on its own, would it?" Vince asked.

"No," Malone said with a slow shake of his head. "But they had a poor man's fuse down there as well. That's what they were trying to do, blow the car up."

We were all on our feet now, standing by the window, watching the police do their work. Logan whined and restlessly wandered around the house. No one really paid him any attention.

"What's a poor man's fuse?" I asked.

"Different things can be used. This looked like a full

book of matches wrapped around a lit cigarette. In theory, when the cigarette burns down far enough, it will ignite the matches. Under ideal circumstances, that sudden burst would have touched off the gasoline, which would have blown the car up," Malone said quietly.

"But it obviously didn't work," Vince said.

"They didn't take into consideration the wind. It was enough to put out the ember on the cigarette." Malone put an arm around my shoulders and pulled me close. "So when it didn't blow, they decided to smash the windows and spray paint the car."

"Why would they want to hurt Vince?" Linda asked softly, her eyes staring at the floor.

Malone took a deep breath and let it out slowly. "Maybe they don't really want to hurt him. Maybe they just want to scare him away."

"Scare him away from what?" I asked.

There was a moment of silence while we all considered possibilities. But I sensed we all knew the answer to my question.

"Not what, Jamie, who," Linda said quietly, slowly raising her head. "They want to scare him away from me."

\* \* \* \*

Linda tried to send us away after that, but neither Malone nor I was going to budge. We waited until the cops finished examining the car. A flatbed tow truck came in and winched the Mercury away. Two of the cops went around the neighborhood, talking to the other residents to find out if anyone heard or saw anything during the night.

Vince had stepped into the kitchen to make some calls. He alerted his insurance agent of the vandalism and made arrangements for a rental car. It wasn't clear at this time whether or not his Mercury was repairable. I don't think any of us was thinking beyond the moment. He came back from the kitchen and sat on the end of the sofa. Linda was pacing the floor. I had never seen her so angry in my life.

"This is ludicrous," Linda snapped. "This is the twenty-first century. If I want to spend time with Vince Schulte, it's nobody's business but ours."

"It's starting to look like someone is making it their business," Malone said. "It could be the same person who has been following you."

Linda's resolve seemed to melt into the floor. She lowered her chin to her chest. Without a word, she turned around and went to where Vince was sitting. The confusion was evident on his face.

"I didn't want to trouble you," she said quietly. "I thought at first it was you, or maybe someone just playing a little joke on me."

"What are you talking about?" Vince asked, his eyes growing wide with concern.

Linda slowly sat beside him. Without even realizing it, I noticed how their hands interlocked. "For about three weeks now, I've been finding little gifts in the strangest places. There was a bag of gummy bears under the windshield wipers on my car when I came out from school. And one afternoon, there was a travel magazine tucked in the mailbox. It didn't have my address on it, like a subscription. It was something someone purchased at a store and left for me. And last week, someone left a Valentine's card on my windshield at school. The day before yesterday, I found two sweetheart roses on the front porch."

"Has anything like this ever happened before?" Vince asked quietly.

Linda slowly shook her head. "There were no notes, no messages, nothing to give me a clue as to who was leaving these things. Obviously they know where I live and where I work."

"But there was nothing threatening," Malone said.

Vince swung his head in Malone's direction. "You knew about this?"

Malone nodded.

"And of course, Jamie knew as well," Vince snapped angrily. "But for some reason, you didn't want to tell me."

He started to rise from the sofa, but Linda refused to let him go. "I didn't want to worry you. At first with the candy, I thought it was one of my students. I just put the bag in the car and threw it out on my way home. I wouldn't eat something like that, especially if I didn't know where it came from."

"What about the other gifts?"

Malone pushed away from the wall. "The magazine was one of those travel books about things to do in the Southwest. That was a while ago."

"And I thought the flowers might be from you," Linda said, still squeezing Vince's hands. "It was two tiny red roses, with a piece of red satin tying them together."

"How romantic," Vince said sarcastically.

"But don't you see, that's why I thought they were from you," Linda said. I could see her eyes welling up with tears. "Because you are the most romantic man I've ever known. And I don't care what other people say or think. Whoever I spend my time with is my choice. And I choose you."

From my perch on the chair, I watched Vince's anger dissipate. He was looking into her baby blue eyes. Tenderly, he wiped the tears from her cheeks. Then he drew her close and held her. Linda buried her face in his chest as more tears came. His right hand was lost in that jumble of curls, slowly wading through her hair. Malone started walking toward the kitchen, pausing just long enough to grab my hand and pull me along. Even Logan followed us. This was not a time for a discussion. It was time for them to be alone.

# CHAPTER ELEVEN

It seemed like hours had passed since Malone and Vince left. Linda and I were in the kitchen watching Logan pace around the house. Even the dog knew things were not settled. I tried to get her to eat some toast, but Linda wasn't interested. I offered to make her some eggs and was rewarded with a smile.

"I'm not that desperate, Jay Kay, just upset."

"I can tell you're feeling better when you revert to my nickname."

"What do you think is taking the guys so long?"

I shrugged. "Malone said he was going to take Vince to pick up his rental car and run a quick errand. But he said it wouldn't take him long."

We both looked up as Logan started barking. He raced to the door, his bushy tail wagging furiously. He only does that when it's someone he knows. Through the window I could see Malone and Vince ascending the stairs. Linda went to unlock the deadbolt and let them in. Vince was carrying a large brown paper bag. Malone had a toolbox in one hand and a cardboard box in the other. They weren't exactly smiling, but their faces weren't etched in gloom and doom either. Vince set his bag on the kitchen table and quickly shed his coat and gloves.

"Malone is a very wise man," he said as he began unpacking the bag. I glanced at Malone, who dropped the box and his tools by the front window. He winked at me as he pulled off his coat.

Suddenly, the table was filled with food. Not just any food either, but delicacies I have only found one place on earth.

"You went to Toot's Deli?" I asked in amazement.

Linda stared at the small mountain of food that materialized from Vince's bag. "Do I smell pastrami?"

For the first time that day, a smile crossed Vince's face. "We have pastrami with hot mustard and Swiss on French bread, rare roast beef with lettuce, tomato, and horseradish on a Kaiser roll, smoked turkey with provolone cheese and garlic mayonnaise on rye, and a triple salad on an onion roll. There are enough dill pickles in here to feed an army. And she threw in two quarts of matzo ball soup to take the chill off."

Since the sandwiches were so gigantic, we could each take a quarter of each one. I had no idea what a triple salad was. Turns out it was egg salad, tuna salad and chicken salad. As we feasted on the soup and sandwiches, we were able to put the morning's events behind us. The meal gave us all fuel. We didn't talk about anything specific until we were done eating. Linda and I wrapped up the extras. I saw Vince swipe a piece of roast beef and slip it to Logan. I swear the dog smiled in delight as he gulped it down.

When we were back at the table, I turned my gaze to Malone. "So what's in the box, Damien?"

"I picked up a few little goodies that will give Linda some peace of mind and might just help us put an end to this nonsense."

Malone looked over at Vince, who nodded sagely. Apparently they had gone shopping for more than just food.

"Tell me what you're talking about," Linda said. I

noticed that she had one hand linked in Vince's and the other was resting on Logan's head. Her two guys were staying close by.

Malone pushed away from the table. "It will be easier if I show you."

He went to the cardboard box by the window and opened it. The three of us followed, although I was pretty sure Vince already knew what was inside. Malone began setting out the equipment on the carpet. I had no idea what I was looking at.

"I reached out to a friend who is a private investigator. He has quite a supply of gadgets available and offered to loan me a few things," Malone said as he looked up at our curious faces.

"Damien, what in the world are you talking about?"

He winked at me. "We're going to take the offensive. We all want to make sure Linda will be safe. These little gadgets will help."

Malone held up two tubes that looked like heavy magic markers. "These are spy cameras. We already know this guy has left gifts for Linda on her car. So we're going to set it up with video cameras. These are equipped with motion sensors and strong batteries. We'll clip one on the visor by the driver's seat, facing forward. The other will go on the passenger side, facing the rear." He looked right at Linda. "If anyone approaches your car, we'll capture them on video. When you come home at night, we'll check that day's activity and see if you spot anyone hanging around your car that's not supposed to be there. We'll also recharge the batteries each night."

"Thanks, Malone," she said softly. I could tell she was relieved by the idea of taking action.

"What else do you have there?" Vince asked.

There were several other cameras. These were heavier, outdoor models that he could plug into an outlet. He explained they also had a battery backup, in case for any reason the power went out. Two of them looked like outdoor spotlights, which he could easily screw into existing light fixtures. It was Malone's intent to cover both the front and the back of the house. He explained that it wouldn't take him long to set everything up.

Logan chose that moment to wander in and curl up at Linda's feet. Automatically, she reached down and tugged at his ears.

"How is Logan with strangers?" Malone asked.

Vince answered quickly. "He is loud and obnoxious, especially if Linda isn't present. It's taken him weeks just to get used to me."

"Did he make any noise last night?" I asked.

Linda thought about it for a moment then shook her head. "No, he was fine. Usually, if someone comes to the door or even up the driveway, he hears it and will go check it out. That's one of the reasons I have him."

Malone nodded and was quiet for a moment. I could sense he wanted to ask her something else, but was trying to figure out the best way to do it. Instead of asking the question, he pulled on his coat and grabbed the two spotlight shaped cameras. Vince went through the kitchen and opened the overhead door to the garage. A few minutes later, we watched Malone set up a stepladder and quickly change the regular light bulb for the camera at the front of the house. He came back inside after installing the camera in the rear light fixture. He and Vince set up the other two cameras at opposite ends of the house, to cover the full exterior. They went into the garage and prepared Linda's car as well. Malone also explained that he had borrowed two more of the marker style cameras for Vince to put in his rental car. At last he shed his coat and looked at us.

"I'd like to talk to Linda alone."

Vince and I sat on the sofa. The coffee had me so amped up. It's a wonder I was able to sit still. Logan followed Linda and Malone down the hall to the small bedroom she called her studio. Linda's talents extended to music. She played keyboard and the violin. I didn't think we'd be hearing any performances today.

I realized Vince was staring at a picture on the table at the end of the sofa. It was of Vince and Linda at the New Year's Eve party. They had just come off the dance floor. Vince had his arm around her, his head turned to hear something Linda was saying over the noise of the crowd. Both of their faces were beaming. It was a great shot. I thought of it as a new beginning.

"Do you think I'm nuts, Jamie?" Vince asked quietly.

I bit back a laugh. "Vince, you are one of the least crazy people I have ever met. Why would I think you were nuts?"

He gestured at the photo. "I'm an old man, Jamie. What in the world am I doing with such a beautiful young woman?"

"From where I stand, you're having a wonderful time." I reached over and lightly punched him on the shoulder. "And she is, too. Don't you think Linda wants to be with you? Weren't you listening earlier?"

"That might have just been bluster on her part," Vince said.

I shook my head. "For such a smart man, you can be pretty stupid when it comes to matters of the heart."

He turned on the sofa so he could face me. "It has been a long time since I have had any romantic inclinations. But from the moment I saw Linda on New Year's Eve, it was as if those feelings were rekindled. My body may argue, but my heart feels like a teenager whenever I'm with her."

"That sounds like a pretty good thing to me."

"I'm not going to question why she wants to be with me. I am just very glad that she does."

"Linda has always been independent. And I know that she treasures the time you two are together. I think the fact that you're both comfortable in your own lives is a big part of it. She's not looking to be the good wife, rushing home to clean your house, do your laundry, cook your meals and have your slippers and beer waiting when you come home."

Vince chuckled. "I could never picture her in that role."

"So stop questioning your sanity, Doc. Enjoy the romance."

"When did you become so knowledgeable on matters of the heart, Jamie?"

I took a moment to consider it. "I think it was when I started dating Malone."

\* \* \* \*

Malone and I were just about to leave when a sedan pulled up to the curb in the spot where Vince's car had been vandalized. After his private conversation with Linda, Malone was being awfully quiet. Linda and Vince were in the kitchen talking about the new security measures. Vince didn't think it was enough. Linda was adamantly refusing to be driven out of her own home. My attention had been on their conversation as I struggled to zip up my coat. Malone gave me a gentle nudge and tipped his head toward the window.

The sedan was obviously an unmarked police car. I watched a guy struggle to get out from behind the steering wheel and head up the driveway. I noticed he wasn't wearing boots, but leather shoes, dark slacks and an overcoat. He wore no hat or gloves. As he got closer to the house, I noticed that it looked like he hadn't shaved in a few days. Malone opened the front door and ushered him inside.

"I'm Detective Ruzzio with the Farmington PD. Sorry I didn't get here earlier, but we're running a little short-handed."

Malone handled the introductions. Ruzzio pulled a notebook from his pocket and checked off the names on a printed form. He talked to us as a group, and then asked to speak with Vince in private. A few minutes later, he talked to Linda. After that, he came back to the group.

"The lab rats will be going over the car. With any luck, we'll find a fingerprint or something that will lead us to whoever was misbehaving. And we might even be able to match it to a print on that magazine."

Malone nodded. "I've contacted the forensic lab at the post. They will have the magazine and whatever prints they were able to lift delivered to your office."

Ruzzio scratched at his beard stubble with his pen. "I've already checked with the watch commander. We're going to add some extra patrols in this area. You see anything weird, you just call 911 and we'll have units here faster than I get heartburn from Italian sausage and peppers."

"If it gives you heartburn, why do you eat it?" I asked, unable to stifle my curiosity.

"My mother would never speak to me again if I didn't eat it. That would be sacrilegious. Although now that I think about it, that might not be such a bad thing."

"Is there anything else we can do, or any other precautions we should take?" Vince asked.

Ruzzio gave it some consideration then looked directly at Linda. "I'm sure Sergeant Malone has told you this already, but it's worth repeating. Keep your eyes open. Your cell phone should always be in one hand, your car keys in the other. If your car has a remote device with a panic button, make sure it works and don't hesitate to hit it. If you're out, go with a friend or several friends. Don't take chances."

"Malone did tell us the same things," Linda said quietly.

"And you can't think of anyone who would want to bother you like this?" Ruzzio asked, more to himself than anyone else. Linda just slowly shook her head. He let the quiet settle around the room. But his next question shook us all up.

"Tell me about your ex-husband."

I don't know which one of us was the most surprised. The fact that Linda had been married and divorced wasn't a secret. But I had not thought about Derek Bishop in a long time. And from the look on Linda's face, it was obvious that neither had she. Ruzzio gathered us all around the kitchen table for what looked like a friendly conversation. He was leaning against the counter, watching the four of us react.

"What could Derek possibly have to do with this?" she asked quietly. "I haven't spoken to him in months and haven't seen him in years."

Ruzzio scratched at his stubble some more. "I don't know who might be involved, but I've got to look at every angle. People do strange things. Maybe he never got over losing you."

"He's the one who left me," Linda said softly and I could see the painful memory reflected in her eyes.

"How long were you married?" Ruzzio asked.

"About eighteen months," I said, jumping into the conversation. "It was a real whirlwind courtship."

Ruzzio turned his bleary eyes in my direction. He reminded me of a basset hound. But before he could say anything, Linda confirmed my assessment.

"Derek was all flash and glitter. Of course, I didn't realize it back then. He was a little older than me, with a decent job as a purchasing agent for one of the automotive companies. He did a lot of traveling." Linda had dredged all these memories up now, and was calmly describing the situation as if she was merely an innocent bystander.

"So why did he leave you?" Ruzzio asked.

Vince interrupted, obviously aware of how painful this was for Linda. "Are you sure this is relevant to what's been happening lately?"

"Detective Ruzzio can't tell what is relevant and what isn't at this point. So he has to ask all kinds of questions, as difficult as they may be," Malone said.

Ruzzio nodded. "Thanks, Sarge. I know this isn't easy, but it may give me a lead. Or it may help rule out someone like your ex-husband. So can you tell me, why did he leave you?"

Linda gave a little shudder before responding. Then she reached over and found reassurance in Vince's hands. *Three months ago those would have been my hands she would have been reaching for. Part of me was a little sad, but I pushed those thoughts away to concentrate on her response.*

"Derek dazzled me when we met. There was a little bit of the bad boy in him that I thought was just an act, but it turned out to be a glimpse of the real deal. He could be sweet and charming when it suited his purposes, but he was as hollow as a chocolate Easter bunny.

"Derek came from a large, boorish family. They measured success two ways: by the amount of money you made and the number of children you sired. We never talked about having kids when he seriously started pursuing me. And Jamie's right, it was a real whirlwind courtship. Less than three months after we met, he proposed. Derek gave me two options, either a big, gaudy wedding with a zillion people or an elopement." Linda paused at the memory.

"But she held her ground and it was an elegant, tasteful ceremony," I said, filling the silence and giving her a chance to gather her thoughts. Ruzzio bobbed his head in acknowledgment. I sensed he didn't really want this much detail, but he was willing to let her answer the question her own way.

"In the beginning, it was a nice marriage. We went on trips and he lavished presents on me all the time. He wanted me to get pregnant right away, but I just started teaching at the high school and wasn't ready for a family. For a while I resisted, but Derek became more demanding. So, I went off the pill. But even after six more months, I still didn't get pregnant. We went to a series of doctors and they ran a series of tests." Linda paused as if she had run out of steam. There wasn't a sound in the room. Logan must have sensed her discomfort because he came over and laid his snout on her leg. Absently she rubbed his head with her free hand.

"And the test results?" Ruzzio asked quietly.

"Confirmed what I had already known, or at least guessed at. I couldn't have children. I had some problems when I was younger, cysts on the ovaries, among other things. So, I couldn't get pregnant. Part of me was relieved. I really loved my job working with the kids and didn't want to lose what I had to start my own family. But Derek didn't see it that way. He started looking at me as if I was less than a woman. He got bad. He would drink more. He started getting rough with me, insulting me when we were with his family and friends, accusing me of tricking him into marrying me.

"I tried to talk to him about options, like adoption. But Derek wouldn't hear of it. If the child couldn't be his biologically, he didn't want anything to do with it."

"So he left you," Ruzzio said.

Linda bobbed her head in reply. "He started staying out more and more with his friends. Then there would be days when he wasn't traveling but he wasn't home either. His clothes always smelled like booze, sweat, and perfume. I heard through some friends that he was involved with a couple of other women. I tried to get upset, but by that time, I'd fallen out of love with him. I couldn't get mad. I was just...disappointed. Then one day I heard that he'd gotten one of those women pregnant. Two days later, I got served with papers for the divorce." She gave her shoulders a minute shrug. "He was done. I got a generous settlement, bought my own house, and got on with my life."

Ruzzio took out his notebook again. Linda took her address book from the counter and gave him Derek Bishop's contact information. He left to do his detective work, which left us all wondering the same thing.

# CHAPTER TWELVE

Somehow we all made it through the rest of the weekend. Malone and I left shortly after Ruzzio did. Linda's two guys stayed by her side until it was time for her to go to school Monday morning.

I did my best to work, doing revisions and writing a draft for a couple of scenes that I had been struggling with. With the problems Linda was having, it was becoming impossible for me to concentrate on anything else. I couldn't seem to get into the creative flow. Realizing that the afternoon had slipped away, I suddenly had a case of cabin fever, so I grabbed my coat and gloves and got out of the house. Since I was out running a few errands anyway, I swung by the post. When I start finding excuses to stay away from my computer, that's when I need a kick in the motivation. I was hoping to find that in the form of Malone.

It was almost six o'clock. I knew the administrative staff was long gone. Malone would be overseeing the shift. One of the troopers at the front desk waved me through to the bullpen area.

Malone was leaning against a desk, quietly talking with two other people. I hesitated in the background until I caught his eye. He smiled and waved me over and introduced me.

"Jamie, this is Sergeant Jefferson Chene and Detective Megan McDonald. They work with the multi-jurisdictional investigative squad."

Chene gave me a thin smile and shook my hand. "We prefer Squad Six. It's a lot less glorified, but it gets the job done." His voice was low and deep.

"I've heard about you," Megan McDonald said. "You're the one who cracked the Kleinschmidt shooting. That was good work."

I smiled at the compliment. "According to Malone, it was just a stubborn redhead with an active imagination. Hope I'm not interrupting anything."

Chene easily shook his head. "No, we were just on our way across town from Ann Arbor. Thought I'd stop by and pick up the fifty bucks Malone owes me from the Patriots and Broncos game."

"I told him not to bet against New England, but he wouldn't listen," I said.

Malone shrugged. "Hey, I'm a Denver fan. What can I say?"

While the cops bantered, I took a moment to study them. Chene was a light-skinned black man, close to six feet in height, with a solid build. His black hair was clipped short. He was clean-shaven, with piercing, dark eyes. He had a short, jagged scar on his left cheek. McDonald was almost too pretty to be a cop. She had shoulder length blonde hair and hazel eyes. She was about my height. Her frame was muscular, but she still looked feminine. I had no doubt she could hold her own with the male officers.

"So what does a multi-jurisdictional investigative squad do?" I asked.

Megan gave me a wink. "We catch the bad guys. We can't leave all the work to the civilians."

"Most of our cases span different communities," Chene said. "Sometimes they are in the same county, other times, it can involve several counties."

"Do you collaborate with the different communities in your investigations?" I asked.

"Well, in some cases we do," Megan said, "but usually they turn to us to take over the case. Sometimes it's a matter of manpower or experience. Our boss kind of likes it when we're left to work on our own."

"Without the help of any nosy civilians," I said.

"That goes without saying," Chene said with another thin smile.

I looked at him closely. He reminded me of someone, but I couldn't make the connection. "Your name is Jefferson Chene. Isn't that an intersection in Detroit?"

Chene nodded once. "Yes, that's right."

I waited for him to elaborate, but there was nothing else coming.

Malone paid his debt. Chene made a show of holding the bill up to the light, as if to make certain it wasn't counterfeit. Then he and McDonald headed out. When we were alone, Malone pulled me close for a hug. After a while we separated and I boosted myself up on the desk, letting my legs dangle.

"What brings you by, Jamie?"

"I can't just swing by to say hello when I'm driving past?"

He gave me a soft smile. "You can stop in anytime. But it's only been about four hours since I left home."

Already he can see right through me. "I'm worried about Linda. It's creepy to think someone's following her around like that."

"The Farmington Police are looking into it. There's nothing else we can do officially. It's their jurisdiction."

Exasperated, I drummed my heels against the desk. "I know, Angelo, but that doesn't mean I like it."

"I did a little background on Detective Ruzzio. He's got a good track record and has cracked some difficult cases. We need to give him some time."

"In something like this, Malone, I don't have very much patience."

Malone nodded in agreement. "Neither do I, Jamie. But maybe there's something we can do unofficially."

Malone encouraged Linda to stick with her usual routines. In the meantime, he had some ideas he wanted to follow up on. The rat wouldn't tell me what they were. I got the impression he was going to do something that might be a little bit shady. So it was up to me to help keep Linda going.

* * * *

"I don't really feel like going to the gym," she said Tuesday afternoon.

"Tough shit, Algae, you got me started on this exercise routine. We can't quit now. So get your cute little ass over here or should I pick you up?"

"Jay Kay, I just don't want…"

"I'm on my way. I've got my gear on and I'm walking out the door. And you know damn well, I can be as stubborn as you are."

She sighed in my ear then started laughing. "Okay, pick me up."

"See how easy it can be?"

Linda was ready when I arrived, so she jumped into the Honda. She had a smirk on her face and playfully slapped my leg as I was driving away.

"What was that for?" I asked innocently.

"You're pathetic. I almost believed for a moment that you would be disappointed if we didn't go to class tonight. You, the girl who thinks shopping for clothes qualifies as a form of physical fitness."

"Shopping does count. When you're trying clothes on, that's when you decide whether or not your body needs some attention."

"That makes no sense," she said with a grin.

"Yes, it does. If I'm shopping for jeans and the size I always wear seems to be too tight, I know one of two things has happened. Either I've been eating too much or the jeans were mismarked."

She was laughing now. "You are so pathetic."

"I resemble that remark." At least I had her in a good mood. I parked at the gym and we ran inside. Cramming our coats into a locker, we headed for the aerobics room. Madeline was already warming up with a few stretches as the students wandered in. She smiled widely and encouraged us to loosen up. The class started right on schedule and she proceeded to put us through our paces. The combination of kickboxing and yoga moves was a good mixture for us. Most of the students were regulars now, so we had the same dozen or so women every week.

As the class was winding down, Madeline walked around the room checking our poses. She had a funny smile on her face. She ended class a couple of minutes early and asked everyone to gather around.

"Some of you may have heard that I've also started teaching some other classes. These are not ones that are offered here at the gym, but it's another form of exercise that you might find to be challenging and a lot of fun."

Most of us exchanged skeptical looks. I noticed Madeline watching a couple of the older women in the group. She waited a moment before continuing.

"What I'm talking about is a pole dancing class. They have been very popular on the West Coast for a number of years," Madeline said, still keeping that funny smile on her face.

"A class for pole dancing, like what they do at a strip club?" one of the older women asked loudly.

"That's right," Madeline said. "It can be a very vigorous workout. And it can also be very sexy. Some of my students say it can really spice things up in the bedroom."

One of the older women turned and left the room. In a way, it didn't surprise me. A woman in her late twenties also chose to exit at that time. Maybe her bedroom was spicy enough. The rest of us looked at each other, then back to Madeline.

"I'm not trying to get you to do something that you're not interested in. This will be an all-female class. It can be fun, but it is also a very strenuous workout. You might be pleasantly surprised."

Linda piped up beside me. "Where do you teach these classes?"

Like her bedroom needed any extra attention!

"We don't have a studio nearby yet, but we are looking at several locations. In the meantime, some people have hosted parties in their homes. I also have my basement set up. I'm going to hold a class there in a couple of weeks. If any of you are interested, please let me know." Then she smiled brightly and told us all to have a good night.

Linda grabbed my arm and dragged me toward the corner where Madeline was standing.

"How much does this class cost?" she asked.

Madeline considered it for a moment. "Since we're going to do this at my place, I'll charge you twenty bucks each. You should plan on a two-hour session."

"What do we wear?" Linda asked. "I don't have any stripper outfits in my closet."

I started to interject something, but she wagged a finger at me. The smile on her face was the best I'd seen in days. I decided to keep my mouth shut.

"You can wear the same gear that you do for this class. Bring along a pair of shorts, too. And bring whatever shoes you'd normally wear for dancing." She gave Linda a card with her address and phone number on it.

"Sign both of us up, Madeline," Linda said. "We'll definitely be there."

I could feel my chin drop. "Are you crazy? You want us to take pole dancing lessons?"

Linda tucked Madeline's card inside the spandex strap of her top. "Yes, I think it will be fun. And it will certainly keep my mind off of anything else. Besides, it will be worth twenty bucks just to see you swinging from a pole."

"You can be so cruel."

As we left the aerobics room, Linda guided us over to a pair of stationary bicycles. Since it was Tuesday, we would extend our routine. Apparently the idea of the pole dancing class bolstered her spirits. She kept laughing as we peddled. I sensed she was imagining what I would look like swinging from a silver pole.

From the corner of my eye, I saw one of the regular guys heading our way. There was an empty bike beside me, but the one next to Linda was occupied by a high school girl whose legs were churning so fast she could power a race car. I caught Linda's eye in the mirror as the guy came forward. A smirk crossed her face.

This guy was at the gym every time we had been here. He wasn't as pushy as some guys, but I always seemed to notice his eyes on us. I watched him in the mirror as he moved to the bike beside me.

"Hi," he said, giving me a nod as he adjusted the seat and started pedaling.

"Hi," I said.

Linda started talking about a project she wanted to assign to her class. I turned most of my attention to her, but kept an eye on the mirror. The guy seemed to have found his rhythm and his eyes were focused on the television monitor mounted on the wall above the mirror. I took advantage of the situation and took a quick look at him.

He was taller than Malone, probably about six-two, and stockier. I guessed he was about the same age as Malone, but I noticed that his blond hair had a lot of gray streaks in it. I wondered for a moment if he colored it and was due for a tune-up. Linda asked my thoughts about her project.

We talked for a while about school and the book I was working on. At the advice of Shannon, my literary agent, I'd taken the events of the Kleinschmidt shooting and was turning this into a mystery. I was fictionalizing some of the parts, but a lot of it was going to be exactly how it happened. I didn't need to go into a lot of specifics with Linda, since she'd already heard the story. About the time we were finishing up our session, I noticed the guy beside me step off his machine and walk over to the water fountain.

We stopped pedaling and climbed off. On the wall near the water fountain was a canister with alcohol wipes, which they encouraged you to use on the machines to clear away any sweat and germs you might have left behind. Linda and I had just finished sanitizing our bikes when the guy came back around.

"You girls done for the evening?" he asked, standing directly behind our machines.

Linda gave him a slight smile. "Yes, we're all set."

His eyes were latched onto her now. "It's pretty cold outside. Would you like to go get some coffee?"

"Sorry, but we already have plans for tonight," Linda said.

He took this into consideration for a moment. "We'll have to do it some other time then," he said, nodding his head.

"We'll see."

He started to turn away, then swung back around and extended his hand. "I'm Bob. I'm here about this time every weeknight. I work out Saturday mornings, too."

Linda gently took his hand and introduced both of us. As an afterthought, he turned and squeezed my hand briefly, pumping it up and down three times, like a used car salesman.

"I'll see you around," he said. Then he spun on his heel and headed toward the locker room.

"Do you ever get tired of that?" I asked as we gathered our coats.

"Tired of what?" Linda asked coyly.

"Do you ever get tired of being the object of such

blatant masculine desire?"

She batted her lashes as we stepped outside. "It's the price one must pay with such an adoring public."

"Algae, you can be so full of shit!"

* * * *

It was more than two weeks since Vince's car was vandalized. Linda was trying her best to keep things going, but I could see the strain starting to get to her. She confided in me that Vince had suggested they not see each other until this problem was settled, but Linda adamantly rejected that idea. To prove her point, she had showed up at his house wearing a long woolen winter coat, her boots, and a smile. All of Vince's objections disappeared as soon as she'd gotten inside and he'd learned that was all she was wearing besides a little perfume.

Malone made it a part of his daily routine to stop by Linda's school and view the footage from the security cameras. One of the vice principals, who also oversaw security, started to look forward to his visits. I might have been jealous if he hadn't pointed out that she was in her early sixties, almost as round as she was tall, and had spiky, white hair. So when he called me just before his shift was about to start, I didn't think much of it.

"Jamie, is tonight one of your workout nights?"

"Yes, Lamont, it is. Linda usually picks me up on her way there."

"That's what I thought."

I detected a little glimmer of energy in his voice. "Malone, what's going on?"

"I was just checking on you, Jamie. I like the idea that you're getting regular exercise, beyond the bedroom."

"Are you sure that's all it is, Lamont?"

His voice remained calm. "Jamie, on the nights that you work out, you usually go home take a long, hot shower, splash a little perfume in all the right places, and are very amorous when I arrive. That's the kind of reception a man can definitely look forward to at the end of his day."

"I'm glad you get to reap the benefits of my exercise routine, Lamont. But are you sure there's not some other reason why you called?"

"You just have to trust me. You do trust me, don't you, Jay?"

I let an exasperated sigh escape my lips. "Mostly," I said.

"That's good enough." And with that, he hung up.

I tried to put that conversation out of my mind when Linda showed up. Fortunately, she was in a talkative mood, telling me about a particularly good group of students and an enthusiastic discussion that had taken place during one of her last classes of the day. We got to the gym and both got lost in our workout.

But in the back of my mind, I kept wondering if there was something Malone wasn't telling me.

\* \* \* \*

We stopped for tea and pastries on our way home. It was not exactly the healthiest of dinners, but neither one of us had much of an appetite after our workout. It was warm in the coffee shop, with a number of people camping out, and a steady stream of patrons coming and going.

I never really saw him until he was standing beside our little table. We had been talking quietly, bits of cranberry muffins on the plates before us. Linda had taken off her jacket and draped it over her chair. She had pulled the clips from her hair and shaken out her cascade of curls. My jacket was draped over my shoulders, since my back was toward the door and there an occasional gust of winter air would snake its way through the bodies and find my bare arms. I had been telling Linda about the progress on my research when we realized someone was standing there.

"You're my goddess," he said in a voice that creaked. "I'm here to serve you, to worship you, to honor you."

Linda jolted back in her chair as if she'd been slapped. The guy had a thick, brown envelope in his hands and he extended it toward her. I noticed his hands were rough and chapped and the nails were torn and ragged. He looked vaguely familiar. He was of medium build with dishwater blond hair that hung in his eyes. He could have been anywhere from sixteen to thirty. She opened her mouth, but no sound came out.

"You will always be my goddess," he said, his voice leveling out. "And you will be mine, only mine. No one else deserves you."

He dropped the envelope on the table. I realized he had a knife in his palm, a nasty looking thing with about a six-inch blade. The envelope had covered it. I was starting to bolt out of my chair, when suddenly he was spun around by the shoulders and slammed face first against the wall across the aisle. His head came back once as he struggled. Blood streamed from his nose. Then his right arm was yanked behind his back, the wrist moving high between his shoulder blades. The knife clattered to the floor. I stared in amazement as a heavy, black boot pinned the blade in place. The noise level in the coffee shop immediately dropped. And in the sudden quiet, a voice I knew so well reached my ears.

"That lady is a friend of mine," he snarled. "And you have bothered her for the last time."

With a quick move, Malone snapped handcuffs on the guy's wrists. I stared in amazement as he spun him around and pressed his back against the wall. From my seat I could see Malone's face. The intensity boiling in his eyes was something I had never seen before. And I hoped to never see that look directed at me.

Martin Van Allen, one of the troopers from the post who worked with Malone, appeared behind him. "I'll take him, Sarge."

"She is my goddess," the guy shouted. "You cannot interfere with the goddess. It is forbidden."

Malone roughly pushed him to Van Allen. As the other trooper began to inform the guy of his rights, Malone pulled an evidence bag from his pocket and gathered up the knife. Only then did he turn to the two of us.

"It's over."

Just like that?

\* \* \* \*

We were gathered in a conference room at the Farmington Police Station. Detective Ruzzio was interrogating the suspect. Neither Linda nor I had a clear idea what the hell was going on. Malone went out to make some calls. He returned as the detective was entering the conference room.

"Okay, Malone, now it's your turn," Ruzzio said, running a palm over his bald head. "You want to tell me how you tracked this nutcase down?"

"It was a combination of dumb luck and timing," Malone said. "I kept looking for a pattern with this guy and he finally returned to it."

Ruzzio settled into a chair, propped an elbow on the table, and rested his chin on his knuckles. Once again it looked like he hadn't seen his razor in a couple of days. Maybe he was one of those guys who had five o'clock shadow an hour after he shaved. "So enlighten me."

Malone said that two of the gifts for Linda had been left on her car while it was at work. He instructed Linda to always park in the same block of the parking lot, where the security cameras could see her vehicle. He figured the stalker would leave his gifts near the end of the day, so they wouldn't be out in the weather for too long. In addition to the school's security cameras, Malone had installed the spy camera on Linda's car. He described the little camera to Ruzzio and the detective gave him a nod of acceptance.

Earlier today, he checked the security footage at the school and saw someone approach her car on foot. They hesitated by the windshield for a moment then hurried away. Apparently, he was planning to leave her another gift, but someone entering the lot scared him off. Malone used the spare key to Linda's car to grab the spy camera. Then it was simply a matter of hooking it up to a computer through the flash drive attachment. Now he had a clear picture of the stalker.

Malone explained that he notified the post that he would be taking some personal time off. He thought it might only be a few hours. Then he followed Linda, making certain she wasn't bothered. While in the parking lot of the gym, he saw the stalker circling the lot, staying close to her car. He followed us to the coffee shop, unaware that Malone was following him.

"I contacted one of my men on patrol in the area. He came to the coffee house to back me up. I watched him approach the table and saw the knife." Malone glanced at Linda and me before continuing. "I wasn't taking any chances that he might harm them. So I grabbed him."

Ruzzio looked around the table at each of us. "Nice work, Malone."

"Did he make any kind of a statement?" Malone asked.

"Oh, yeah, once he got started, he wouldn't shut up. Says he was only trying to serve his goddess. That it's his role in life to take care of her. Nothing else matters." Ruzzio gave his head a shake. "His name is Daniel Kennison. He has worked odd jobs since he got out of high school a couple of years ago. Lately he's been working the early morning shift at one of those coffee shops just like the place you nailed him." Ruzzio scratched his chin and stretched. "I'm waiting for a search warrant to be authorized. Then I'll go to his place and see what we can find. But I wouldn't worry anymore. This guy's at least one cannoli short of a dessert platter and he'll be staying right here for a while."

Linda and I had already given our statements to a uniformed officer. Malone looked at Ruzzio and raised his eyebrows.

"Take them home, Malone. I've got all your numbers. If I need anything or learn anything else, I'll call you."

"Thanks."

Linda stood up and numbly shook the detective's hand. Then she stared at me for a moment and reached for Malone. He came around the table and pulled her close for a hug. She clung to him for a bit, and then let him go and reached for me.

"It's finally over."

# CHAPTER THIRTEEN

Malone had gone to work after the excitement. Linda and I went back to my place, where she called Vince to give him the good news. Shortly after that, she left to go home. I got the sense she wasn't going to be alone for long.

It was after one before Malone came home. I was still awake, propped up on the 'aunt' with the latest mystery by James W. Hall. He packs so much into his novels it is incredibly easy to lose yourself in the story. It was the style of writing I always wanted to achieve in my own work. I had lit the birch logs in the hearth a while ago and was enjoying the warm glow. Malone looked tired but handsome as ever as he stepped into the room. He didn't say a word; he just came over and flopped down on the cushions beside me.

"You're running late, Lamont," I said, marking my place with a forefinger while leaning over to kiss him.

"I had some paperwork that I needed to catch up on. And I had a very interesting call from Detective Ruzzio," he said through a yawn.

"So what did he have to say?"

Malone shook his head. "I'm tired, Jamie. Let's talk in

the morning."

I rudely shoved him off the 'aunt' and he fell to the floor in surprise. I followed and landed on top of him, pressing my nose against his. "Bullshit, Malone. We can talk right now."

"You can be so demanding," he said with a laugh.

"You've never complained before. Start talking, Lamont."

"Ruzzio got a search warrant and went to the kid's place. Turns out, this guy was completely overboard with Linda. He had pictures of her plastered on the walls. These were all winter shots, so it looks like he's been following her since she came back from Raleigh."

Apparently Ruzzio also brought along a couple of Farmington technicians from their cyber-crimes unit. A preliminary examination of Kennison's computer revealed a role-playing game called Exaltation. One of the key characters in the game was the Goddess. According to Ruzzio, the graphic art for this character was incredibly similar to Linda. Everything from the shape of her face, her eye color and her mane of curls were all very close to that of the Goddess.

"From what Ruzzio can put together, Kennison was working at the coffee shop that Linda goes to some mornings before work. He wasn't the guy taking the orders, but the one making the flavored coffees and lattes. Once he saw her, he became obsessed with her," Malone said, still sprawled on the floor beneath me.

"But how did he know where she worked, or where she lived?" I asked.

Malone shrugged. "Work was easy. Linda wears one of those lanyard things with the name of the school system on it and her ID badge is clipped to it. Chances are she had it on one morning when she stopped in. All Kennison needed to do from that point was to spot which car she drove off in and put the two together. From there, it was simply a matter of getting up the nerve to approach her."

"But why did he have the knife? I mean, if she was his goddess, why would he harm her?"

"I don't think the knife was any danger to her," Malone said thoughtfully, "but rather to dissuade you or anyone else from interfering with him."

It took a moment for that to sink in. "Do you really think he was going to stab me, Malone?"

"I don't know, Jamie." He reached up and ran a hand through my hair. "Nothing about this guy shows violence toward a person before, unless you think about what he did to Vince's car. But that was an inanimate object. He could have just used the knife as a means of chasing you away. He'd finally worked up the nerve to approach Linda and he didn't want anyone to dissuade him."

"So what was in the envelope he was carrying?"

"More pictures of Linda, taken from a distance and some of the artwork from that video game. There were a few where he cut and pasted his own picture in along with hers, but usually it was his head cropped onto someone else's body."

"What happens next?"

Malone told me that Ruzzio would be holding Kennison until they could bring him in front of a judge for arraignment. He was also requesting a psychiatric evaluation, so they could see if he was crazy or just obsessed.

With Malone smothering yawns, I realized it was time for bed.

* * * *

That Wednesday, there was a whirlwind of activity. With the worries about Linda removed from my shoulders, I suddenly found the energy and enthusiasm to write. Once I got to the keyboard, it was like catching up with an old friend. My fingers danced across the keys, racing to get the ideas and dialog and settings down on the page, struggling to keep up with my buzzing brain. It was as if a dam had broken and now I had to make coherent thoughts out of everything.

Malone left shortly after nine. Detective Ruzzio called him about the arraignment hearing for Kennison. Malone wanted to attend, just in case there was a need for any clarifications. From there, he planned on going to the gym, then to the post for his shift. I didn't try to dissuade him. I knew we'd get together later that evening for our own form of celebration.

Linda called me before school started. Her voice was filled with the usual excitement and laughter that I always associated with her. She would be stopping by after work. We both wanted to relax, to put this nasty business behind us.

It was after one when I took a break. I had just popped a bagel in the toaster and was warming up a mug of tea when Malone called.

"Hey, Jamie." His voice was back to its usual deep tone with just a hint of that gentleness I'd grown accustomed to. I felt the trace of a warm glow inside, realizing I had been missing him all morning.

"Hello, Ludwig. What's going on?"

He laughed softly in my ear. "Ludwig? Really?"

"It's variety, Malone. I've got to keep guessing. Did you call because you missed our morning snuggle time?"

"Guys don't snuggle, Jamie, they spoon. I called to give you some news. And I promise to not roust you out of bed before ten tomorrow morning."

"So what's the news?"

"Ruzzio got word from his forensic people just before the hearing. Turns out they were able to lift some fingerprints from that tape that was used on Vince's car and from a few other spots on the vehicle. It's a perfect match for Kennison. So those charges will be added to the stalking. That should be reassuring to both Linda and Vince that we got the guy who was causing all this trouble."

I beamed a smile at the phone. "Ludwig, I will have to find some very special way to show my appreciation for your ingenuity and hard work."

"Well, if you run out of ideas, I may have a couple of suggestions for you."

"Malone!" I wondered if he could imagine how flushed my face was.

"Got to run, Jamie. I'll see you tonight."

"Until tonight, Ludwig, until tonight."

* * * *

With Malone's encouragement, Linda and I resumed our normal schedules. So Thursday night, we went back to the gym to work out. As we were heading toward the aerobics room, I noticed a guy walking toward us. Linda, who was full of positive energy and enthusiasm now, actually slowed down as we reached the lockers and smiled at him.

"Hello, Bob," she said, giving him a nod of recognition.

"Hi, Linda, it's good to see you tonight."

Obviously I was non-existent in his eyes. But I'm used to that when she's around, especially when she's dressed in spandex and Lycra.

"Maybe we could grab coffee after your workout," he said.

She hesitated. There was a flicker of consideration in her eyes. "Well, Jamie and I always ride over together. So if we went for coffee, it would be the three of us."

He looked over at me as if I had suddenly been beamed next to him by Scotty from *Star Trek*. I nodded and shoved my coat in the locker beside Linda's.

"Sure," he said with a shrug, "that's fine with me. I'll be done in an hour."

"That's when our class ends. We'll meet you right here."

We watched him stride away. He seemed to walk taller, as if he had just conquered an opponent. I was a little surprised at her reaction.

"You really want to go out with this Bob guy?"

She tossed her head and gave me a reassuring look. "Jay Kay, I am in such a good mood, I couldn't see the harm in it. Besides, we're just talking coffee here. And you'll be my chaperone. We'll have a little conversation and I'll politely thank him for his interest, but tell him that I'm involved in a very serious relationship. What harm can there be in simply having coffee with the guy?"

I had no response to that and considering how good she was feeling, I didn't want to be the one to bring her down. So I shrugged and pointed at the door to the aerobics room. "Let's go get sweaty."

True to his word, Bob was waiting for us when we came out of the room an hour later. He had a heavy down parka on over his exercise gear. We grabbed our jackets from the locker and headed toward the exit. When we were in the parking lot, I noticed Linda kept me between her and Bob. So maybe she wasn't feeling quite so devil-may-care after all. Bob stopped beside a big Cadillac sedan and motioned toward the doors. Linda gave him that sweet smile and shook her head.

"We'll just take my car and meet you. Where would you like to go?"

If he was disappointed by this change in plans, he hid it well. Bob mentioned a small coffee shop on Six Mile Road, only a few miles from the gym. It was also a halfway spot between my house and Linda's, but I didn't think much of it at the time. We followed him down the road. About the time the heated seat in Linda's car was just starting to toast my buns, we pulled into the parking lot. I noticed she didn't park alongside Bob's car, but pulled into a space across the aisle from it. He was standing by the rear bumper of his Caddy, his head swaying to some internal music as we joined him.

No one spoke until we were inside and lined up by the counter.

"Remember, this is my treat. So anything you'd like, feel free to order it," he said, sweeping his arm toward the menu board and the pastries lined up in the display case. Although he sounded friendly enough, I caught a forced quality to his speech.

"That's very magnanimous of you, Bob," I said, after selecting a cup of herbal tea and a lemon poppy seed muffin.

"It's no problem, Janey. It's not often I get to enjoy the company of two lovely ladies."

We took our orders and moved to a corner of the store where a table for four was available. I was always surprised at how busy these places could be, even on such a cold and dark night. Once we were settled in, I leaned back and observed this attempt at a dating ritual. Linda was very adept at steering the conversation and Bob didn't seem to notice how smoothly she did it.

"So what type of work is it that you do, Bob?" she asked sweetly while lightly blowing some of the heat from her tea.

His chest seemed to expand as he talked about himself. "I like to think of myself as an entrepreneur. I dabble in different things. Product sales, real estate, equipment leasing, whatever it is, I can make a buck at it. But in the end, I always get what I want. So what about you, Linda, how do you spend your days?"

Linda smiled, tore off a corner of her scone, and popped it into her mouth. "Oh, my life is pretty mundane. Tell me more about your ventures."

Bob shrugged out of his parka and let it fall over the back of his chair. From my position I could see one of the sleeves was resting in a puddle of snowmelt. Bob made no move to straighten his coat, so I ignored it and turned my attention back to the conversation.

"Real estate is my thing right now. Well, that's my

sideline. I'm a sales rep for a janitorial supply company, so I'm always on the road during the day, meeting people, taking them out for lunch and stuff. But I just know I'm going to make a fortune in real estate. It's the perfect time for it."

"Isn't the real estate market in bad shape as a result of the economy?" I asked.

A brief scowl crossed his face. "Nah, that's what all the punks want you to believe. It's a great time to buy up property that's been foreclosed. You can get some of it at auctions or directly from the banks for next to nothing."

Linda propped an elbow on the table and cupped her chin in her palm. I noticed that neither one of us had removed our coats, despite the warmth of the coffee house. It gave me the indication that she was not planning on staying here very long.

"So how will you make your fortune, Bob?" she asked quietly.

He turned his full attention on her. "Well, like I was saying here before Janey interrupted, I can get some properties for next to nothing. But I'm not buying just any piece of crap or some rundown dump in the ghetto. I'm focusing on vacation properties. You know the type, nice getaway cabins near the lakes or up where the crazies go skiing and ice fishing and shit like that."

"So will it take a long time to capitalize on your investments?" Linda asked, maintaining a very interested and concerned look on her face. I took a large bite out of my muffin to keep from saying anything.

"The market will come back around, within two years tops. Once people start getting a little comfortable again, they're gonna want to find a nice place to go away for the weekends. I've got a couple set up just north of Saginaw on one of the lakes. And I just found one out on Harsens Island. These places may need some work, but if I say so myself, I'm pretty handy when it comes to fixing things up. I save a lot on the labor that way. Most of those contractors will screw you over every chance they get." He paused to take a healthy gulp from his coffee. "So I buy the place on the cheap, spend a few bucks on supplies and a few hours of my time, and the next thing you know, I've got a place ready to sell."

Linda bobbed her head gently in agreement. "That sounds like a very good plan. Have you sold any of these vacation homes yet?"

"Nah, it's too soon for that. And like the one on Harsens Island, it needs some work to get it ready. And while I'm doing the work, it gives me a place to stay. This one is right on the river, so I know it will sell quickly when I'm ready. Unless I decide to keep it for myself, have a place to go and relax."

"Sounds nice," Linda said.

"Oh, hey, I got pictures of it," Bob said. He fumbled around with his parka for a minute and pulled a worn envelope from his pocket. There was an address on the front that read 'Green Drive'. He flipped it over and dug some prints out of it. He passed them to Linda for her approval. I leaned over close to her so I could see them at the same time.

The cottage didn't look like much. It was a small, one-story cabin with weathered boards. It looked like it hadn't been used in several years. It was close to the water and you could see it was probably less than thirty feet from the front of the house to the river. There were other shots as well, including one from the rear of the house, facing toward the road. There was a highway sign, pointing off to the right, and a dead end road sign leading to the left. The property that the house was on looked pretty good in size, maybe as much as an acre, but I'd always been a city girl and that was just a guess. I did notice that the pictures were well worn, as if they had been handled a lot.

"See," Bob said, "this place has got lots of potential. I can work on fixing it up in my spare time."

Linda nodded in agreement. "I'm sure your wife must

be very proud of your efforts."

A look of disgust crossed his face. "I'm not married. Well, not anymore. So it's just me. But I wouldn't mind having the right woman to keep me company up there. Maybe work alongside me, fixing the place up."

Somehow the pictures had ended up right in front of me. Not wanting to interrupt, but hoping to wrap up this conversation, I smoothed the stack together and tucked them back in the envelope. Then I placed it on the table between Bob's hands. I noticed how scarred the knuckles were and how the skin looked dry and chapped. From the corner of my eye, I saw Linda finish her tea.

"Well, Bob, I wish you the best of luck with your project. But it's getting late and my sweetheart will be wondering where I am." She turned her attention to me. "Ready to go, Jamie?"

"Sure. Thanks for the tea and the goodies, Bob. It's been nice chatting with you."

I kept my eyes on his as I pushed back my chair. There was a brief flicker of confusion, but then he blinked and nodded.

"Yeah, it is getting late. It was nice talking with you, Linda. You too, Janey. Maybe sometime you'd like to take a drive out to the lake, get a closer look at that cottage."

Linda gave him a soft smile as she got to her feet. "I'll think about that, Bob. Thank you for the refreshments. I'm sure we'll see you at the gym."

He made no move from the table. Bob looked up at us and I got the sense he was seeing us for the first time.

"Yeah, I'm sure you'll see me at the gym. Good night, Linda, Janey."

Neither one of us bothered to correct him. We turned and walked out into the cold, winter night.

"I don't think that guy is wrapped too tightly," I said as Linda drove me back home.

"Jamie, be nice. He's just a little rough around the edges."

"That's putting it mildly. I'd say he's quite a dumb ass."

Linda let loose with a laugh that I hadn't heard in a long time. "Dumb Ass Bob is perfect. You just gave him the name that fits."

"He certainly gave me the impression that he's not open to scintillating dialog. It's all about him. For a minute I pictured him as a caveman, dragging the woman behind him by her hair. Did you take a good look at those pictures?"

"That cabin certainly needs a lot of work. But it might turn out to be something nice if he puts the effort into it."

I thought about that for a moment. "Somehow, I picture Dumb Ass Bob going on the cheap side of things. If he were painting the inside, he wouldn't bother with sanding down the walls or taping off the ceiling in order to do a nice job. He strikes me as the 'quick and dirty' kind of guy, where the moldings won't meet up in the corners and if he can get a bargain on moldy carpet, he'll go for it."

"Jay Kay," she said, choking back another laugh, "that's not very charitable."

"I get that way when people don't get my name right."

We were quiet for a few minutes, each of us thinking about the strange guy we'd just left behind. It made me realize how lucky I was to have a guy like Malone in my life. I got the sense Linda was thinking the same thing about Vince. I glanced up as Linda pulled the car into my driveway.

"So are we still set for that 'special class' with Madeline tomorrow night?" Linda asked.

My puzzled expression must have given it away. I didn't have a clue what she was talking about. She just kept staring at me with an innocent look on her face.

"Algae, with everything that's been going on lately, I don't have the slightest idea what you're referring to."

She sat there patiently, a mischievous gleam dancing in her eyes. Obviously she was determined that I would figure this out. But I was still at a loss. Our workout schedule hadn't varied, no matter what craziness was going on. Tuesday and Thursday evenings and Saturday mornings were the only days we ever went to exercise. So I had no idea what she was…then it hit me.

"Oh, shit!"

Her face lit up as if I had somehow pulled a switch. "See, I knew you'd remember Madeline's *special class*. I already paid her, so we're all set. I'll pick you up and…"

"Linda, if you think I'm going to learn to pole dance, you really are crazy."

"Jay Kay, don't think of it as something dirty. Think of it as a form of exercise. It will be a nice break from the routine. And I know Malone is working tomorrow night, so you've got absolutely no excuses. We're going."

"But Linda…"

"No buts, Jay Kay. Now get out of my car. I want to go home and soak in a nice, hot bubble bath before my sweetheart comes over."

There was nothing else I could say. I leaned over and gave her a hug, then jumped out of the car. I watched her drive away. A long soak in a very hot tub suddenly sounded like a wonderful idea.

# CHAPTER FOURTEEN

When Linda showed up Friday afternoon, I was actually starting to look forward to this 'special class'. Malone had been very attentive when he'd gotten home from work and found me curled up beneath the quilts, reading a Harlan Coben thriller. I had soaked forever in the tub, then slipped on a red silk negligee, splashed a little perfume in a few strategic places, and was feeling quite warm and sexy by the time he arrived. Malone's reactions caused me to lose my place in the book and to forget all about anything beyond the four walls of the bedroom. I have no idea when we finally drifted off to sleep. And truth be told, I really didn't care.

On weekdays, I normally stay focused on work after Malone goes to the gym or the post, but today he suggested we go out for brunch. So we splurged on baked French toast, sausage, and coffee. I'd swear they used an entire loaf of bread just for our two portions. Amazingly, we ate everything. An active sex life must lead to a healthy appetite.

When he left for work, I turned my attention to the computer and put in over four straight hours without a break, letting the words jump from my fingertips. I didn't even bother editing; I just let the story flow. Sometimes it just works that way.

I was more than ready for a break when Linda arrived. I was still in jeans and a sweatshirt, but it only took me a minute to change into workout clothes. She reminded me to bring a pair of shorts to change into, and heels for dancing. Feeling a little foolish, I slipped two pairs of high heels into a bag along with the shorts. I think we were both a little nervous as we climbed into her car and drove to Madeline's house.

There were half a dozen cars parked in the driveway and in front of the house, which was a small bungalow set back from the street, only about five miles from the gym. I recognized a couple of the other women from our aerobics class heading up the walk. We got out of the car and when I hesitated, Linda playfully pushed me from behind and threw a snowball at me. Before I could retaliate, she linked her arm in mine and dragged me toward the house.

Madeline was greeting everyone as they came in the front door. She instructed us to drop our coats in the living area. Downstairs we found a finished basement, brightly lit with a small bar in the corner, a tile floor, and a large mirror that ran nearly the length of one wall. About six feet from the mirror was a pole secured to a beam in the ceiling. There were chairs grouped around the pole in a semi-circle. Next to the bar were coolers filled with bottled water, soft drinks, and beer. There were a dozen women milling about. I recognized a few more of them from our classes.

"Okay, ladies," Madeline said as she entered the basement, "let's all relax. We're going to have a few laughs and learn some things. I guarantee you will feel like you've had a good workout when you're done, along with a good time. Help yourself to a drink and find a seat."

Once we all settled into a chair, she began the lesson.

"No matter how old you are or how flexible you are, everyone can do these moves. It just takes some practice.

It's a lot like being a kid, playing on the jungle gym or the swing set."

Linda gave me a look. "I recall you always falling off the swing set, Jay Kay."

"Hush. That was years ago. I'm much better at it now."

Madeline picked up on our exchange. "Falling is part of learning. You'll notice that in the beginning we're going to take it slow and I'll be right next to you. And remember that falling is inevitable. What's important to remember is that when you do land on the floor, you get back up sexy."

Bernadette, one of the older women from our class, roared with laughter. "Get up sexy? At my age, I'm lucky to get up at all."

Madeline beamed a smile. "Trust me. By the time we're done tonight, even if you trip over your own feet, whoever you're dancing for will not notice that you fell. They will be too focused on the way you get back up. And it will be sexy."

With that, Madeline turned on the stereo and flipped on a song with a slow, sultry beat. She began to move around the pole, explaining how she placed her hands and where. All the laughing and comments faded away quickly as we watched her move. She was graceful, using the pole as a dance partner, swaying against it. When Madeline lifted both feet off the floor and wrapped her legs around the pole, every one of us was watching intently.

After showing us some basic moves, we each got a turn on the pole. At one point, it looked like a chorus line as Madeline had us line up in front of the mirror and practice some of the steps. There were moments of nervous laughter. I noticed a couple of the women taking beers from the cooler, which seemed to give them the courage to try these new steps. Linda's face was flushed and she couldn't stop laughing.

"You know, Jay Kay, this really is a good workout."

I agreed. "I thought we were in pretty good shape, but we're using muscles I didn't even know I had."

Madeline encouraged us to change into our shorts and heels. There was a great deal of laughter now as we each learned new dance steps, some of which involved the pole, others a chair. As each of us took our turn with the pole, we did, in fact, end up on the floor and find a way to 'get up sexy'.

When it was Linda's turn with the pole, she yanked the clips from her hair and shook out her curls. Then as she did each move, she would toss her head. When she was on the floor, she tipped her head forward and her eyes were hidden by that luxurious wave of hair. Slowly, she wiggled forward and got back to her feet. Everyone was cheering and applauding. I could only imagine a guy's reaction to that pose. I hoped Vince was taking his vitamins.

Inspired by her efforts, I tried my best to master the dance steps. I thought I did fairly well, but my version of the 'get up sexy' move definitely left something to be desired. A few of the women cheered. A few more were laughing. And Linda did her best to be supportive. She gave me a hug after my routine and spun me around.

"You did it, Jay Kay. I can't believe it, but you did it."

"What did you think of my moves?"

She couldn't help but laugh. "When you use those on Malone, maybe you should make sure the lights are off."

After our workout, we stopped for soup and salads at a local deli. Linda was glowing as she recounted the events of the class.

"I never would have thought that dancing like that could be such a vigorous workout. Or that it could be so much fun," she said with a devilish smile on her face.

"Does this mean that you might be considering a career change?"

"Hardly. Dancing like that in front of a bunch of strangers has absolutely no appeal for me, no matter how much money they might throw my way. I'm only thinking of a private performance for a very special man."

"Just make sure you put Logan in another room or the

poor dog might think something's wrong with you."

She flicked a grape tomato from her salad at me. I caught it as it rolled across the table and popped it into my mouth.

We joked and laughed some more about our efforts that night. When Linda suggested we try it again sometime, I was surprised at how quickly I agreed. Her good mood was contagious.

After she dropped me off, I wandered the house for a few minutes. I descended the stairs into the basement, still wearing my workout clothes. There was a washer and dryer in the basement and earlier today I had pitched a couple of loads of laundry down the chute. It was my intention to throw a load in. As I piled jeans into the washer, I realized there was still a little bit of room. Emboldened by my dance steps this evening, I stripped down to the buff and threw everything in the washer. The floor was cold, so I slipped my tennis shoes back on.

Leaving the corner where the washer is, I noticed one of the support pillars for the basement was about the same size as the pole that Madeline used in her basement. With a broad smile on my face, I made my way upstairs for a long, hot shower and to prepare for my inaugural dance.

* * * *

I was sitting on the rocker when Malone came home that night. He stood in the entrance from the kitchen, looking at me for a moment without saying a word. I set my book down on the table and, with what I hoped was a fluid movement, slid from the rocker to my feet.

"Good evening, Bartholomew," I said in my best attempt at a sultry voice.

Malone drew me close for a kiss. "You're all dolled up, Jamie. Were you out on the town?"

I stepped back and took his hand. Then I did a slow pirouette so he could get the full effect of my outfit. I was wearing what Linda called my slave girl sandals, the ones with high heels and straps that laced up above the ankles. My legs were bare. I was wearing a jet-black wraparound skirt that was a good four inches short of my knees, a white silk blouse that had a plunging neckline, which was very daring for me, and large hoop earrings. Now standing at arm's length from Malone, I arched an eyebrow at him in what I hoped was a sexy look.

"Do you like my outfit?" I asked coyly.

"Most definitely."

Without another word, I led him back to the kitchen and then the stairwell. I kept him close enough so I knew he was getting a whiff of my perfume, something called "Enchanted" that he had given me for Christmas. I hoped its name was well deserved.

In the basement, I guided him to a folding chair and an old table. On the table were a wine glass and a chilled bottle of sparkling grape juice left over from the holidays. I pushed Malone gently down on the chair and instructed him to open the bottle. With a quizzical look on his face, Malone decided to play along. While he was fiddling with the cork, I went over to the corner where I had set up a portable stereo. I switched it on along with two floor lamps that I had arranged on either side of the support pole. With the bright lights shining and the music cueing up, I turned toward Malone. I couldn't look at his face for fear he might start laughing. As soon as the first song started, I began to dance, swaying to the beat, using the tricks Madeline taught us just a few hours before. Halfway through the first song, I managed to glance at Malone. His eyes were wide with delight as I took three quick steps and grabbed the pole, swinging around it.

Things progressed quickly from there. I felt daring, sexy, and idolized. Knowing it was inevitable I'd end up on the floor, I had placed an old yoga mat near the pole, in the hopes that it would cushion my landing. Somehow, I maintained enough control to slide gracefully down the pole and land gently on the mat. And just as Madeline had taught me, I managed to 'get up sexy' as the song was ending.

As the next song started, I moved closer to Malone. Standing beyond his reach, my body was moving in time with the music, swaying and twisting. Remembering some of the more advanced moves Madeline had done, I let myself go. Still moving with the music, I dared to step closer. Gazing into Malone's eyes gave me the confidence to keep going. I ran my hands up my body, fluffing out my hair, shaking everything I had. There was no way I could keep going if I tried to talk, so I didn't. My fingers slid down my sides and came to the little belt that held my skirt in place. Undoing it, I extended one end to Malone. He pinched the end between his thumb and forefinger. And then I slowly turned away from him, letting the wraparound skirt unwrap.

I continued to dance, to move to the music. I had my back against the pole now, with my arms reaching above my head as the song faded. My eyes closed for a moment and suddenly I felt Malone's hands on me. I was in the air, in his arms as my body shuddered to catch my breath. He was carrying me up the stairs as if I weighed no more than a feather.

"Did you like my dance, Bartholomew?" I whispered.

"That was the sexiest thing I have ever seen, Jamie."

"But I wasn't done yet."

We were moving through the kitchen now and he paused to give me a long, hot, passionate kiss. "You can always do an encore performance later, Jay, but I couldn't sit still any longer. Let's just say this is my version of a standing ovation."

\* \* \* \*

So there I was almost a week after Linda's stalker had been arrested. The pole dancing lessons and Malone's positive reaction to my performance were all the incentive I needed to try something else. It was Malone's day off and he was sleeping late. Two days ago, I discovered a guy who sold firewood and ordered a cord of birch logs, which he had kindly delivered and stacked neatly at the back of the house, under a heavy tarp. I'd stocked up the bin beside the fireplace. Last night after our exercise class, I'd stopped by one of those fancy markets and picked up a few delicacies that would be perfect for what I had in mind. I'd been focusing on my writing for the last week, so there was laundry to do and the house needed cleaning. Now as Malone dozed, inspiration struck and I quietly moved around the house, making my preparations.

I stood in the doorway to our bedroom and watched him. Even asleep, Malone could affect me like no other man I'd ever known. Not that there were that many. He stirred and reached across the bed for me, instinctively seeking that physical contact. I leaned against the doorframe and sipped from the mug of tea I was holding in both hands.

"Hey, Jamie," he said, his voice a bit raspy. He stretched beneath the quilts.

"Brunch is ready, Vasily. But first you need to shave and shower."

"I was hoping to spend a very lazy day with you, Jamie."

I could feel my eyes twinkle with delight. "That's exactly what I had in mind too, Vasily. But first you must shave and shower." I set the mug on the dresser and leaned over, rewarding him with a long, lingering kiss. When he tried to pull me down on top of him, I stepped back and pointed toward the bathroom. Grudgingly, Malone slipped out of bed and headed for the shower. When I heard the water running, I returned to the living room and urged myself to be patient.

A little while later, Malone stood before me. He was wearing a thick terrycloth robe that reached almost to his knees. And I knew that was all he was wearing.

"Jamie, what did you do with my clothes?"

Innocently, I batted my lashes at him. "What clothes, Vasily?"

"All the clothes from the closet and the dresser that belong to me are gone. The only thing in the bathroom or the bedroom is this robe."

I moved from the rocker to stand before him. "Today, Vasily, you will not need clothes. We have a sumptuous feast awaiting us. There is a nest of blankets and pillows to sprawl upon in front of a roaring fire and soft music playing on the stereo. And if you get chilled, I promise to keep you very, very warm."

Malone's gaze shifted from me to the array on the coffee table. There was a plate of shrimp, a bowl of hummus, crackers, chunks of dark rye bread, several different types of cheese and dips, a platter of fresh fruit, and two steaming mugs of hot and sour soup. Then he looked briefly at the fire. Gradually he turned his gaze back to me. I was wearing a black satin robe, some of Malone's favorite perfume, and nothing else.

"Welcome to a lazy day, Vasily."

He drew me into his arms and we slowly sank to the nest of pillows. He didn't say a word, just gently began kissing me. As he worked his way down my neck, I felt his fingers slowly untie the sash on my robe.

"I'll give you back your clothes tomorrow, Malone," I managed to gasp.

He paused and leaned back to look at me. "Suddenly clothes don't seem very important, Jay."

# CHAPTER FIFTEEN

Maintaining our routine when it came to our exercise schedule, Linda and I went to a couple of elliptical machines after our workout Tuesday night. Her mood was upbeat and positive and I had to admit it was somewhat contagious. It was one of those nights where there was a parading cast of characters, those we had dubbed with goofy nicknames. She had me laughing so hard I was having difficulty maintaining my balance on the machine.

"Look in the mirror to your right, Jay Kay," she said in that sultry voice. "You can see Mikeus Interruptus has entered the building."

I followed her directions and recognized the fellow who looked like a monk and had forced his way into our conversations on more than one occasion. We both acknowledged him with a simple nod of the head. He was already involved in a discussion with several other guys who seemed receptive to whatever it was he had to say.

"Check out the No Sweat Trio," Linda said, inclining her head in the opposite direction.

There were three women, somewhere in their late forties, walking toward the group of men. We noticed them here on many of the nights we worked out. Although they were often dressed for exercise, they never seemed to do enough to break a sweat. When Linda passed them one night on her way to the water fountain, she realized all three were wearing makeup and perfume. That was when she dubbed them the "No Sweat Trio" as it was obvious they were not there for an actual workout, but for the social interactions. This helped confirm my theory this was their version of group dating.

"Algae, isn't that the Screamer?" I hooked a thumb at a young woman in purple and black workout gear with extremely short black hair.

"Good eye, Jay Kay. How could we forget the Screamer?"

One of our Thursday night classes, Madeline was out sick. Since there wasn't enough time to notify everyone and cancel the class, the gym provided another instructor. Neither one of us could remember her name, but we would never forget her style. She had a tendency to shout out a countdown, encouraging us to hold each position for as long as possible during the stretches. At one point we were all inclined on our backs, balancing on those inflatable exercise balls, feet planted on the floor and arms reaching above our heads, so we looked like we were doing backbends. As she counted down from ten, the instructor would follow each number with a grunt and a groan.

It was during this segment of the workout that Linda began to quiver. Unable to hold the pose, she rolled off the ball onto the floor and curled up on her side. The group took a quick break at the end of that stretch. I turned to Linda, who was mopping the sweat off her face with a towel and a sparkle in her eyes.

"Are you okay?" I asked.

"I'm fine. I just suddenly had the image of her doing that countdown while she was having sex, screaming out when she was getting close to a peak."

"Algae!"

She looked at me and started laughing. "You were

probably thinking the same thing, so don't even try to give me that innocent look."

I knew there was no arguing the point, so I didn't try. We had just come up with the perfect nickname for the young substitute instructor.

Now Linda was grinning wickedly as we watched her proceed to a treadmill in the corner and crank up the speed.

We took turns identifying the other characters and the crazy names we had bestowed on them. Together we spotted Dumb Ass Bob, the Psycho Blonde—whose peroxide locks might have convinced more people it was her natural color if her roots didn't show and her eyebrows weren't so black—and Motor Mouth, a young woman who worked at the gym, showing new members how the various equipment worked. When there were no new people around, she would begin talking to anyone who would listen, about anything under the sun. No matter what the situation, she never stopped talking.

We quickly finished our extra workout and headed for the door.

* * * *

It was after five on a snowy Saturday afternoon when an electronic buzzing by my ear shattered my plans for a peaceful evening. I had been dozing on the 'aunt', dreaming of tropical paradise vacations with Malone, and it took me a minute to realize it was my cell phone, perched on the table, chirping away. I snagged it just before it went to voicemail, not even bothering to look at the screen.

"Hullo," I mumbled in the gap between sleep and coherency.

"Sorry to bother you, Jamie," that cultured male voice sounded in my ear, "but I was wondering if Linda happened to be with you."

My eyes snapped wide open. "What do you mean,

Vince? I thought you two had big plans for the evening. She said something about a fancy dinner and that was just for starters."

"Yes, we did have rather elaborate plans for this evening, but she isn't answering her phone and she's not here at the house."

I could feel my heart hammering double-time against my ribs. This couldn't be happening! The creep that had been stalking her had been caught weeks ago. As far as I knew, he was still in jail, unable to scrape together enough cash to put up his bond for bail and there were still questions about his mental stability. There had to be some logical explanation. My mind couldn't slow down to consider it.

"Are you inside the house?" I asked.

"Yes," Vince answered tensely, "she gave me a key a few weeks ago. I've checked every room. Her car is not in the garage. The house was dark, except the one light on the timer."

My stomach dropped to my ankles. "What about Logan?"

As if hearing his name, I heard the dog bark in the background. "He's here, Jamie. I let him out when I arrived. He acted like he's been cooped up all day."

I didn't remember getting up off the 'aunt', but I was moving quickly now, pulling my winter coat from the closet, grabbing my purse, gloves and keys. Wedging the phone against my shoulder, I yanked on my heavy boots.

"She wanted me to pick her up at five," Vince said. "We have reservations for dinner then we were going to see a play downtown. We were going to celebrate the end of this craziness, a chance to get back to a normal life." He hesitated and I could hear the anxiety rising in his voice. "Dear God, Jamie, if anything has happened to her…"

"Vince! Slow down. You stay at her house. I'm on my way. But I want to call Malone. And Vince…"

I heard him draw a long, deep breath and let it out

slowly. "Yes, Jamie?"

"Don't touch anything."

By the time I reached Linda's house, Malone was there. He had commandeered one of the state police cruisers and raced over, red lights flashing. As I bounced the Honda roughly against the curb, I saw a flash of colored lights in my rearview mirror. A Farmington police car sped down the street, spraying snow behind it like a hydroplane's rooster tail. Malone must have had the presence of mind to call them in. He and Vince were standing just inside the doorway, waiting for me. Malone caught me by the arms and pulled me close.

"Let's wait for the uniforms to get inside."

I was amazed at how calm his voice was. But when I looked at his eyes, I could see the worry that mirrored my own. Where the hell was she?

It was a male-female team from the patrol. I recognized the man, Wheeler. He had been here back when Vince's car was vandalized. His salt and pepper hair was cropped close beneath his hat. He was older than Malone and he exuded a sense of professionalism. I got the sense he didn't miss much. The nametag on the female cop was Haridy. She was letting Wheeler take the lead.

Malone quickly filled them in on Linda's disappearance. Both cops were aware of the situation with the stalker and the recent arrest. Wheeler used his radio and got the dispatcher to confirm that Kennison was still being held in the Oakland County Jail. Haridy was busy jotting down notes, getting our names and contact information.

"Who saw her last?" Wheeler asked, directing the question to all of us. The guys looked at me.

"I did. We went to our aerobics class this morning as we normally do. Then we ran out for coffee."

"What time was that?" Haridy asked.

"Class was at ten for an hour. We had something to eat and she dropped me off around eleven-thirty."

"What was she wearing?" Malone asked.

I remembered that she had brought a duffel bag with her into the gym. She didn't want to shower there, but she had wanted to change clothes. "Black jeans, a pair of black winter boots, a white hooded sweatshirt over one of her exercise tanks. And a bright red ski jacket."

"Was she headed home?" Wheeler asked. I noticed his voice was raspy and I caught the faint scent of tobacco. For some ridiculous reason, I wondered how much he smoked.

I was about to say she was coming back here when I saw Vince move out of the corner of my eye. Seeing him in a suit and tie reminded me of their date. "No, she was going to get her hair done. There was a new place she wanted to try."

"Do you remember the name of it?" he asked.

I slowly shook my head.

Malone gave Haridy the description of Linda's car and the license number. She called the dispatcher and requested all units to look for it. Malone stepped outside. I wondered what he was doing. I didn't have to wait long to find out.

He ducked back inside. "It started snowing this morning about ten. There are no tire tracks in the driveway, beyond where Vince's car is parked. If Linda had come home, there would be tread marks in the snow. She hasn't been back."

Wheeler glanced at me. "If she was just going to run in for a minute, would she park in the street?"

I shook my head. "Linda always pulled into the garage and used the connecting door by the kitchen."

The cops checked all the doors and windows. There was no sign of forced entry. Malone pointed out that the locks had been recently changed. After Kennison had been arrested, Malone had removed the security cameras.

While the cops searched the house, Malone and Vince stood by the front window and talked softly. Logan came up and nuzzled my hand. He could sense things were wrong. He wanted to be reassured just like the rest of us. I walked him into the kitchen and filled his dish with food. Then I topped off his water dish. As I turned, I noticed the phone book on the shelf by the counter.

On a hunch, I opened the book to the commercial listings. There were more than twenty hair salons in the area. I slowly ran my finger down the list, looking at the names. Nothing clicked. I sensed someone at my shoulder and glanced up. Haridy was nodding in agreement.

"I was just thinking the same thing. Too bad she didn't circle one."

"None of these names are familiar. She used to go to a place in Northville, but the owners sold the business and moved out of state."

Haridy took the book from me and lifted her radio. She called the dispatcher and suggested they assign different units to check the parking lots for each salon. At the same time, she was informed that no one fitting Linda's description had been admitted to any of the hospitals in the area. And there were no reports of accidents in the area involving her type of car.

There had to be something I was missing. Closing my eyes, I leaned against the counter and slowly scratched Logan's head. I kept trying to replay our conversation from earlier today. One of the skills I'd honed as a reporter was recall. Concentrating, I focused on what we'd talked about this morning. My best friend had been back in all her glory. Gone was the stress from the last few weeks. There was laughter in her eyes. She had been looking forward to a night on the town. She talked about a gourmet dinner at the historic Whitney Restaurant downtown. Vince had scored tickets to "Romeo and Juliet" at the Hilberry, Wayne State University's theater that featured a mixture of professional actors and graduate students. Linda had been animated. She planned on bringing Vince home and not letting him go until sometime Monday morning.

So where the hell was she?

Frustrated, I turned away from the counter and nearly knocked Haridy on her ass. She was a little shorter than me, but it was hard to tell if she was solid or thin with the bulky winter coat she wore. I hadn't realized she was standing so close.

"Sorry," I mumbled.

"No worries," she said with a grin, "I'm used to getting bumped around. Maybe you should sit down. You look a little wonky."

"I'm okay." I was too restless to sit. I walked down the hall to the main bedroom. Logan padded along beside me.

Linda was the most organized person I'd ever known. Before she left for the gym this morning, she had taken the time to arrange her outfit for tonight on the valet stand by her dresser. Knowing Vince would be dressing up she had pulled out a gold and black dress that was one of her favorites. It had a subtle diamond pattern to it with a cinched bodice that accented her curves. Like her curves needed accenting. The dress had long sleeves to keep her arms warm and a short pencil skirt that would allow her to flaunt those fabulous legs. On her dresser was a pair of dangling earrings that she would wear, white gold ones that I had given her for a birthday a few years ago. There was a matching necklace on the dresser as well. A new pair of stockings was on top of her lingerie for the evening. Shiny black boots with two-inch heels were leaning against the dresser. I knew that she would have a bottle of perfume on the counter in the bathroom, along with her makeup kit.

She wouldn't have gone to this trouble if she'd had a change of heart about tonight. It was obvious she was planning to come home from the salon and get ready.

I sat on the edge of the bed. Even her bed was made. I smoothed out the comforter as Logan came over and put his head on my thigh. Something tugged at my memory. I looked down at his big brown eyes and stroked his head. What was I missing? I sensed it was close. But what was it?

I turned my head to look at her outfit again. And there it was.

"Diamonds!"

Logan raced into the living room ahead of me. Malone and Wheeler had been brainstorming about possible places to look for her while Vince stood by the window and listened. Haridy was coming out of the kitchen, having heard the noise of my approach.

"It's called Diamonds, or something very similar. It's a new place, which is why I didn't see it in the phone book."

Vince faced me, his eyes briefly flaring with hope before the realization hit and that worried look returned. "If it's new, Jamie, we'll never find it."

Before I could reach him, Haridy laid a reassuring hand on his arm. "We'll find it, Dr. Schulte. Just you watch."

She pulled a personal cell phone from a pocket. It was one of those Blackberry clones that had Internet connectivity. In less than a minute, she had typed in a name and a general location. The screen flashed and there it was.

"There's a Diamond Girls Salon on Grand River near Drake," she said, turning to Wheeler to show him the screen. He nodded and grabbed his radio. Haridy hit a button and called the salon. My eyes went to the clock in the kitchen. It was almost six. I hoped they were still open.

And just like that, we all seemed to breathe a little easier. Wheeler radioed the dispatcher and requested that a patrol unit go directly to the salon. Then Haridy gave a shake of her head and disconnected the call. It was a long five minutes until Wheeler's radio squawked. The shop was already dark and closed up tight for the night. Wheeler instructed the officer to search the parking lot for Linda's car. The salon was in a large, busy strip mall featuring a variety of stores and a bar and grill on the corner. With all the snow that had fallen during the day, and was continuing to fall, we weren't going to get a quick response.

I gave Malone a pleading look. He knew I wanted to go there. But he stepped over and drew me close. "Let's wait, Jamie, and see what they find."

Logan kept pacing between Vince and me, wearing a path in the carpet. If Malone hadn't been holding me, I would have been doing the same thing. After an eternity, Wheeler's radio chirped.

"We got it!"

Wheeler confirmed that the details on the car matched. The officer had even cleared enough snow from the windshield to verify the VIN with the dispatcher, so it wasn't a chance that someone switched her plates with another similar car. The officer explained that the car had been there for several hours, judging by the mound of snow on the roof, trunk and hood. Malone and Wheeler exchanged a glance.

"What was the name of the detective handling the investigation of the stalker?" Malone asked.

"That would be Ruzzio. He's off duty tonight."

Malone nodded slowly. "If it was me, I'd be calling him on this. And I'd have that car impounded."

Wheeler considered it for a heartbeat. He turned his eyes to Haridy. "Do it. I'm going to request another officer to the scene."

So now we knew where her car was. But had she kept her appointment? And if so, where had she gone without her car. I whispered these thoughts to Malone.

"That's a good point, Jamie," he said, giving me a little squeeze. There were not enough words in the world to tell him how much I needed that contact right now. I looked over at Vince. He seemed to have shrunken inside his suit. I nudged Malone and inclined my head. Gently he released me.

I went to Vince and wrapped my arms around him. "We are going to find her, Vince. Don't doubt it for a minute."

He looked at me for a moment then gave me a fierce

hug. "I hope you're right, Jamie. If anything has happened to her…"

"Don't even think it, Vince." From deep inside, I summoned every ounce of conviction I had. "We will find her."

Malone joined us. "Farmington PD is tracking down the owner of the salon. They'll find out if she kept her appointment or not."

"What difference would that make?" Vince asked.

"It can give us a time frame," Malone said. "Then we can check the various security cameras at the strip mall. They may have some in the parking lot, along with whatever we can find from stores near the salon or near where she parked her car."

These were all good ideas, but none of them could answer the million-dollar question. Where the hell was she?

# CHAPTER SIXTEEN

It was well past midnight but I was too keyed up for sleep. I sat on the rocker, nervous energy slowly moving it back and forth. I hadn't bothered to light the fire. I didn't want to get lulled into a false sense of security, of feeling safe and warm in my own little house while my best friend was missing. Instead, I replayed the events of the last six hours.

There had been plenty of activity, but nothing to show for it. Malone notified the post that he was taking personal time and to call in another sergeant for the remainder of his shift. That spurred me to call Bert and tell him what was going on. Ten minutes later, he was at Linda's house with us. Although it was not his jurisdiction, Bert quickly took charge of the situation. He didn't step on anybody's toes ---he just went right over the heads of every cop there. By the time he entered the house, Wheeler had been contacted by his police chief and told to cooperate fully with whatever Bert wanted done. No questions asked.

Bert and Malone had gone to the strip mall. One of the Farmington cops contacted the property manager and the security company. They reviewed the feed from the cameras, looking for any sign of Linda. But the afternoon's snowstorm wasn't helping matters. Most of the images, which were grainy to begin with, were even fuzzier with the heavy snow.

At Haridy's suggestion, I sent a picture of Linda from my cell phone to hers. She forwarded this to the cops on the scene. They were going through each store, interviewing people who worked there, looking for anyone who might have seen her.

Bert worked with the security people, reviewing the footage from the day. Malone met with the salon owner. It was confirmed that Linda kept her appointment. She had chatted with the owner, who was also her stylist, left her a big tip, and been pleased with the new look. The owner remembered Linda saying she was going home to soak in a warm tub and get dolled up for a night on the town. It had been around three o'clock when she left the shop.

When Malone called me with this update, he seemed surprised it had taken so long. I had him give the phone to the owner, who confirmed my suspicions. Linda had gone for the works—shampoo, trim and some highlights in a few strategic places. No wonder she was there for a while. But at least that helped establish when she left.

Unfortunately, that was where the trail ran cold. The cops could find no witnesses. They checked every shop, and the bar that shared the big parking lot. And once Bert had a time frame, they narrowed the search of the video and took it frame by frame. Nothing. We had run out of ideas.

Vince refused to leave her house. I knew he wouldn't sleep. He wanted to be there, just in case she called or showed up, and he wouldn't leave Logan behind. Bert coaxed me into going home. Farmington PD was going to keep an officer parked outside her house, just in case anything happened. Malone left when I did, taking the police cruiser back to the post where he would change and pick up his Jeep.

I knew that Vince wasn't the only one about to have a

sleepless night. I kept trying to think if there was something that had happened today that I missed. Linda had been full of energy this morning when she picked me up. It was the best workout we'd had in weeks. She kept cajoling me, urging me to move faster, kick higher, and to dance, dance, dance. I'd swear half the class was laughing right along with her.

So what happened when she left the salon?

I knew that I wouldn't really rest until I found her. And somehow I knew she was counting on me to figure it out.

Sunday was a slow-motion agony. When Malone had gotten back to the house, he hadn't said a word. He just pulled me up from the rocker and held me for a while. Then he led me into the bedroom and propelled me toward the shower. Thankfully, he wasn't expecting any sexual activity. We showered together. There, in the hot steam with his arms wrapped around me and my body covered with lather, I finally lost it. I think I cried until the water started to run cold. Malone just kept holding me.

Later, wearing thick flannel pajamas, I curled up beside him, my head resting on his chest.

"Why is this happening to her?" I whispered.

Malone slowly shook his head. "Once we find her, we'll know the why and all the other answers. But we need to stay focused, Jamie. And we need to stay strong."

"Vince must be going out of his mind. To think all this nonsense was behind them and then to have her disappear, it just doesn't make sense." I bit back a yawn. How could I sleep at a time like this?

Malone snuggled me closer, slowly smoothing out my hair with his hand. "It's like some kind of magician's trick, a regular vanishing act. One minute she's getting her hair done, the next, poof! She's vanished into thin air."

But who was the magician? And what did they want with her? There had been no call yet, no ransom demands. How much money could a schoolteacher be worth?

With those questions bouncing around in my head,

exhaustion claimed me. When I awoke six hours later, I still didn't have any answers.

Malone and I got to Linda's house around eight. Vince met us at the door with a haggard look on his face. If he had slept, it hadn't been for long. He was still wearing his suit with the tie yanked down and the top button of his shirt undone. Malone handed Vince a duffel bag and pointed him toward the shower. He looked a bit better when he came out wearing a pair of Malone's jeans and a thick wool sweater. I had fed Logan and taken him for a walk to burn off some nervous energy. While I was gone, Malone whipped up a large skillet of eggs and potatoes. Although neither Vince nor I seemed interested in food, the three of us ate it all.

"We need to keep up our strength," Vince admitted. "Linda would be very upset if she knew how much this was bothering us."

"She'd probably kick my ass for worrying so much," I said.

Malone filled our coffee cups. "Have you checked the machine?"

Before leaving for the night, Bert made sure that Linda's answering machine was turned on. He instructed Vince to let any calls go to the machine so they would have a recording of it. Although someone had been here the entire time, we never bothered to check it. Now Vince got to his feet and looked. There were no messages. He hit the playback button and we all heard her sultry tones on the prerecorded message.

I felt a little tug at my heart just listening to her voice.

"Where are you, baby?" I whispered.

I was perched on one of the chairs at her kitchen table when an idea hit me. Why didn't I call her? Maybe her phone was on the fritz. I hadn't thought of my phone since I'd called Malone early last night on my way over here. It took me a few minutes of searching before I tugged it from the pocket of my winter coat.

And just like that, my heart almost stopped.

My legs folded underneath me and I dropped in a heap on the floor. Logan must have thought I wanted to play because he bounded over and pushed his head in my lap. Malone was standing in the kitchen doorway, his eyes filled with concern.

It took me a moment to find my voice. "She sent me a message," I mumbled, extending my phone to him.

Malone dropped to his knees beside me and gently pried the device from my fingers. Silently, he read the text. Vince joined us on the floor. He looked anxiously at both of us. Malone took a deep breath and read it aloud.

"Jamie, I need to take some time for myself and sort things out. Don't worry about me. I will be fine."

Malone raised his eyes from the screen to look at me. "The time stamp on there is around four-thirty yesterday afternoon. You didn't have the phone with you?"

It took me a minute to recapture my movements from yesterday. "I had just come back from the produce market. Before I put the groceries away, I hung up my coat and dropped my purse and my phone by the 'aunt'. Then I was in the kitchen. When I get a text, it just chirps one time. It's a feature I rarely use. And Linda hates texting."

"This doesn't make any sense," Vince said. "Why would she need time for herself? Going out last night was her idea. She wanted to celebrate."

Malone glanced back to me. "Could she have changed her mind?"

"No way, Malone. She was all pumped up about going out. And why would she bother to get her hair done if she had changed her mind?"

I didn't trust myself to take the phone. "Read it again."

He did. But those cobalt blue eyes never left my face.

"There's only one answer, Malone."

"What's that, Jamie?"

"Linda didn't send that message.

My response was met by a heavy silence from the two

guys.

"What do you mean, Jamie?"

"First of all, Linda would never send me a text. She would call me and if I didn't answer, she'd leave a message on voice mail. When it's just us, she never calls me Jamie. Secondly, she was so excited about her date with Vince that there's no way she had a change of heart." I turned to look at the two guys kneeling beside me on the floor. "Then there's Logan. I don't believe for a minute that she would go away and not take him with her, or make arrangements for someone to care for him."

"She's right," Vince said with a nod, "the dog is always with her. Whenever she's spent the night at my house, she's brought Logan."

"So we're in agreement that the message is bogus," Malone said quietly as he climbed to his feet. He reached down and took my hands and brought me up to stand next to him.

"But what does this mean?" Vince asked.

"It means we now have a clue that might give us a lead."

Malone walked into the other room and drew his own cell phone from his coat. He hit a number on the speed dial and was immediately connected. After a brief conversation, he snapped the phone shut and gave me a short version of his low voltage smile.

"Help is on the way."

\* \* \* \*

Help arrived in the form of Bert less than twenty minutes later. Right on his heels were Detective Ruzzio and a member of the Farmington PD cyber squad. Malone had given me an idea as to what was happening, so I dug through Linda's desk and found the details they would need. Malone pulled Vince aside as the others gathered around the kitchen table.

"I should have thought of this last night, "Malone said, "We may be able to use Linda's cell phone to pinpoint her location."

"How in the world can you do that, Malone?"

He nodded toward the table. "Most cell phones are equipped with a GPS system. That way if there is an emergency, say a 911 call, authorities can determine where the call is originating. If Linda's cell phone is still on, we can track her that way."

The sound of a hand slapping the surface of the table got everyone's attention. Bert was scowling. He had both fists planted on the table and towered over the two Farmington cops.

"Sorry, Captain, but it looks like her phone is switched off," the technician stammered.

"Not your fault, son. I was really hoping you'd have better luck." Bert turned his head in my direction. His expression was speaking volumes.

"It's not on, but I can give you a general vicinity as to where the phone was when that text message was sent," the technician, whose name was Williamson, was rapidly typing on his laptop computer. Then as the screen changed, he spun the computer around so everyone could see it.

It was a section of a map. The city highlighted was New Baltimore, and it looked like it was near a body of water. But this was Michigan and there are lakes everywhere, in all shapes and sizes. I had never heard of New Baltimore. I glanced from the screen to Bert and then Malone's face. There was no recognition showing from either of them. Williamson then expanded the map to show an area north and east of Detroit, up near Lake St. Clair.

Ruzzio was digging a notebook from his pocket. "Wait a minute. This area isn't far from Port Huron. In fact, it's kind of on the way there."

"So what's the connection?" Bert asked sullenly.

"Her ex-husband is working in Port Huron. And he lives not far from New Baltimore."

I was stunned. Why would Derek Bishop kidnap Linda? Before I could find my voice, Malone asked the same question.

"It seems that Bishop's life hasn't been all champagne and caviar since his divorce," Ruzzio said. "He got married right away and had three children by wife number two, but it didn't last. Apparently, he started to slap her around a bit. Now he's paying alimony and child support and his career has taken a dive. He's also gotten hit with a paternity suit."

"How do you know all this?" Bert asked.

"I tracked him down and interviewed him when we were trying to get a line on the stalker," Ruzzio said. "He told me at the time, that things hadn't exactly worked out like he planned. He made some comment about how life was so much better when he and Ms. Davis were married." Ruzzio shrugged. "I believed him. So maybe he thought this was the best way to get back together with her."

"You got an address?" Bert asked.

Ruzzio tapped his notebook. "Right here."

Bert hooked two fingers in his direction. "Let's roll."

Before turning for the door, Bert stepped over and enveloped me in his arms. "We will find her, Jamie. You have to believe that."

"I do, Bert. I just hope you find her soon."

\* \* \* \*

Waiting was a study in frustration. Everything seemed to be happening in slow motion. Vince was doing his valiant best, but I could see that not knowing what was going on was hitting him hard as well. Malone persuaded him to take a walk and get Logan some exercise. The two of them bundled up and marched out into the drifts of snow, the dog bouncing between them. I settled back on the sofa and tried to put everything together.

Derek Bishop was a jerk. This wasn't a completely objective opinion, but one that I had culled over the years. Yes, he could be charming when it suited his purposes. But deep down, the guy had all the substance of a used tissue.

I was not a big fan of coincidences. Maybe that has to do with Bert's influence during my formative teen years. Bert always said there was no such thing as a coincidence and for the most part, I've come to agree with him. Even so, I was having a difficult time tying Derek to Linda's disappearance.

Linda mentioned that her last conversation with Derek had been when her mom, Gracie, broke her hip back in October. Because Linda always tries to give everyone, even slimy, unfaithful ex-husbands, the benefit of the doubt, she had called him to let him know about Gracie. She told him that she was on her way to care for her mother. For some reason, Gracie always liked Derek. She recognized the high level of bull that he was constantly flinging, but still liked him. By the time Linda got to the hospital in Raleigh, she found a bouquet of flowers in Gracie's room from Derek, wishing her a speedy recovery.

So *why* would Derek kidnap her? He must have known that things were long over between them. They had been divorced for nearly seven years. From Linda's description, his second wife had also been very pretty, but I doubted she was of the same caliber as Linda. There just aren't that many women around who have her combination of physical beauty, intelligence, and sense of humor. And she had given Derek the one thing that Linda was unable to—children. So why would he come back into Linda's life now? She would have no interest in getting back together with him, of that I was certain, especially when things were going so well with her relationship with Vince.

Try as I might, I just couldn't come up with a scenario where Derek would want to get involved with Linda again.

And there was no way I could picture her being interested in him. Despite all my musings, I still couldn't answer the million-dollar question.

Where the hell was she?

It was a couple of hours before Bert called me. Bert had met Derek a few times over the years. He hadn't wasted any time on formalities. While Bert and Ruzzio were driving in that direction, Bert had contacted a nearby State Police Post and instructed a couple of troopers to go to Derek's house. He was brought into the post for questioning and left alone in a conference room until Bert arrived. Bert decided to forgo the standard interrogatory practice and use a more direct approach. I didn't learn this right away. Ruzzio filled us in when they returned to Linda's house.

"He almost put him through the wall," Ruzzio said, a wide smile on his face and a satisfied gleam in his eyes. "Twenty-two years on the job and I've always wanted to do something like that. Never had the stones to try it myself and it was a pleasure to witness."

I was surprised to hear about this, but Malone didn't register any reaction at all. We all looked at Bert for clarification.

"I'm not in the mood to waste time. I wasn't going to let that worm get cute and try to manipulate the situation. So I went right at him," Bert said. He accepted a mug of coffee from me and was leaning against the kitchen counter.

Ruzzio filled in the other details. Bert had stopped him outside the interrogation room and sent the Farmington cop into the observation area. Bert then walked into the room where Derek was waiting. Bert removed his overcoat and hung it over the camera in the corner of the room that was pointed at Derek. Bert then turned, grabbed Derek by the neck, and slammed his back against the wall. Derek was a decent sized guy, but Bert probably had thirty pounds of muscle on him. The guy never had a chance.

It was an unorthodox approach, but it was definitely effective. One look into Bert's eyes was enough to convince anyone that he wasn't screwing around. Ruzzio described the terror etched on Derek Bishop's face as Bert asked his questions. There was no chance Derek wouldn't tell the truth. Even when Bert repeated his questions, or rephrased them, Derek gave the same responses. He had not seen Linda in several years, and the last time he had spoken to her was when she had called about Gracie. While Bert was conducting the questions, Williamson ran a complete background on Derek's cell phone history. He was able to confirm that there had been no other calls to or from Linda. Derek had been clueless when she'd returned from Raleigh, or that anything unusual was going on until Ruzzio interviewed him.

"So it's a dead end," Vince said softly.

"Derek's involvement sounds like a dead end," Bert said sternly. "I still don't like the idea she was near his home when she sent that text. I've got a couple of guys watching him, just in case."

"Where do we go from here?" I asked.

Malone reached over and gripped my hand. "We wait."

The rest of Sunday slowly passed. Ruzzio left a patrol car in front of her house, just like on Saturday. In the event anyone should call, we rigged Linda's home phone to forward any calls to Vince's home where an answering machine was already switched on. With the guys gathered around the table, I made the difficult call to Gracie, Linda's mother. We had to let her know what was going on. I was able to persuade her to stay home, promising to call the moment we learned anything. Bert encouraged us to go to our respective homes and get some rest. Malone had to cover a shift at the post and Vince had a full slate of patients on Monday. Without hesitating, I grabbed a large bag of chow for Logan and his leash. There was no way I was going to leave him alone. He had to be with someone and I was the most logical choice.

Back at the house I was too antsy to sit still, so Logan and I went for a long walk in the twilight. The cold air made my nose run. Sometimes, it made my eyes water too. This must have been one of those times. At least, that was what I kept telling myself.

We finally headed back to the house when my ears were tingling and my fingers were getting cold, even inside my gloves. Logan bounded in the side door and even waited patiently for me to wipe the snow from his paws. Once I unclipped his leash, he headed for the living room and his favorite spot by the hearth. I filled a dish with water for him, made myself a cup of tea, and went to join him. Still feeling the chill from outside, I lit the fire and sat in the rocker, thinking of Linda.

That's how the evening passed. I stirred only twice, once to put more logs on the fire, the other when Logan kept bumping my leg in an effort to get me to feed him. I had no appetite. The dog was curled in front of the hearth when Malone came home. I was still in the rocker. He walked over and pulled me from the chair and just wrapped his arms around me.

"Where could she be, Malone?" I mumbled into his shoulder as he held me close.

"I don't know, Jamie. I know that she is a very determined woman. And I know that she won't ever give up until we find her."

"We're all she's got, Malone. You and me and Vince and Logan and Gracie are her whole family, her whole world. If anything happens…"

He silenced me with a tender kiss. "No more talking, Jamie. It's time to rest."

When he started to pull me toward the bedroom, I declined and moved to the 'aunt'. Malone studied me for a moment, and then piled a couple more birch logs on the fire. He pulled a thin blanket from the closet and grabbed two pillows from the bed. We snuggled down fully clothed, and I found a temporary peace in his arms.

Eventually I drifted off to sleep.

When Monday arrived, I felt like I was just going through the motions. I walked and fed Logan and forced myself to eat some brunch with Malone. He left early because he had to be in court. I made him promise repeatedly to call me the moment he heard anything, no matter what.

Waiting was driving me crazy. I needed to do something. The computer held no appeal. I couldn't concentrate on the story, or revisions, or even reading over my notes. I clicked on the folder with digital pictures and tried to get my mind on happier times. But every other picture was of Linda, or me and Linda. There were a number of recent ones, since she'd come back from Raleigh. I stared at the one from New Year's Eve, where the four of us were together, beaming smiles and enjoying life. My heart ached for Linda.

I missed her. I was worried about her.

All right, I'll admit it. I was scared about what might have happened to her.

Logan must have sensed my discomfort. He raised his head from the dog bed that Malone had tucked into the corner of the office. Those brown eyes pleaded with me. I got up and went into the kitchen for some tea. Logan padded after me. I knelt down and hugged him.

"Where are you?" I whispered.

He didn't answer.

Back at my desk, I switched to a mapping program on the computer and brought up the New Baltimore area. According to the techno-wizard with the Farmington Police, this was where that message had been sent. It still didn't make sense. Linda was a west side girl. She was born and raised over here, just like me. She used to joke that if you went east of Woodward, you needed to take your passport with you. I don't think she knew anyone over there, unless you counted Derek Bishop.

Staring at the map wasn't getting me anywhere. I

moved the mouse to go back to my homepage, but somehow clicked on the icon to change the view of the map. Curious, I waited to see what was around there. Maybe New Baltimore wasn't their destination. Maybe it was just a spot where they were driving through.

The screen refreshed. When it did, I jumped so fast my mug of tea went flying across the room.

I knew where Linda was.

And I knew who had taken her.

# CHAPTER SEVENTEEN

I sat anxiously for a moment, trying to recall the conversation. He hadn't been talking to me. I was in the background, listening to him go on and on while he was trying to impress Linda. Soon I remembered enough of the details to know that I was on the right track.

Malone was in court, so there was no way I could reach him. Sometimes he got done with his cases early. It depended on the judge. I tried his cell phone anyway, but it went right to voicemail. "Call me, Malone. I think I figured out where Linda is."

I pulled on hiking boots, my old down jacket, and my gloves. Logan was padding anxiously back and forth by the door. He knew I was going out. But I didn't feel right taking him with me. I made sure he had plenty of food and water, then gave him a hug and headed out the door. I jumped in the car and headed northeast.

I tried to reach Ruzzio, but he was out of the office. Malone would be pissed. There was no way I could sit still though. I needed to take some sort of action. He would be pissed to the tenth power if he knew what I'd taken with me.

Before leaving the house I'd opened the strongbox he'd

mounted inside the closet in the master suite. I'd pulled out the Beretta I had purchased back in December. I put a loaded clip into the gun and for some reason, grabbed a spare magazine as well. I put everything in a small nylon bag and then dropped it in the trunk next to the little emergency kit I kept there.

It was almost three by the time I got off the freeway at Twenty-Three Mile Road. I had the map open on the passenger seat and was following the automated directions from the Honda's navigation system. I kept going east, following the curve of the lake. Just in case Malone called, I propped my cell phone on the dash, so I wouldn't have to fumble around for it.

It took half an hour to cruise along Twenty-Three Mile Road before I saw the sign for Harsens Island. A car ferry sat at the dock, creaking back and forth. I looked at the gray sky, the swirling gray waters, and wondered again what the hell I was doing. I asked the deckhand if he knew where I could find the sign I'd seen in the picture. He gave me directions as we began to cross the channel. The wind picked up and began roughly tossing the ferry about. If I had eaten lunch, I probably would have lost it by then.

Some way, somehow, we made it across the channel and reached dry land. The heavy ramp on the car ferry slammed down on the dock with a clang. I followed the cars in front of me as we eased off, timing my departure with the rocking motion of the boat. Firm ground felt reassuring beneath my wheels.

I followed the deckhand's directions, turning left, then right, and let the road take me where it must. The scenery wasn't much to look at. It was the beginning of April. Ice was the most popular element available. There were some small patches of snow here and there. The trees were all bare. The two-lane road followed a canal that seemed to cut through the center of the island. From my brief research, I had discovered there was a game reserve in the middle of the place. I didn't have a clue as to what kind of game would be there.

As the road turned, I saw a row of houses. These were the vacation cottages that would be open in the summer months, where people could come up from the city to enjoy the sunshine, fresh air, and the water. More than likely, there would be clear blue skies and even bluer water in those days, not the lifeless gray color I saw now.

I turned right and followed the road past more cottages and a small town that had several stores and a bar. Some people live here all year long. I wondered if it was enough to keep any business profitable. I kept going. The road dipped and twisted and turned. Somewhere out here, there was a sign I was looking for.

And then I saw it.

I drove past it, then pulled off the road and turned the car around. There was absolutely no traffic on the road, which could be helpful. Or maybe not. Years ago, a friend at the newspaper where I used to work as a reporter gave me a stadium blanket and a pair of binoculars when I was doing a feature on a deaf football player. I'd kept the bundle in the car ever since. Now I used the binoculars to study the area beyond the sign.

The house was set back from the road quite a ways down a long gravel driveway. It was close to the water's edge, probably no more than fifty feet from where the channel lapped against the seawall. It was probably an idyllic setting during the summer, where you could lounge about and watch all the boat people, the ore freighters, and the sailboats going by. Now it looked like something out of a bad Dickens novel.

This house was in dire need of fixing up. The paint was peeling and from where I sat, even I could see a number of shingles were missing from the roof. Plywood covered some of the windows, whether out of necessity or just to keep the elements at bay for the winter was anyone's guess. There was no sign of activity at the house. The other building caught my attention.

About halfway down the gravel drive was a small building off to the left. There was a canal that stretched from the channel, ran alongside the house, and went about fifty yards beyond the smaller building. I guessed this was a garage or storage shed. It was a wooden structure, probably not as old as the house, and in slightly better condition. There was a door that faced the gravel. It was mostly wood with a small, half-moon window about shoulder height. There were no other windows that I could see. A small chimney jutted out of the roof on the right and thin wisps of smoke curled slowly out of the pipe.

About midway between the house and the shed was the old Cadillac sedan. It was one of the big, four-door jobs, a veritable land yacht. Just the kind of thing to boost a salesman's self-esteem. Or maybe it was helpful to influence potential clients.

I'd been watching for about five minutes, trying to make up my mind about approaching the house, when the door on the shed opened and out stepped Dumb Ass Bob. He turned around and waved his arm back inside. I couldn't see his face or hear what he said, but from his body language, I could tell he didn't look happy. He slammed the door. Hard. Then he stomped over to the Cadillac and climbed behind the wheel. Gravel spun from behind his tires as he shot out of the driveway and onto the main road. The Caddy fishtailed as he hit the blacktop. He quickly got it under control and zoomed away.

Now was my chance.

It took me all of ten seconds to jump out of my car and pop the trunk. From the small bag, I pulled the Beretta and the spare clip. I put the gun in the right pocket of my jacket, the clip in the left. Then I ran the zippers down, so they wouldn't fall out as I ran. I pulled a wool cap tightly over my head, shoved my keys into the pocket of my jeans, and tugged on my gloves. As an afterthought, I grabbed the big flashlight from the toolbox and the Honda's tire iron. A quick look up and down the highway proved I was still alone. Who knew for how long?

I didn't hesitate. I started running toward the driveway. My heart was racing. All those exercise classes were paying off. I reached the building without feeling like I'd just been in a marathon.

Up close, I realized it was a boathouse, about the same size as a one-car garage. I peeked through the window, but it was dark inside. There was a hasp set into the doorjamb and a loop on the door to accommodate a padlock. There was no lock in place. Taking a deep breath, I wrapped my hand around the doorknob and turned it. To my surprise, it rotated and the door opened. I stood there for a second, trying to peer inside. Something moved back by the far wall. I looked over my shoulder to make sure I was still alone. Then I stepped over the threshold and snapped the flashlight on.

What sounded like a groan came from the back wall. I took another step. Now the beam from the flashlight reached all the way in. Something moved. I could hear fabric brushing against the wall. I took another step. The groan was louder now and the movement became more frantic. Suddenly I realized I was in the shadows and she couldn't tell who it was. I turned the flashlight around and pointed it at my chest.

"Linda," I said as calmly as I could, "it's me. Jamie."

She groaned again and sobbed. I moved to her quickly now, setting the light on the floor.

She was chained to the wall. A rag was jammed in her mouth and tied behind her head so she couldn't scream or cry out. I eased it from her mouth, brushing some of her hair back from her face.

"Oh, my God, Jamie, it's really you! He's insane. I think he's going to kill me." She was sobbing now, hopefully in relief. The tears were flowing down her face. She must have been terrified.

"I'm not going to let that happen, Linda. I'm going to get your out of here." I put my arms around her and held her. We both needed that contact for a few minutes.

Raising the light now, I took a better look at her and the situation. Her left eye was swollen shut and there was a nasty purple bruise on her cheek. There were scratches on her right cheek. Her nose was caked with dried blood. I wondered for a moment if it was broken. Her lips were swollen and split. She was sitting on the floor with her hands in her lap. There was a length of chain wrapped around her wrists. I followed the chain to a strut on the wall where it was secured with a bolt. I wondered if I could splinter the wood with the tire iron.

Taking Linda's hands, I lifted them up. There was a small bolt with a wing nut through the links. Where it was positioned, there was no way she could reach it with her fingers. But I could. Within seconds, I had spun the nut free, slipped the bolt through the links and had unwound the chains from her wrists.

"How did you find me?" Linda asked, biting back another sob.

I threw a glance over my shoulder at the door. "I'll tell you later. Right now, we need to get out of here. Can you walk?"

She struggled to her feet, wincing as I helped her up. Her left arm was pressed close to her side. Linda tried to take a step and cried out, falling against me.

"What did he do to you?" I asked.

"He beat me. When he got tired of using his hands, he kicked me a few times in the ribs. He wanted what I wouldn't give him." Her voice was a whispery gasp. "What I couldn't give him."

I moved to her right side and got her arm around my shoulders. My left arm circled her waist. We needed to get out of here. For a moment I debated running back to the car and driving it closer. There was no way I'd leave without her. Slowly, we took a step. I saw her wince in pain. Maybe talking would keep her distracted.

"He wanted sex?" I asked, gently urging her forward.

"Oh, yeah, he really wanted sex. He even went so far as to pull it out and wave it in my face. I told him I'd bite it off if he came any closer. He still wanted it until I kicked him in the balls."

I could see the flash of determination and anger in her right eye.

We had taken two more steps toward the door. Suddenly something blocked the gray light outside. It took me a second to realize what had happened.

"You bitch," he snarled. "Why couldn't you leave us alone? Don't you remember me telling you, I always get what I want?"

Dumb Ass Bob reached in and grabbed the doorknob. Then he slammed the door shut, sealing our fate.

Linda slumped toward the floor. There was a stack of equipment, tattered lawn chairs, and boxes here and there. Along the opposite wall was an old sofa, closer to the small heater. I helped her to it, realizing how cold her fingers felt. I needed to get her out of here and get her some medical attention. The flashlight had been forgotten on the floor. I snatched it up and gave it to Linda. Then I moved to the door and tried the handle. It would turn, but the door didn't budge. Looking out the window confirmed it. He'd snapped the padlock in place through the hasp.

"Shit!" I muttered.

"Can you call Malone, Jamie?"

I patted my pockets, realizing my cell phone was still propped on the dashboard of the Honda. "Shit," I repeated, telling Linda where it was.

Now I felt like the dumb ass. He must have seen my car and circled back. Then he'd approached the boathouse on foot, so as not to alert me. Now we were stuck here. There was no way to get through that window. Maybe when we were six, we might have been able to fit, but not now. The door was sturdy. I turned to consider our options.

I remembered this was a boathouse. Listening closely, I

could hear the water sloshing against the pilings beneath us. Yet there was no opening for a boat. Taking the light from Linda, I shined it along the floor, walking slowly toward the center of the room.

While the wooden floor along the perimeter and by the door was made of thick planks, thin sheets of plywood covered the center. I bent down and thumped one panel with my fist. It reverberated with the pressure and wobbled, but held. I moved the light to the back wall and stepped closer. This wall was actually a door, about the size of a small garage door. Somehow this would be rolled to the side in order to accommodate a speedboat or a rowboat in better weather. I pressed against it. The door didn't budge.

"Shit."

"You said that already," Linda said quietly.

I had to think of something. There must be a way to get out of here. Or maybe we could just wait him out? Malone would start to worry when he got my messages and couldn't reach me. I realized that I had never given him any specifics about where I thought Linda was. Suppressing a groan, I moved back to Linda and sat beside her on the couch.

"What do you think he's doing?" she asked.

"I don't know. All he said was he always gets what he wants. Then he slammed the door and locked us inside."

She shuddered. I put my arm around her.

"You know what he wants. It was more than just sex." Her voice was hoarse and she had to clear her throat a couple of times. "He wants to dominate me. He wants to take away my freedom, my choices, take away my whole life."

There was an old blanket on the sofa. I wrapped it around her, trying to warm her. There must be a way out of this.

Linda kept talking, sharing with me what had happened. "He didn't believe me when I told him I wasn't interested. That I couldn't give him what he wanted. That he might as well kill me, because I couldn't do it. I couldn't give in to him." She turned her head, and I could see that her right eye was filling with tears again. "He's going to kill us, Jamie."

"Not if I have anything to say about it."

It was almost an hour before he returned. This time he pulled the old Cadillac down the driveway, crunching the gravel beneath the tires. I'd used the time rummaging through the boathouse, trying to find anything useful. The best I had done was to discover some granola bars, a six-pack of water bottles, and a small package of Oreos. He hadn't been feeding Linda. Maybe he thought hunger would weaken her resolve. I had gotten her to eat the Oreos and one of the granola bars. She savored the water as if it was fine Italian wine.

He parked the Caddy at the end of the driveway, about midway between the boathouse and the house. Linda remained on the sofa. I stood by the door, watching him through that half-moon window. He marched up to the door and stood there, fists on his hips, defiantly glaring at me.

"You bitch," he snarled. "Do you have any idea what I went through to get her alone? How long it's taken me to plan this?"

I couldn't believe this guy. "You kidnapped her! This isn't a fucking prom date!" I snapped savagely.

His eyes narrowed at me. He was clenching his jaw, trying to hold the anger back, but from here even I could tell it wasn't going to last. "I get what I want. I always get what I want."

"Not this time, Bob. I'm sure you've had to deal with disappointment before." My eyes flicked from him to where Linda was perched on the sofa. We had granola bars and water. I wondered how long we could hold out.

He stepped to the door and punched the wood with his fist. "Yeah, I've been disappointed before. But you ain't gonna like how I deal with it."

The look on Linda's face scared me more than anything else. She was slowly shaking her head.

"I'll give you one last chance, Linda," he shouted at the door, knowing she was inside, but not sure exactly where. "You've got one last chance to give me what I want."

"I can't," she whispered, "I can't."

"Forget it, Bob," I shouted. "Your party's over."

He thumped the door again. "You're wrong, bitch. My party's just getting started. You're gonna get to see firsthand how I deal with things when I don't get what I want."

He punched the door once more and tugged on the padlock to make sure it was in place. Then he stomped back toward the Cadillac. This time, he went toward the trunk and pulled out two gas cans. With the last of the afternoon light fading behind him, I could just barely see the determined look on his face.

"Shit!"

The boathouse was an old, wooden structure, probably built in the late sixties. It had a short peaked roof. The small gas heater in the corner had been a more recent addition, something to take the chill off the room during the winter months. Perhaps the previous owner liked to work on his boat during the off-season. About three feet in from the door, I got the sense that we were still over dry land. Anything beyond that, the structure rested on stout, wooden pilings, driven deep into the mud and muck beneath the water. There was no insulation, no internal drywall or paneling. I could put my hands on the wall struts and touch the exterior walls. The boards may be old, but they were definitely thick enough to keep us inside.

Linda stirred from the sofa. "What's going on, Jamie?"

"He's got two big gas cans, Linda, and he's bringing them this way." My voice caught in my throat.

Linda summoned all her strength, all her courage and determination, and pushed off the sofa. Wincing in pain, she limped toward me. As she moved alongside me, I pulled her good arm across my shoulders and helped steady her. Linda turned her good eye to the window. I followed her gaze.

Dumb Ass Bob had unscrewed the cap on one of the five-gallon cans. Now he was splashing the fluid on the boathouse wall. He stepped around the corner of the building, out of our line of sight. But I could hear it. And I could smell it. Definitely gasoline.

"What are you doing, Bob?" Linda called out. "Why can't you just let us go?"

He came back around the corner of the building and threw the empty gas can in the general direction of the Cadillac. He considered it for a moment then walked closer to the door.

His voice was a guttural snarl. "I get what I want, Linda. Are you ready to give it to me?"

Linda turned slightly to face me. "I can't let him kill you, Jamie," she said softly. Then she turned back to the door. "Will you let Jamie go?"

He shook his head once. "It's too late for that, Linda. The nosy bitch is gonna get what she deserves. But you can live. You just gotta give me what I want."

"I can't let you kill her, Bob. But you could keep both of us." She was shaking now, whether in fear or desperation I couldn't tell. Not that it mattered.

There was a snort of derisive laughter from the other side of the door. "I don't think I could get it up for that skinny bitch. I like my women with some curve to them." With that, he trudged over to the other can and unscrewed the cap. Now he was splashing gasoline on the front of the building and moving to the corner by the door. The odor of the gasoline was overpowering, seeping underneath the gap between the floor and the door.

We watched in disbelief as he poured the rest of the can on the wall. Then he turned and pitched the empty can back toward the other one, resting on the gravel driveway by the Cadillac. From the pocket of his coat he dug out a Zippo lighter. With his thumb he flipped the top open then closed. Open, then closed. Open, then closed. He stepped close to the door so he could stare through the window at both of us.

"He is insane," Linda whispered. "He's going to burn us alive."

"You can't do this, Bob!" I yelled, pulling Linda back. I realized now she had grabbed the doorknob, as if she expected him to release us.

"Don't see where you can do fuck-all about what I do," Bob said. "I told you time and time again. It's my motto. I always get what I want."

There was only one thing I could do.

"What did you say, Bob?" I asked loudly, keeping my eyes on his through the window.

He gave his head a disgusted shake. "Damn, you must be dense. I said I always get what I want."

My eyes were boring into his. "Yeah, well *get this*!"

The roar was deafening.

# CHAPTER EIGHTEEN

I'd jammed the Beretta's muzzle up against the door, almost shoulder high on me. Then I'd squeezed the trigger twice. I only hoped that the gunshots would not ignite the gasoline vapors that had to be drifting heavily on the other side of the door. Linda screamed and dropped to the floor. My ears were ringing. There was a hole the size of my fist in the door. Outside I could hear Bob shouting now, cursing in pain and disbelief.

Tentatively I peeked out the window. He was on his back on the ground, floundering about. He was groaning and cursing up a streak. His hands were empty. Try as I might, I couldn't see the Zippo anywhere. I pulled Linda to her feet.

"Jamie, where did that gun come from?" she asked, her voice trembling from shock. "Did you kill him?"

"If I did, he is one noisy ghost."

I got her back to the sofa and pressed a water bottle in her hands. Outside Bob's cursing was growing softer. Had I killed him? I tried to picture where the bullets might have struck him. He's taller than me, so shoulder height on me might have been in his stomach or his chest. Had both bullets hit him? Or had the force of the first one spun him away? It had happened so quickly, I couldn't be sure.

I moved back to the window, still clutching the Beretta in my right hand. I was amazed at how natural it felt as I had drawn it from my jacket and racked the slide. I never thought I would fire this gun at someone again, but Dumb Ass Bob certainly seemed determined to burn us alive. My actions bought us some time. Sooner or later, Malone would find us. I had to believe that. I really had to keep believing that.

I took a glimpse out the window and froze. Bob was no longer on the ground by the door. Somehow he had crawled or squirmed his way back to the Cadillac. I tugged again at the door. It didn't budge. For a nanosecond, I considered shoving the barrel of the gun through the hole in the door and trying to blast away the padlock. But I rejected the idea almost as quickly. For one, I'm no Annie Oakley and I couldn't even see the hasp of the padlock. For two, what if I missed and the bullet sparked off something on the ground and ignited the gasoline? For three, I needed to figure out what Bob was up to.

It was hard to see him clearly in the fading light. I could only see the general shape of him, hunched over the trunk of the Cadillac. There was a small light on under the trunk lid. It didn't illuminate much. I could just see him fumbling around there. He staggered a bit, thrust both arms into air, and let out a howl that chilled my bones.

Linda had somehow materialized beside me. She was clutching the flashlight. Now she pointed it out through the hole in the door. The beam was strong enough to reach him. Just as we realized what he held, Bob managed to ignite one end.

"Emergency flares," Linda said with a groan.

I tried to pull her away from the door so I could take another shot at him. But Bob fell to his knees at that point and pitched the flare in our direction. It bounced across the gravel and came to rest near the corner of the building. And just that quickly, the flare ignited the gasoline.

Malone was going to kill me.

There wasn't a doubt in my mind. He was going to kill me.

I knew it in my heart, in my soul, right down to the marrow of my bones. From the top of my wavy red locks to the bright red polish on my toenails, I knew without a doubt it was a sure thing.

Malone was going to kill me.

That was provided I got out of this alive, of course.

He'd warned me time and again to mind my own business. Why couldn't I listen to reason? How could it be that less than four months after I narrowly escaped certain death at the hands of a psychotic bikini-bar waitress, I find myself in another situation where chances of my survival were so slim? Only this time, it was not just my life on the line. I had somebody else counting on me.

Now it was up to me. I needed to figure out a way of getting us out of here, fast, because right now, time was rapidly running out on me. Make that us. There was no way I was leaving alone, but there sure as hell was no way I wanted to stick around. Right now, all I really wanted was to be back in my cozy little home, curled up on 'The Jewish Aunt', waiting for Malone to come home from work. But I knew that was not going to happen.

We were trapped. And waiting on the other side of that wall was someone who would rather see us sliced open on a coroner's slab than walking out the door. And to help them make that wish come true, they were setting the wall on fire.

Malone may have to wait in line to kill me.

Some of the gas vapors may have evaporated or been diminished by the wind outside, but there was still enough to help encourage the fire. I could feel the heat coming through the door. I wondered if the smoke would get to us first.

"Jamie, we're going to die."

I turned my full attention on her. She was my best

friend, my unofficial sister, my life. If we were going to die here and now, I wasn't going to make it easy. I forced the determination into my voice. "We are not dying here, Linda Gail. We've got too much to live for."

With that, I grabbed her good arm and led her to the center of the room. Then I had her stand so we were back to back. I didn't know how much time we had.

"Whenever I take a step, you do the same. Keep your back tight against mine."

Her voice was a tremble, barely audible over the noise of the fire. "Jamie, I'm scared."

"So am I, baby, but we're getting out of here. We're getting out right now!"

With that, I aimed the Beretta at the floor and began firing. Take a shot, take a step. Take a shot, take a step. I finished the first clip, ejected it and slapped the second one home. I racked the slide and kept going. Every time I fired, Linda gave a little start, but she kept her back pressed against me. I figured I had about three shots left when I stopped. There was a complete circle in the floor now. The thin plywood was creaking beneath our feet. I tucked the gun back in my pocket and zipped it shut. Then I had Linda turn around to face me.

The smoke was getting thick in the boathouse. I could no longer see the window or the door. I could also feel the heat. I couldn't think about those things right now. I took her hands in mine.

"Think of it as an aerobics class. We're going to jump together and break through this floor. Then when we hit the water, we'll move away from the building, back toward the road."

Linda was shaking, but she nodded her head in agreement. "I love you, Jamie."

"I love you, Linda. Now on the count of three, we jump."

Together we counted it off. We both jumped. I slammed my boots against the floor with everything I had.

It held. We did it again. This time there was a loud creak beneath us. I locked eyes with Linda.

"One more, baby, third time has gotta be the charm."

"If it's not, Jamie, I'm gonna keep jumping."

We bounced off the floor and slammed our feet down together. The plywood snapped beneath us, like a trapdoor swinging open. We were free.

We skittered off the plywood and hit the water awkwardly. The water was so cold it was like ten thousand tiny needles were jabbed into my skin. The intensity of the cold took the breath out of my lungs. I knew we would never score points for synchronized swimming, but right now, I didn't care. We were out of the boathouse. I was still holding Linda's hands. Kicking our legs, we moved out from under the boathouse to the edge of the canal. To our right there was deeper water and the channel out front. To our left were the end of the canal and the road. I hoped we'd be able to find something to help us climb out of the frigid water.

"Jamie, what are we going to do now?" Linda asked. I could see the exhaustion on her face but I knew she wasn't giving up.

"We go toward the road. Maybe somebody will see the smoke or the flames. Or maybe they heard all those gunshots."

I guided Linda along the seawall. The fire in the boathouse was roaring now. Tilting my head back, I could see flames shooting up at least thirty feet into the sky. And a column of thick, black smoke was billowing out of there as well. There was the dull whoop of an explosion and part of the back wall blew out into the canal. I remembered seeing a propane tank and a couple of gallons of paint thinner on the shelves. The heat must have ignited them. I was glad we weren't in a direct line with the building any longer.

Linda had to be exhausted. I was worried about her injuries. If Dumb Ass Bob had splintered or broken one of her ribs, it could move and puncture her lung, or even her heart. I shook that image from my mind. I needed to get her out of this water and get the medics on the scene. Once we were out of the water, I could put her in the Honda and call up the Marines.

I studied the seawall. It was wood planking, thick and solid. The top of the wall was about two feet above me. There was enough light from the fire now that I could see most of the way along the wall. I'd been hoping there might be a ladder extending from the land into the water but there was no such luck. I had another idea.

"Linda, we need to get out of this water now."

"I'm open to suggestions, Jamie."

"That's good, because here's what we're going to do. I'm going to put my back against the wall and form a stirrup with my hands. You put your foot in the stirrup and you can step right up onto the ground."

She looked at me like I was crazy. "You make it sound so easy, Jay Kay."

I grinned at the sound of my nickname. "That's exactly how it is gonna be, baby."

Our clothes were getting waterlogged. I didn't know how much longer adrenaline would keep us going. I pressed my back to the wall, knowing full well that when she stepped up, I might be submerged in the freezing water. That didn't matter. I had to get her out.

I laced my fingers together. She leaned close and kissed my cheek. Then she whispered in my ear, "I will always love you, Jay Kay."

"I will always love you, Algae. Now get your cute little ass out of this water so we can go home."

She put her right foot into my hands. Together we counted to three. Linda reached up with her good arm for the top of the seawall as I lifted my arms with everything I had. As I expected, the force of her weight and the sodden clothes drove me under. Suddenly, it was as if she was light as a feather. Her weight was gone. Yet I was sinking deeper into the cold, dark water.

Strong hands grabbed the shoulders of my ski jacket and plucked me out of the water like a puppy from a washtub.

"You picked a hell of a time to go swimming, Jamie. This ain't exactly beach bikini weather."

I shook the water out of my eyes and looked at him. He was sprawled on the ground, his arms hanging out over the edge of the seawall, holding my upper body out of the water. It took a second before I recognized him.

"You gonna pull me in, Chene, or leave me dangling like a marlin?"

"I've got to get a better grip, Jamie. It's nothing personal." He slid one hand down to my armpit, and then the other one.

"You get me out of here, Chene and I'm going to kiss you."

A flicker of a smile crossed his face. "Don't think Malone would be too keen on that. Brace your feet on the wall. Then when I straighten up, just walk up."

He must have thought I was one of the Flying Wallendas or part of a circus act. I did as he said and the next thing I knew I was on the ground. I lay there, relishing the feel of the frozen ground against my cheek. Turning my head, I saw a black Pontiac sedan in the driveway. It was running and all the lights were on. A door slammed and someone appeared above me.

"You keep this up, Jamie, and you'll start giving civilians the idea they don't really need cops to protect them."

I rolled over and sat up. Megan McDonald, the other detective I met recently with Chene, squatted beside me and wrapped a heavy wool blanket around my shoulders.

"What's the score?" Chene asked.

"I called it in. I requested a medical helicopter to fly these two to the nearest hospital. I'm worried about hypothermia. Linda needs a doctor to check out her injuries. I've got some of her wet clothes off. We wrapped her in your overcoat."

Chene nodded. I realized he wasn't wearing a jacket, just a thick sweater. I jerked my head toward the Cadillac.

"What about Dumb Ass Bob?"

A smirk crossed Megan's face. "Now that's an appropriate name. I think he'll live. He's lost some blood but I don't think it's fatal. I slapped a couple of pressure bandages on him and dragged him away from the fire. He's out cold."

So I hadn't killed him. I didn't know whether to be happy or not.

"What's the timeframe on that helicopter?" Chene asked.

Megan checked her watch. "It should be here shortly." She jerked a thumb in the direction of the Caddy. "That guy has got bullet holes in him, Jamie. Don't suppose you had anything to do with it?"

I tried to reach for the pocket, but my hands were shaking too badly. Chene took one look at me and scooped me up, blanket and all, and carried me over to the Pontiac. Linda was in the front passenger seat. Megan opened the rear door and Chene slid me inside. I tapped my right pocket. He undid the zipper and withdrew the Beretta. Quickly he ejected the magazine and popped out the round that was in the chamber. He handed it all to McDonald, who was slowly shaking her head. Chene closed the door.

I reached over her shoulder and found Linda's hand. She squeezed it tightly. We sat there in silence, the car's heater running full blast, waiting for the helicopter to arrive.

\* \* \* \*

Nobody parties in the hospital. Okay, maybe when babies are born there can be a little celebration. But really, can you think of any other time that people would be in a festive mood in a hospital?

I was wearing a pair of dark green hospital scrubs, which really looked good with my red hair. The emergency room doctors had checked me out. Apparently when we had crashed through the boathouse floor, a nail or screw had been driven into my right calf and left me with a ragged gash that required about a dozen stitches and a tetanus shot. Beyond that, I was pronounced good. It hadn't taken much to persuade the docs to let me take a long hot shower and rinse off the smoke and cold. Now I was wearing the scrubs and a pair of thick slipper socks to keep my feet warm.

Linda was being cared for. The examination determined that she had three cracked ribs, a broken nose, and some fractures to the left orbital bone around her eye. Her left shoulder had been dislocated as well. She was dehydrated and undernourished, but her prognosis was good. They were going to keep her overnight for observation. She was in the bed by the window. Although there was no medical reason to keep me, I was going to stay with her.

Somehow the nurses managed to wash Linda's hair. Her left arm was in a sling, giving her shoulder a chance to heal. She was sitting up in bed while I brushed her hair, letting the brush ride through the curls and clear out the snarls.

"Jay Kay, I need to call Vince. He must be worried sick," Linda said.

"Baby, neither one of us has a phone. I'm sure Malone is on his way."

There was a knock on the door. McDonald and Chene stepped inside.

"Just wanted to check on you two," Chene said quietly, "and make sure the hospital was still standing."

Megan handed me my purse, car keys and my cell phone. She had driven my car here. I flipped the phone open to contact Malone, and saw the look on Linda's face. I passed her the phone so she could call Vince. I motioned the two cops out into the hallway to give her some privacy.

There was a little waiting area just down the hall, with a couple of sofas and chairs and a television mounted high on the wall tuned to an all-news channel. We walked down there. Megan found the remote and silenced the screen.

"So exactly how did you two just happen to show up when you did? Not that I'm complaining. I'm just very curious," I said.

Jefferson Chene was now wearing a chocolate brown leather jacket. He must have kept a spare set of clothes in the trunk of his car. He and Megan were sitting on the sofa adjacent to the chair I had flopped into.

"Malone called us," Chene said in that low voice. "We're based near Mt. Clemens, so we were a lot closer than he was to the scene."

"But how did he know where I was? I never got specific with my messages."

Megan gave me a wide smile. "He used the same thing you did to find Linda. We pulled the GPS coordinates for your phone. We figured where ever the phone was, you couldn't be too far away. Of course, once we got onto the island, that smoke signal certainly helped us find you. We arrived just as you were lifting Linda out of the water."

No wonder she had been light as a feather. Chene must have grabbed her as soon as I went under.

"Malone told me how stubborn you are," Chene said. "He also said you adamantly believed that Linda would never take off without telling you. Also she would never leave her dog behind."

"So you just dropped everything and took a drive, looking for Malone's girlfriend?" I asked.

Megan started to laugh. "We're not a dating service, Jamie. Malone said you've got pretty good instincts. When he couldn't reach you, he thought you might be in trouble. So he reached out to us."

I took a few moments to reflect on that. "How's Dumb Ass Bob doing?"

"He's in surgery, but the prognosis is good. He'll live to go to trial. Based on what you've told us and what he did to Ms. Davis, I'd say he'll be going away for a long time," Chene said.

A thought meandered across my mind. "He said something about how he deals with disappointment, just before he torched the building. It made me think he's done something this drastic before."

The look on Megan's face was incredulous. "You're serious, aren't you?"

I shrugged. "It might be worth looking into his background. If you believed the lines he used, he dabbled in real estate, buying up foreclosed properties, and then fixing them up to turn a profit. He used to be married. Maybe his ex-wife could confirm the story. And that was just one of his...businesses."

Megan nodded. She pulled out her phone and sent a quick text message to someone, probably requesting more information on Dumb Ass Bob. I got to my feet. I wanted to get back to Linda, to make sure she was okay. Chene and Megan also stood. I realized in all the activity getting us into the helicopter and then to the hospital, there was something I'd forgotten.

"Hey, Chene," I said, standing right before him.

"Yes, Jamie?"

"Thanks for showing up when you did." I reached up and put my hands on his face. In my peripheral vision, I could see Megan's eyes widen in surprise.

"What are you doing, Jamie?" Chene asked.

"I'm paying my debt. Now pucker up, Chene." I rose up on my toes and kissed him on the lips. I kept my eyes open and he did, too. His hands moved to my hips but only to steady me, not to pull me closer.

"You're getting awful friendly with my lady, Chene."

I jumped and saw Malone standing there. Megan

started laughing and Chene took a step back, shaking his head. I rushed into Malone's arms. He bent down, finding my lips with his and rocking me with a very passionate kiss. After a moment he relaxed his grip but didn't let me go. Malone leaned back and looked deeply into my eyes.

"Are you okay?" he asked quietly.

"So much better now." I turned and looked at Chene and Megan. Malone nodded at the two cops.

"It must be my animal magnetism, Sarge. Women just can't seem to keep their hands off me."

"You wish," Megan muttered.

Malone embraced me again. "This one can be a lot of trouble, Chene. You might want to think twice."

"I was just thanking him for coming to our rescue, Malone."

"I didn't see you kissing Megan."

I pushed him away. All three cops were laughing now. I reached over and hugged Megan, whispering my thanks in her ear. Then the four of us returned to Linda's room. And the party atmosphere was enhanced.

# CHAPTER NINETEEN

I pushed open the door, leading the others. I thought she might be resting but she was holding court. Vince was sitting on the edge of her bed, lightly holding her right hand. They were talking quietly. One of the nurses was bustling about, checking the IV tubes and adjusting the bed. She spotted a bouquet of flowers that Vince brought and ducked into the bathroom, filling a plastic vase with water and arranging the flowers. Somebody else was leaning against the window.

"Bert!" I said in surprise, running over and being engulfed in his arms. "What are you doing here?"

He gave that snort that could be a laugh or disgust. "Where else would I be, Jamie? My daughter and her best friend end up in the hospital. You don't think I'm going to come check things out?"

I was dumbfounded. Of course he would be here.

Bert nodded in Malone's direction. He was talking quietly with Chene and McDonald. "When Malone couldn't get through to you on the phone, he came to me. We listened to your message. It was his idea to check your location. We figured out Chene was closer. So I reached out to his boss and asked for a little assistance. Once we heard that Chene had found you, we headed over. Malone had Vince meet us. We all wanted to make sure both of you are okay."

"I'm sorry, Bert."

He was still holding me in that fatherly embrace. "Sorry for what, Jamie?"

"For putting you guys through all this."

"You got there in time to save your best friend's life. You caught the bad guy. You were right about Linda being abducted. Jamie, you have nothing to be sorry about."

"Guess all those years of living with you rubbed off on me, Bert."

He smiled. "Glad to hear something good came out of that."

The nurse gave us all a scolding look as the noise level in the room was getting to be a bit much. Malone was still in uniform and the other three cops seemed to convince her with their presence alone that she would be overruled. She made a comment about visiting hours ending and ducked out of the room.

Chene and McDonald started to head for the door, but Linda called them over. She kissed both of them on the cheek and gently expressed her thanks. McDonald made a comment about all the women kissing Chene, which seemed to fluster the guy. They shook hands with Vince, Bert, and Malone. I hugged them both before they left.

Bert, Malone, and I were gathered around the foot of Linda's bed. She and Vince seemed to be oblivious to us.

Malone nudged me. "It seems to me I saw a pizza place just down the street. Is anybody else hungry?"

Before I could answer, Bert spoke up. "Now that you mention it, food does sound pretty good. You think they deliver?"

Malone grabbed my hand and led me out of the room. "Let's go find out."

* * * *

It was a couple of hours before the guys left. The three of us sat in the little lounge area. Malone had persuaded one of the nurses to call the pizzeria for us. He ordered two large pizzas with mushrooms, pepperoni, sausage, ham, and green peppers. They delivered it along with a couple of large bottles of Diet Coke. I had taken some slices for Vince and Linda, but never got beyond the door. We gave the rest to the nurses on duty.

Malone took the Honda. The plan was he would return in the morning once Linda was released and drive us all home. Bert lived closer to Vince, so he was going to drop him off.

Now with the lights off and the guys gone, the room was quiet and peaceful. After being examined by the doctors, Linda called her mother. While she refused to go into details, Linda was able to reassure Gracie. She promised to call again tomorrow with an update. It wouldn't surprise me if Gracie came to visit. Linda had asked me to roll the little table between the two hospital beds out of the way, and then slide my bed closer. I remembered doing this when we were small, so the two beds could touch and we could hold hands and whisper when we were supposed to be sleeping.

"You need to rest, Algae."

"Jay Kay, I can't believe everything that's happened lately."

"With time, it will all be forgotten." I shifted onto my side so I could see her face. Even in the dim light from outside, I could see the bandages on her nose. Her lips were still puffy and split. "Vince sure seemed glad to see you."

A flicker of a smile crossed her lips. "Yeah, well, let's see what his reaction is in the daylight. I've got to be looking pretty scary right now."

"I don't think he noticed."

"Jay Kay, you wouldn't believe what he was saying. He kept saying '*mio bel tesoro*', which means my beautiful darling. It was as if he couldn't see all these bruises, stitches, and bandages on my face."

I reached over and took her right hand. "That's all just temporary, Algae. Vince knows that you are still his beautiful darling. I think he's just happy to have you back. We all are."

She smiled and snuggled down in the bed as best she could. I knew they were giving her some painkillers to take the edge off. Her shoulder was bandaged and so were her ribs. What she needed now was time and rest. I watched her. Her breathing was slow and steady and her eyes were closed. Just when I thought she'd fallen asleep, she whispered my name.

"I never said it. Thank you for saving my life, Jay Kay."

"You're very welcome, Algae. Now go to sleep."

"Okay."

The next morning we were waiting for Malone. The doctors had done their follow up examinations on Linda and deemed that she could leave. I was given pages of instructions on how to take care of her. One of the nurses had shown me how to wrap the bandages on her shoulder and her ribs. There was no doubt Vince would also be assisting in this area, but I kept those comments to myself.

Linda was dozing on the bed. Malone was supposed to be bringing clothes for both of us, along with jackets and shoes. It turned out the police had taken all of our clothing as evidence to be used in Dumb Ass Bob's trial. Briefly, I wondered when I would get the Beretta back. Not that I had any plans to use it anytime soon, or ever again for that matter. Yet...

I heard a funny noise in the hallway. Turning away from the window, I saw the door slowly open and heard the click of nails on linoleum. Linda stirred and opened her eyes.

"Oh, baby," she said softly, reaching out with her good

hand.

Logan jumped up and put his front paws on the bed. He nuzzled her hand with his snout. Linda scratched his head. I could see she was fighting back tears. Malone was standing there, holding the dog's leash in one hand and a small suitcase in the other.

"Good morning, ladies. Your limousine awaits you."

I went over and greeted him with a kiss. "Jasper, how did you ever get that dog into this hospital?"

He winked at me. "Wasn't hard, Jamie. I have a prescription in my pocket from a physician who is treating Ms. Davis. This dog has very therapeutic powers."

"That is absolutely true," Linda said. She had swung her legs over the side of the bed and was vigorously rubbing Logan's fur. "I'm feeling better already."

I took the suitcase from his hand and chased Malone from the room. I dressed quickly, and then helped Linda into her clothes. Logan was our guide as one of the nurses brought a wheelchair to take Linda outside. Malone pulled the Cherokee up to the doorway so we could quickly tuck Linda and the dog in the back. He had the heater running full blast.

We had talked a lot this morning. I was going to stay with her for the next day or two, until her strength returned. Whatever appointments she might have, I would be happy to drive her to them. I think Vince was planning to clear his schedule for the rest of the week, so that he could take care of her. Linda would make the final decision. It didn't matter to me. I was just happy to have her back. I turned and propped my back against the door so I could look at the two most important people in my world. Malone caught me staring at him and winked at me. In the back seat, despite the ordeal she had been through over the last forty-eight hours, despite the bandages, bruises, and stitches, Linda was smiling. She had her good arm wrapped around Logan's neck and I don't think she was ever going to let him go.

Malone's cell phone began to chirp. He answered, listened quietly for a moment, and then had a brief conversation. I watched his eyes flick to the rear view mirror to check on his passengers before he glanced over at me. One of those low voltage smiles crept into the corner of his eyes. "No, I won't be there, but I have no doubt they can handle this on their own. Thanks for the heads up." He folded the phone and set it back on the dash.

"What's all that about, Jasper?"

"That was Megan McDonald. She and Chene want to meet with the two of you to get formal statements. They've been in touch with Ruzzio and he was planning on coming by Linda's house around four, so they will join him." His eyes again flicked to the mirror and he watched Linda's features for a moment. "McDonald asked if I was going to be there."

Linda spoke up from the rear seat. "That's when you told them we can handle this on our own."

He nodded. "It will be easier for you to only have to go through this once, with the cops from both departments. Jamie will be there to provide her part of the story. I figured you were in good hands."

Linda reached across and squeezed my shoulder. "You've got that right."

\* \* \* \*

Linda napped for several hours before the trio of cops arrived. Malone stayed with her while I ran out to the market to stock up on many of her favorite foods. Now the five of us were settled around her kitchen table. I had a momentary flashback to several conversations that had taken place right here over the weekend with different players. As if to confirm that this setting was now real, I bumped Linda's leg with my knee and maintained physical contact.

228

McDonald and Ruzzio placed tape recorders on the table. The cops had conferred earlier and Ruzzio was going to lead the interview. If Chene or McDonald had any questions, they would interject.

Ruzzio walked her through Saturday's events. I was impressed by how calmly she could tell the tale.

"I came out of the salon and it was snowing pretty heavy. Fortunately, my car wasn't far away. I put my hood up to cover my hair, but that blocked my peripheral vision. So I didn't see him come up alongside me until he grabbed my arm and spun me around."

"This was Fitzroy who grabbed you?" Ruzzio asked as she paused.

There was brief look of confusion on her face. "I never heard his last name. I only knew him as Bob or as Jamie and I referred to him, 'Dumb Ass Bob'. He is the one who kidnapped me."

"What happened next?" Ruzzio prompted.

"He put some kind of a cloth over my mouth and nose. It must have been something like chloroform because the next thing I knew, I was in the front seat of his car and we were driving into the storm."

"Crime scene technicians found a rag in the back seat of his car that still had traces of ether on it," Chene said quietly.

"He kept saying that I should have been more cooperative, because he always gets what he wants. He really didn't like to do it this way, but he wasn't giving me any choice. My wrists were tied together and it was so tight I couldn't feel my fingertips. I tried to talk him out of his plan. I told him that there was no way that I could just disappear, too many people would be looking for me." Linda paused and looked right at me with her good eye. I could see the determination, the understanding and knowledge that I would have never stopped trying to find her. She resumed her narrative.

"He made a comment about how he'd never been able

to get me alone before, I was always with that damn redhead. I told him she was expecting to hear from me that afternoon. I told him she'd be calling soon. That got him angrier. So I told him that if I didn't call or text you soon, you'd start to worry. He chewed on that for a minute, and then he pulled into a parking lot by the freeway and sent Jamie that text. After that he turned off my phone and kept driving.

"I had no idea where we were going. He kept talking the whole time, telling me all his plans for the two of us, how we would be so happy, living in this beautiful house and have everything we'd ever need. I was numb. I just sat there listening to him, trying to think of a way to escape. He'd gone so far as to tie my ankles together too, so even if I could get out of the car, I couldn't very well run."

"What about when you went across the ferry. Didn't anyone see that you were tied up?" Ruzzio asked.

Linda shook her head. "You have to remember it was snowing pretty heavily and the wind up there by the water was really blowing. The deckhand collected the money and hurried back into the cabin with the driver. He never got close enough to the car to take a good look at me. When we got on the island, I still didn't know where we were. I hadn't been paying attention to my surroundings; I was just trying to think of a way of getting out.

"When we got to his cabin, he dragged me into that building where Jamie found me. At first, he untied my wrists and ankles and when I tried to run, he blocked me. He knocked me down a couple of times. He said the island was pretty deserted this time of year, so it wasn't like I could run next door to the neighbors and they would help me. He even let me go outside the building and look around. It was bleak. There was no sign of life anywhere. No smoke rising from a chimney, no cars in sight, no people walking around. It's like we were the only people for miles around. There was nobody to hear me scream. It was cold, windy, and dismal. I knew I couldn't get the car keys from him, but I wasn't giving up easy. He had to drag me back into that building and when I struggled, he hit me again."

There was silence around the table. Linda took a sip of water, drew a deep breath, and continued.

"He tried to undress me but I kept fighting him. I got in a few good kicks and punches, which probably made him madder, but I didn't care. After a while, he took a different approach. He chained me to the wall and left me in that building by myself. I guess he had food and a bed in the house, but I never went in there. I tried to undo the chains but they were too tight and my fingers were numb. When he came back he must have thought that I would change my mind and give in, but I'm too stubborn. I knew there were people out there looking for me."

She went on to describe the beatings, how he had punched her in the cheek, closing one eye, kicking her in the ribs and chest. Dumb Ass Bob only saw the exterior beauty of Linda and didn't realize that her spirit and determination helped to manifest her true beauty. He obviously didn't see the irony of the situation, where his physical assault was damaging the outer beauty that he was driven to covet, to own.

At length, the cops turned their attention to me and I told my side of the story; I started from the discovery of the area around New Baltimore to the memory of the conversation over coffee with Dumb Ass Bob, and my efforts to find her. Chene had me repeat the part about being locked in the boathouse, the threats, the gasoline, and shooting Bob twice. McDonald raised her eyebrows in what I took to be a look of approval or admiration, when I described shooting a trapdoor into the plywood floor so we could break out with the building burning down around us. The two state cops knew the rest of the story and had already filled in Ruzzio on it. Once we were done, they put their coffee mugs in the sink, gathered their coats, and headed for the door. Ruzzio and McDonald were already outside when Chene turned back to us.

"Linda, I'm glad that you're home, safe and sound. Jamie, what you did was very brave, but you were damn lucky. I'm sure Malone has probably told you the same thing more than once."

I nodded. "I couldn't just sit around and wait. She's my friend. And good friends will go to great lengths to help each other."

He took a moment to consider that then gave me a slow nod of his head. "It seems to me we could all use friends like that."

"I owe you, Chene."

"You don't owe me anything, Jamie. Just take care of yourself. And Linda."

* * * *

Friday afternoon, my cell phone rang just as I was about to leave Linda's house. Vince was going to stay with her. I was pleased to see that her bruises were fading and she was gradually regaining her strength. What really impressed me was her spirit, how resilient she was. I got a fierce, one-armed hug before heading out. Now I glanced at the phone and saw Bert's number on the screen. He asked me to swing by the post when I had a few minutes. I told him I was on my way.

I was escorted back to Bert's office. He was just finishing up a call and he motioned me into the room with two fingers. When I started to sit down, he shook his head, racked the phone, and moved from around his desk. There was no hesitation as he wrapped his arms around me for a fatherly bear hug.

"What am I going to do with you, Jamie Rae?" he asked after a moment.

"Well, you could buy a girl dinner."

He snorted that laugh of his and slowly released me. "Have to give you a rain check. I've got a date."

232

I dropped into one of his visitor chairs and he leaned back against the desk. "What's going on, Bert?"

"I thought you'd like to get an update on Fitzroy. That was McDonald on the phone with the latest details. Apparently your instincts were right about his background. The guy has a history of criminal conduct, including some assault charges, one stalking situation, and a couple of domestic violence beefs. According to the records, his ex-wife has not been seen or heard from in over a year."

I sat up straighter. "As in disappeared?"

"That's hard to say." Bert gave me a shrug of those massive shoulders. "McDonald and Chene are going to do a bit more digging. There is a possibility that Fitzroy was involved in her disappearance."

"Dumb Ass Bob bragged about buying up properties in different areas, some kind of investments in vacation properties where he found one that had been foreclosed and he was going to flip them when the market improved. If these were remote properties, it could be a good place to hide someone. Or their body."

Bert said they were already investigating any real estate holdings Fitzroy had, and would look more closely into the disappearance of his ex-wife. When I asked about his injuries, Bert let a smirk of a grin cross his face.

"He's in stable condition now. A few inches to the right or a few inches lower and it would have been a different scenario."

I was puzzled. A few inches right I could understand, that would have hit him in the heart. But a few inches lower?

"Your first shot hit him just below and to the left of his heart, striking his lung and nicking a couple of his ribs. He was already falling backwards when your second shot hit him in the top of the thigh. A few inches lower and to the right and you would have destroyed his manhood."

I knew I had hit him, but had never given much thought as to where. Knowing what I did now, it was amazing that Dumb Ass Bob had been able to drag himself to the trunk of the Caddy and get the flare. Anger and adrenaline must have been churning in him big time.

Bert pushed off the desk and pulled me to my feet for another hug. "I'm glad you're safe, Jamie. I'm glad that you found Linda and brought her home. I'd really appreciate it if you tried to stay out of trouble for a while, Daughter."

I wrapped my arms tightly around him in return. "I'll do what I can, Dad. But I can't make any promises."

"Somehow I knew that would be your response. And you know, I wouldn't want it any other way."

I left Bert's office and slowly made my way home.

It felt like I'd been gone forever. Even though I'd been coming home each night from Linda's when Vince would arrive after work, my time at home had been unsettled. Deep down, I was still worried about her and the long road to recovery she was facing. Her broken nose had been reset and it would take time to heal, along with the injuries to her shoulder, ribs, and face. Vince assured me that her eye was healing well and that he didn't think there was serious damage to the orbital bone. He knew a specialist who would do a thorough examination once she had gained more strength. She may need surgery. I was also concerned about the emotional and psychological impact the events of the last few months might have on her. So, even when I was here, curled up in bed with Malone, my mind was on my best friend.

After my meeting with Bert, I stopped by to see Malone. Following a welcome kiss, he told me that dinner was waiting for me back home. He also forewarned me that Ian would be coming by in the morning to spend some time with him, but not until around nine.

So when I got home, I was delighted to find a large dish of one of Malone's best recipes in the refrigerator— chicken piccata with lots of mushrooms and capers on a bed of linguine. There was also a bowl of tossed salad and a fresh loaf of crusty, Italian bread on the counter. I scooped out a portion of the chicken and pasta and warmed it in a low oven while nibbling the salad.

After my scrumptious feast, I thought for a few minutes about doing some work on the computer, but I didn't have the ambition. Instead, I put some piano music on the stereo, dug out an old Travis McGee novel and curled up on the 'aunt'. The combination of the great meal, the comfort of being in my own home and the warmth of the fire must have done me in, because the next thing I realized, Malone was sprawled there beside me.

"Welcome home, Jamie," he said, giving me a long, slow, wet kiss that certainly helped wake me up.

"Welcome home, Salvador," I said when I was able to come up for air. Malone's eyes grew wide for a moment and he leaned slightly back.

"What did you call me?"

My heart skipped a beat. Had I finally gotten it right, finally solved the mystery of his first name? I forced myself to be calm and drew a slow breath. "Salvador."

He took a moment to savor it and bent down to kiss my neck again. "That's what I thought."

It took an effort but I pushed him back enough to look at his face. "Am I right, Malone? Did I finally guess the right name?"

One of those low voltage smiles crept into his eyes. "Not a chance, Jamie. Not a chance."

"Then I guess I'll have to keep trying," I said, as I pulled him back to me. "Someday I'm going to figure it out."

"There's not a doubt in my mind."

We stayed on the sofa, kissing, caressing, and very slowly undressing each other. It wasn't a time for talking. It was a time for other, more important things. As I pulled Malone from the 'aunt' and led him back to our bedroom, I knew that after all we had been through in the last few months, things were right with our little corner of the world once again.

MARK LOVE

# THE END

# ACKNOWEDGMENTS

As with any project, this novel would never have been completed without the assistance of others. Some people are growing accustomed to my off the wall questions, trying to understand what the answers have to do with anything, but that's my job to sort it out.

Special thanks to Holly Smith-Vogtman for her insights on various forms of exercise classes, including pole dancing. To Emilia Filocamo, for the clarification on the proper Italian phrasings. To Cameron Love, for helping with the fire scenes and giving me a better understanding of just how hot and how quickly a structure will burn. To the guys at the Spy Shop in Royal Oak for their insight and assistance on surveillance cameras. To Travis Love, Joanna Huestis and Kim Love for proofreading the story and pointing out my many obvious errors.

Any mistakes are mine.

# ABOUT THE AUTHOR

Mark Love (yes, that's really his name) lived for many years in the metropolitan Detroit area, where crime and corruption are always prevalent. A former freelance reporter, Love is drawn to mysteries and the twists and turns that mirror real life. He is the author of "Why 319?" and three books in the Jamie Richmond Series "Devious" "Vanishing Act" and "Fleeing Beauty" and several short stories.

Love resides in west Michigan with his wife, Kim. He enjoys a wide variety of music, reading and writing fiction, cooking, travel, most sports and the great outdoors. You can find his blog at the link below and on Goodreads, Facebook, and Amazon.

http://marklove024.blogspot.com/
https://www.goodreads.com/author/dashboard
https://www.facebook.com/MarkLoveAuthor
http://www.amazon.com/-/e/B009P7HVZQ

# DEVIOUS

## A JAMIE RICHMOND MYSTERY

Curiosity and stubbornness can
be a dangerous mix.

# MARK LOVE

Made in the USA
Monee, IL
07 September 2022

13509848R00142